So Sweet!

THREE BOOKS IN ONE

So Sweet!

THREE BOOKS IN ONE

by Coco Simon

Simon Spotlight

New York   London   Toronto   Sydney   New Delhi

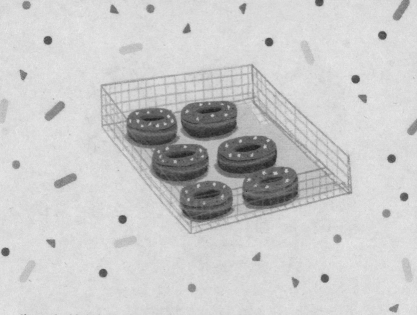

SIMON SPOTLIGHT

An imprint of Simon & Schuster Children's Publishing Division

1230 Avenue of the Americas, New York, New York 10020

This Simon Spotlight edition August 2021

Copyright © 2021 by Simon & Schuster, Inc.

Katie and the Cupcake Cure © 2011 by Simon & Schuster, Inc.

Text by Tracey West; interior designed by Laura Roode

Sunday Sundaes © 2018 by Simon and Schuster, Inc.

Text by Elizabeth Doyle Carey; interior designed by Hannah Frece

Hole in the Middle © 2019 by Simon and Schuster, Inc.

Text by Valerie Dobrow; interior designed by Ciara Gay

All rights reserved, including the right of reproduction in whole or in part in any form.

SIMON SPOTLIGHT and colophon are registered trademarks of Simon & Schuster, Inc.

For information about special discounts for bulk purchases, please contact Simon & Schuster Special Sales at 1-866-506-1949 or business@simonandschuster.com.

The text of this book was set in Bembo Std.

Manufactured in the United States of America 0721 OFF

10 9 8 7 6 5 4 3 2 1

Library of Congress Control Number 2021938707

ISBN 978-1-6659-0166-6

ISBN 978-1-4422-2276-6 (*Katie and the Cupcake Cure* ebook)

ISBN 978-1-5344-1748-9 (*Sunday Sundaes* ebook)

ISBN 978-1-5344-6027-0 (*Hole in the Middle* ebook)

These titles were previously published individually by Simon Spotlight.

CONTENTS

CUPCAKE DIARIES

Katie

and the

cupcake

cure

CHAPTER 1

Who's Afraid of Middle School?
Not Me!

Every time I have ever watched a movie about middle school, the main character is always freaking out before the first day of school. You know what I mean, right? If the movie's about a guy, he's always worried about getting stuffed into a garbage can by jocks. If it's about a girl, she's trying on a zillion outfits and screaming when she sees a pimple on her face. And no matter what movie it is, the main character is always obsessed with being popular.

My name is Katie Brown, and whenever I watched those movies, I just didn't get it. I mean, how could middle school be *that* different from elementary school? Yeah, I knew there would be new kids from other schools, but I figured everyone from our school would stick together. We've all pretty much known one another since kindergarten. Sure, not everybody hangs out together, but it's not like we put some kids on a pedestal and worship them or anything. We're all the same. Back in third grade, we all got sick together on mystery meat loaf day. That kind of experience has to bind you for life, doesn't it?

That's what I thought, anyway. I didn't spend one single second of the summer worrying about middle school. I got a really bad sunburn at the town pool, made a thousand friendship bracelets at day camp, and learned from my mom how to make a cake that looks like an American flag. I didn't stress out about middle school at all.

Guess what? I was wrong! But you probably knew that already. Yeah, the cruel hammer of reality hit pretty hard on the very first day of school. And the worst thing was, I wasn't even expecting it.

The morning started out normal. I put on the tie-dyed T-shirt I made at day camp, my favorite pair of jeans, and a new pair of white sneakers. Then I slipped about ten friendship bracelets on each arm, which I thought looked pretty cool. I brushed my hair, which takes about thirty seconds. My hair is brown and wavy—Mom calls it au naturel. I only worry about my hair when it starts to hang in my eyes, and then I cut it.

When I went downstairs for breakfast, Mom was waiting for me in the kitchen.

"Happy first day of middle school, Katie!" she shouted.

Did I mention that my mom is supercorny? I think it's because she's a dentist. I read a survey once that said that people are afraid of dentists more than anything else, even zombies and funeral directors. (Which is totally not fair, because without dentists everybody would have rotten teeth, and without teeth you can't eat corn on the cob, which is delicious.) But anyway, I think she tries to smile all the time and make jokes so that people will like her more. Not that she's fake—she's honestly pretty nice, for a mom.

"I made you a special breakfast," Mom told me. "A banana pancake shaped like a school bus!"

The pancake sat on a big white plate. Mom had used banana slices for wheels and square pieces of cantaloupe for the windows. This might seem like a strange breakfast to you, but my mom does stuff like this all the time. She wanted to go to cooking school when she got out of high school, but her parents wanted her to be a dentist, like them. Which is unfair, except that if she didn't go to dental school,

5

she wouldn't have met my dad, and I would never have been born, so I guess I can't complain.

But anyway, in her free time she does the whole Martha Stewart thing. Not that she looks like Martha Stewart. She has brown hair like me, but hers is curly, and her favorite wardrobe items are her blue dentist coat and her apron that says #1 CHEF on the front. This morning she was wearing both.

"Thanks, Mom," I said. I didn't say anything about being too old for a pancake shaped like a school bus. It would have hurt her feelings. Besides, it was delicious.

She sat down in the seat next to me and sipped her coffee. "Do you have the map I printed out for you with the new bus stop location?" she asked me. She was doing that biting-her-bottom-lip thing she does when she's worried about me, which is most of the time.

"I got it, but I don't need it," I replied. "It's only four blocks away."

Mom frowned. "Okay. But I e-mailed the map to Barbara just in case."

Barbara is my mom's best friend—and she's also the mom of my own best friend, Callie. We've known each other since we were babies. Callie is two months older than I am, and she never lets me forget it.

"I hope Callie has the map," my mom went on. "I wouldn't want you two to get lost on your first day of middle school."

"We won't," I promised. "I'm meeting Callie at the corner of Ridge Street, and we're walking to the bus stop together."

"Oh, good," Mom said. "I'm glad you finally talked to your old bus buddy."

"Uh, yeah," I said, and quickly gulped down some orange juice. I hadn't actually talked to her. But we'd been bus buddies ever since kindergarten (my corny mom came up with "bus buddies," in case you didn't figure that out already), so there was no real reason to believe this year would be any different. I knew I'd see her at the bus stop.

Every August, Callie goes to sleepaway camp, which totally stinks. She doesn't get back until a few days before school starts. Normally I see her the first day she comes back and we go to King Cone for ice cream.

But this year Callie texted that she was busy shopping with her mom. Callie has always cared a lot more about clothes than I do. She wanted to find the perfect outfit to wear on her first day of middle school. And since we only had a few days before school started I didn't think it was *that* weird that I didn't see her. It was a *little* weird that she hadn't called me back. But we had texted and agreed to meet on the corner of Ridge Street, so I was sure everything was fine.

I ate my last bite of pancake and stood up. "Gotta brush my teeth," I said. When you're the daughter of a dentist, you get into that habit pretty early.

Soon I was slipping on my backpack and heading for the door. Of course, Mom grabbed me and gave me a big hug.

"I packed you a special lunch, Cupcake," she said.

Mom has called me Cupcake ever since I can remember. I kind of like it—except when she says it in front of other people.

"A special lunch? Really?" I teased her. Every lunch she makes me is a special lunch. "What a surprise."

"I love you!" Mom called. I turned and waved. For a second I thought she was going to follow me to the bus so I yelled, "I love you too!" and ran down the driveway.

Outside, it still felt like summer. *I should have worn shorts,* I thought. There's nothing worse than sitting in a hot classroom sweating a lot and having your jeans stick to your legs. Gross. But it was too late to change now.

Ridge Street was only two blocks away. There were lots of kids heading for the bus stop, but I didn't see Callie. I stood on the corner, tapping my foot.

"Come on, Callie," I muttered. If we missed the bus, Mom would insist on walking me to the bus stop every morning. I didn't know if I could take that much cheerfulness before seven thirty a.m.

Then a group of girls turned the corner: Sydney Whitman, Maggie Rodriguez, and Brenda Kovacs—and Callie was with them! I was a little confused. Callie usually didn't walk with them. It was always just Callie and me.

"Hey, Cal!" I called out.

Callie looked up at me and waved, but continued talking to Maggie.

That was strange. I noticed, though, she wasn't wearing her glasses. She's as blind as a bat without her glasses. *Maybe she doesn't recognize me,* I reasoned. *My hair did get longer this summer.*

So I ran up to them. That's when I noticed they were all dressed kind of alike—even Callie. They were wearing skinny jeans and each girl had on a different color T-shirt and a thick belt.

"Hey, guys," I said. "The bus stop's this way." I nodded toward Ridge Street.

Callie looked at me and smiled. "Hi, Katie! We were just talking about walking to school," she said.

"Isn't it kind of far to walk?" I asked.

Maggie spoke up. "Only little kids take the bus."

"Oh," I said. (I know, I sound like a genius. But I was thinking about how my mom probably wouldn't like the idea of us walking to school.)

Then Sydney looked me up and down. "Nice shirt, Katie," she said. But she said it in a way that I knew meant she definitely didn't think it was nice. "Did you make that at camp?"

Maggie and Brenda giggled.

"As a matter of fact, I did," I said.

I looked at Callie. I didn't say anything. She didn't say anything. What was going on?

"Come on," Sydney said, linking arms with Callie. "I don't want to be late."

She didn't say, "Come on, everybody but Katie," but she might as well have. I knew I wasn't invited. Callie turned around and waved. "See you later!" she called.

I stood there, frozen, as my best friend walked away from me like I was some kind of stranger.

CHAPTER 2

The Horrible Truth Hits Me

You might think I was mad at Callie. But I wasn't. Well, not really. For the most part I was really confused.

Why didn't Callie ask me to walk with them? Something had to be going on. Like, maybe her mom had told her to walk with those girls for some reason. Or maybe Callie didn't ask me to walk with them because she figured I would be the one to ask. Maybe that was it.

The sound of a bus engine interrupted my thoughts. Two blocks away, I could see a yellow school bus turning the corner. I was going to miss it!

I tore off down the sidewalk. It's a good thing I'm a fast runner because I got to the bus stop just as the last kid was getting on board. I climbed up the steps, and the bus driver gave me a nod. She was a friendly-looking woman with a round face and curly black hair.

It hit me for the first time that I would have a new bus driver now that I was going to middle school. The elementary school bus driver, Mr. Hopkins, was really nice. And I might never see him again!

But I couldn't think about that now. I had to find a place to sit. Callie and I always sat in the third seat down on the right. Two boys I didn't know were sitting in that seat. I stood there, staring at the seats, not knowing what to do.

"Please find a seat," the bus driver told me.

I walked down the aisle. Maybe there was something in the back. As I passed the sixth row, a girl nodded to the empty seat next to her. I quickly slid into it, and the bus lurched forward.

"Thanks," I said.

"No problem," replied the girl. "I'm Mia."

I don't really know a lot about fashion, but I could tell that Mia was wearing stuff that you see in magazines. She could even have been a model herself—she had long black hair that wasn't dull like mine, but shiny and bouncy. She was wearing those leggings that look like jeans, with black boots, and a short black jacket over a long gray T-shirt. I figured that Mia must be a popular girl from one of the other elementary schools.

"Are you from Richardson?" I asked her. "I used to go to Hamilton."

Mia shook her head. "I just moved here a few weeks ago. From Manhattan."

"Mia from Manhattan. That's easy to remember," I said. I started talking a mile a minute, like I do when I'm nervous or excited. "I never met anyone who lived in Manhattan before. I've only been there once. We saw *The Lion King* on Broadway. I just remember it was really crowded and really noisy. Was it noisy where you lived?"

"My neighborhood was pretty quiet," Mia replied.

I suddenly realized that my question might have been insulting.

"Not that noisy is bad," I said quickly. "I just meant—you know, the cars and buses and people and stuff . . ." I decided I wasn't making things any better.

But Mia didn't seem to mind. "You're right. It can get pretty crazy. But I like it there," she said. "I still live there, kind of. My dad does, anyway."

Were her parents divorced like mine? I wondered.

I wanted to ask her, but it seemed like a really personal question. I chose a safer subject. "So, how do you like Maple Grove?"

"It's pretty here," she answered. "It's just kind of . . . quiet."

She smiled, and I smiled back. "Yeah, things can be pretty boring around here," I said.

"By the way, I like your shirt," Mia told me. "Did you make it yourself?"

I got a sick feeling for a second—was she making fun of me, like Sydney had? But the look on her face told me she was serious.

"Thanks," I said, relieved. "I'm glad you said that because somebody earlier didn't like it at all, and what was extra weird is that my best friend was hanging around with that person."

"That sounds complicated," Mia said.

That's when the bus pulled into the big round driveway in front of Park Street Middle School. I'd seen the school a million times before, of course, since it was right off the main road. And I'd been inside once, last June, when the older kids had given us a tour. I just remember thinking how much bigger it was than my elementary school. The guide leading us kept saying it was shaped like a *U* so it was easy to get around. But it didn't seem easy to me.

14

We climbed out of the bus, which had stopped in front of the wide white steps that led up to the front door. The concrete building was the color of beach sand, and for a second I wished it was still summer and I was back on the beach.

Mia took a piece of yellow paper out of her jacket pocket. "My homeroom is in room 212," she said. "What's yours?"

I shrugged off my backpack. My schedule was somewhere inside. I zipped it open and started searching through my folders.

"I've got to find mine," I said. "Go on ahead."

"Are you sure?" Mia looked hesitant. If I hadn't been freaking out about my schedule, I might have noticed that she didn't want to go in alone. But I wasn't thinking too clearly.

"Yeah," I said. "I'll see you later!"

After what seemed forever I finally found my schedule tucked inside one of the pockets of my five-subject notebook. I looked on the line that read HOMEROOM . . . 216.

So I wouldn't be with Mia. But would I be with Callie? She and I had meant to go over our schedules to see what classes we'd have together. Now I didn't know if we had the same gym or lunch or anything.

Maybe we're in the same homeroom, I thought hopefully. I studied the little map on the bottom of the schedule and went inside. From the front door, it was pretty easy to find room 216. It looked like a social studies classroom, I guessed. There were maps of the world on the wall and a big globe in the corner. I scanned the room for Callie, but I didn't see her, although Maggie and Brenda were there, sitting next to each other. Almost all of the seats were taken; the only empty ones were in the front row, where nobody ever wants to sit. But I had no choice.

I purposely took the seat in front of Maggie— partly because I knew her from my old school, and partly because I wanted to get some info about Callie.

I set my backpack on the floor and turned around. Maggie and Brenda were drawing with gel pens on their notebooks. They were both tracing the letters "PGC" in big bubble print. When they saw me looking, they quickly flipped over their notebooks.

"Hey," I said. "Do you know if Callie is in this homeroom?"

"Why don't you ask her yourself?" Maggie asked, and Brenda burst out into giggles.

"Um, okay," I said, but I could feel my face getting red. Callie and I had never hung out with Sydney, Maggie, and Brenda at our old school, but they had always been basically nice. At least, they'd never been mean to me.

But I guess things had changed.

The bell rang, and for the first time, I felt a pang of middle school fear. Just like those kids in the movies.

It was a horrible thought, but I knew it was true.... Middle school wasn't going to be as easy as I'd hoped!

CHAPTER 3

Humiliated in Homeroom!

$\mathcal{L}$uckily, the homeroom teacher walked in before Maggie or Brenda could say anything else. Mr. Insley had dark brown hair and a beard and mustache.

"Welcome to homeroom," he said, smiling. "This room will be your first stop every morning before you head out to your classes. I can guarantee that this will be your easiest class of the day. On most days, we only have three things to do: take attendance, say the Pledge of Allegiance, and listen to announcements."

"Yeah, no homework!" a boy in the back of the room called out.

"You'll get plenty of that in your other classes," Mr. Insley said, and a bunch of kids groaned. I had to admit that it made me nervous. I had heard that there was tons more homework in middle school, but I hoped it wasn't true.

"Today is your lucky day, because you get to have homeroom with me for an extra ten minutes," Mr. Insley went on. "I'll be giving you some tips about how to get around this place."

There was a loud beeping sound over the intercom.

"Good morning, students! This is Principal LaCosta. Welcome to Park Street Middle School. Please stand for the Pledge of Allegiance."

We launched into the pledge, and after the principal made a few announcements, Mr. Insley took attendance. There were more kids from my old school than I realized, but no Callie.

As Mr. Insley started to explain about how to get around the school, I got this crazy urge to talk to Callie. I carefully reached for my cell phone in my backpack.

I know what you're thinking: *She can't use her cell phone in class!* And you're right. I knew that. But it was like some alien or something was controlling my hands.

Must . . . text . . . Callie.

I slipped the phone under the desk and flipped

it open. I glanced at Mr. Insley and then I quickly texted my best friend.

What happened this morning? R u taking the bus home or walking again?

I sent the text and looked up at Mr. Insley again. He had his back to the class, pointing to a map of the school projected on the screen. So far so good.

I felt the phone buzz in my hands and checked Callie's reply.

Let's talk after

After what? I wondered frantically. After home-room? After school? My alien hands started texting again.

Where r u now? Where is ur homeroom? Should we talk b4 class? Or I can meet u

"Miss Brown, is it?"

I looked up to see Mr. Insley standing right over me! I was so busted. I felt my face get hot.

"Um, yes," I managed to squeak out.

"I should probably remind you of the rule that there is no texting during class in this school,"

Mr. Insley said. "Normally, I'd have to confiscate your phone. But since it's the first day of school, consider this a warning."

I nodded and stuffed the phone in my backpack. I could hear kids laughing behind me.

"Bus-ted," Maggie sang in a loud whisper, then giggled.

Did you ever wish that you could blink your eyes and magically disappear? That's exactly how I felt. I'd even take a time machine—I could go back in time to the start of homeroom and leave my cell phone in my backpack. Or how about wings? I could unfurl them and fly out the window, far away from middle school.

But I was stuck with the awful reality of being humiliated in homeroom. There was nowhere to run.

Fortunately the bell rang. One good thing about being in the front row was that I could make a quick getaway. I dashed into the hallway.

Crowds of kids streamed through the halls. Callie had to be somewhere close by, right? I walked up and down, trying to find her.

Then I noticed that kids were opening their lockers and putting their backpacks inside. I had a feeling I was supposed to be doing that too. *Where*

was that schedule again? It had to be here somewhere. . . .
Found it!

I took it out and tried to find my locker on the map that was on the bottom of my schedule. I had locker number 213. Isn't thirteen supposed to be an unlucky number? But, luckily, it was just down the hallway.

The locker had a built-in lock. I spun the dial, searching for the combination numbers that were printed on my schedule.

26 . . . 14 . . . 5 . . .

The door wouldn't open the first time. The hallway was getting emptier by the second. Panic started to well up inside me.

I took a deep breath and tried again.

26 . . . 14 . . . 5 . . . Click!

The door popped open, and I shoved my backpack inside. I took out the notebook I needed for my next class, science.

I slammed the locker shut and checked the schedule again. Science was in room 234, on the left leg of the *U*. It should have been easy to find, except I wasn't sure what part of the *U* I was in.

I guess if I had been paying attention to Mr. Insley, I would have known where to go. I ran down the hall as fast as I could and turned the corner. Room 234 should have been the first door on the right.

I stepped in the doorway, breathless. I looked around for a seat.

That's when I noticed the chalkboard.

French—Bonjour!

Mademoiselle Girard

I was in the wrong room!

A girl with reddish hair in the front row saw me. "You look lost," she said.

"I am," I told her. "I'm trying to find science. Room 234."

She pointed to the doorway with her pencil. "Right across the hall," she said.

"Thanks!"

I raced across the hallway just as the bell rang.

I was going to be late for my very first class! Could this day get any worse?

CHAPTER 4

Abandoned at Lunch

Okay, so it turned out that I wasn't the only one who was late, and we weren't in any trouble. The science teacher, Ms. Biddle, waved us all in.

"Enter, enter, all you lost souls," she said.

I liked Ms. Biddle right away. She wasn't much taller than any of us students, and her blond hair was spiked on top of her head. She wore a bright blue T-shirt that said EVIL MUTANT SCIENCE TEACHER.

"Welcome to science," she announced. "I am Ms. Biddle, and this is my co-teacher, Priscilla."

She pointed to a plastic skeleton hanging from a stand in the front corner of the room. A bunch of us laughed.

"Based on the existence of Priscilla in this class-room, who can create a hypothesis about what we're going to learn this semester?" she asked.

I raised my hand. "The human body?"

"Excellent!" the teacher cheered. "What a bright bunch of students. I can tell this is going to be a great year."

My humiliating homeroom experience took a backseat in my brain. I really had fun in science class. Science has always been my favorite subject. And I had a feeling that Ms. Biddle could make any subject fun, even math.

When science ended, I resisted the urge to look for Callie in the hallway. I didn't want to be late again. My next class was social studies with Mr. Insley, back in homeroom.

I stopped at my locker and got my social studies notebook on the first try. I made it to the room before the bell rang.

"Hey, it's the cell phone girl," Mr. Insley said when he saw me, and I cringed a little. But I recovered quickly.

"Cell phone? What cell phone?" I joked, and to my relief, he gave me a smile.

Social studies went pretty smoothly too—but still no Callie.

I knew my next period was lunch, and I felt sure I would see her there. I had to. If I didn't talk with her soon, I knew I would go crazy!

I had to stop back at my locker to get my lunch. I swiftly spun the dial.

26 . . . 15 . . . 14.

Nothing happened.

"Okay," I told my locker. "We can do this the hard way or the easy way."

I tried the combination again, and it still didn't work. Frustrated, I pulled my schedule out of my notebook and checked it again.

26 . . . 14 . . . 5. I'd gotten the numbers mixed up.

"Sorry," I told my locker. "My bad."

I grabbed my lunch and raced to the cafeteria but, of course, I was one of the last people to get there.

The cafeteria was twice as big as the one in my old school. Kids sat at rectangular tables that stretched all the way to the back of the room. More kids were lined up in front of the steaming lunch counter along the wall to my right.

It didn't take me long to spot Callie in the crowd. She was sitting at a table with Sydney, Maggie, and Brenda.

Somehow I wasn't surprised. But I wasn't exactly prepared either. What was I supposed to do? Just walk up and sit with them?

Why not? I asked myself. *You and Callie have sat together at lunch every day for years. Why should today be any different?*

I took a deep breath and walked toward the table. There was an empty seat. Perfect!

"Hi," I said, moving toward the seat. But Sydney stopped me with just a few words.

"Sorry, Katie," she said. "This table is reserved for the PGC."

"What's the PGC?" I asked.

"Popular. Girls. Club," Sydney replied, saying each word slowly, to make sure I understood. "You have to be a member to sit here. And you are not."

I turned to Callie. "So, you're a member?"

"Yeah," she said. "It's no big deal, Katie, it's just—"

"Right. No big deal," I said quickly. I didn't want to hear what Callie had to say. I just needed to get away from that table. I felt like I couldn't breathe.

"Hey, Katie!" I heard Callie call behind me. "I'll call you later!"

I walked away and tried to find another seat. I could feel tears forming in my eyes. I could *not* cry in the middle of the cafeteria on my first day of school. I just couldn't.

I saw some kids from Hamilton at other tables, but I walked right past them. I headed for an empty

27

table in the back of the room and sat down.

What had just happened? Callie had joined a club, and I wasn't invited. Fine. But couldn't she at least have warned me before today?

I opened my lunch bag. I didn't feel much like eating, but Mom would be disappointed if I didn't at least try the special lunch she made for me.

Mom had packed carrot sticks with ranch dip (my favorite) and a tuna fish sandwich, plus my aluminum water bottle filled with apple juice. Besides all that, there was a pink plastic cupcake holder, the kind that's shaped exactly like a cupcake. Mom had written on it with a glitter marker, "A cupcake for my Cupcake." Corny, yes, but I knew the cupcake inside would be delicious.

Suddenly I realized I was hungry after all. I unwrapped the sandwich and took a bite.

"Is anyone sitting here?"

I looked up to see Mia, the girl from the bus.

"No, unless they're invisible," I replied. Mia smiled and sat in the chair across from me.

"How's everything going so far?" Mia asked me. She was opening up her lunch bag and taking out a container of what looked like vegetable sushi rolls.

"Let's see," I began. "I got in trouble in homeroom for using my cell phone. My locker hates me.

I keep getting lost. And, oh yeah, my best friend would rather hang out with a bunch of mean girls than me."

Mia raised an eyebrow. "Really?"

"It's all true," I said solemnly. "How about you?"

Mia shrugged. "It's okay . . . just, different. Hey, did you have science yet? Isn't Ms. Biddle awesome?"

I nodded. "I know! I love her T-shirt."

As we were talking, two girls approached our table, carrying trays of food. I recognized one of them as the girl with the reddish hair who helped me find the science room.

"Hi," I said. "Do you want to sit down? There's plenty of room."

"Thanks," said the girl I recognized.

"I'm Mia," Mia said.

"And I'm Katie," I added.

"Hi. I'm Alexis," she replied. "And this is Emma."

"Hi," Emma said shyly.

Alexis's reddish hair was neatly pulled back in a white headband that matched her white button-down shirt. She wore a short denim skirt and ballet flats. I noticed everything matched.

Emma had big blue eyes and straight blond hair. She was really pretty. She had on a sleeveless pink

29

dress with small white flowers on it and white sneakers.

"Did you guys go to Richardson?" I guessed.

Alexis nodded. "Right. Did you go to Hamilton?"

"I did," I replied. "But Mia's from Manhattan."

"Ooh, I always wanted to go there," Emma said. "I heard there's a museum with a giant whale that hangs from the ceiling, and you can walk right underneath it. Have you ever been there?"

Mia nodded. "It's so cool. It's amazing to imagine that something that big lives on the planet, you know?" she said. "You should go sometime. Manhattan's not that far from here."

"Maybe someday," Emma said wistfully.

"So has anyone had that math teacher yet, Mrs. Moore?" Mia asked. She shuddered. "Scary."

"Uh-oh," I said. "I have her next period."

"Me too. But I heard she's not so bad," Alexis told us. "My sister Dylan told me she's strict, but if you just do what she says, you'll be all right."

I finished my sandwich and dug into my carrot sticks. Mia, Alexis, and Emma were really nice, but I couldn't stop thinking about Callie. I glanced over at the PGC table. Callie was laughing at something Sydney was saying. Were they laughing about me?

I didn't realize it at first, but I was accidentally

ignoring the girls at the table, so I quickly tuned back in.

"Earth to Katie," Alexis said. "I was asking you if you had social studies yet."

"Oh, sorry," I said.

"Her best friend dumped her to hang out with some mean girls," Mia explained.

"Really?" Alexis asked. "Which ones?"

I pointed to Sydney's table.

"Oh, I know those girls from camp," she said, shaking her head. "You're right. They are mean. Especially that Sydney."

"I don't know what Callie's doing with them," I said with a sigh.

"Callie?" Alexis said. "I know her from camp too. She always seemed nice."

I reached into my lunch bag and took out my cupcake holder. For a second I forgot about the corny message my mom had decorated it with. I tried to turn it around so the other girls wouldn't see it, but it was too late.

"Aw, that's cute," Mia said.

"Thanks," I replied, relieved. I opened the cupcake holder and took out the sweet treasure inside.

"Wow, your mom packed you a cupcake?" Emma asked. "Lucky!"

The icing was a light brown color. I sniffed it.

"Peanut butter," I said out loud. "With cinna-mon."

"What's inside?" Emma asked.

I took a bite, and a yummy glob of grape jelly squirted into my mouth.

"Jelly," I reported. "It's a P-B-and-J cupcake."

I took another bite, making sure to get the icing and the jelly in the bite at the same time. Like all of mom's cupcakes, it was superdelicious.

At least some things never change, I thought.

I realized that all of the girls were eyeing me a little bit enviously. I couldn't blame them. I mean, who doesn't like cupcakes?

"I've never heard of a peanut-butter-and-jelly cupcake before," Emma said.

"There's a cupcake shop in my dad's neighbor-hood that has fifty-seven flavors," Mia told us. "I bet they have P-B-and-J."

I thought about offering them a bite, but I already had my germs all over it, and the jelly was getting kind of messy.

"The next time my mom makes cupcakes, I'll bring some for all of us," I promised.

"Cool," Mia said.

"Thanks," said Alexis and Emma at the same time.

The lunch bell rang. It was time for my next class.

I stuffed my empty cupcake holder into my bag. My first day of middle school wasn't even half over, but I had a feeling that the only good part of it had just ended.

CHAPTER 5

The Cupcake Cure

So here's what happened the rest of the day:

- Forgot my locker combination after lunch.
- Was late to math class. Mrs. Moore gave me a sheet of math problems to do as punishment. Mia was right! She *is* scary.
- No gym until next week, so I hung out with Emma, who's in my gym class. (Okay, something went right.)
- Had English with Mia, Alexis, and Emma. Good. But left my summer reading report in my locker. Bad!
- Had art as my special class for seventh period. Found out that there's cooking, but I can't take that until January. Rats!

• Spanish is my last class of the day. Then it's *adios*!

• No Callie in *any* of my classes.

When the last bell rang, I stuffed all of my books into my backpack and went outside to look for Joanne's car.

Joanne works in my mom's office. When I was in elementary school, I went to an after-school program until Mom got off of work. But there's no after-school program for middle school. Mom doesn't think I'm old enough to go home by myself. So her plan was for me to hang out at the office every day. Doesn't that sound like fun?

Anyway, she told me Joanne had a small red car, so I started looking around for it. Then I heard Sydney's voice behind me.

"Looking for your former friend?"

I turned and saw Sydney, with Maggie and Brenda laughing behind her. At least Callie wasn't with them. I turned around without answering.

Then I heard a beep. Joanne was waving out of a car window down by the parking lot. I ran to meet her.

"Hey, Katie. How was your first day of middle school? Was it awesome?" Joanne asked.

"Sure," I said, sliding into the front seat.

35

I like Joanne a lot. She's really tall and has lots of blond hair that she piles on top of her head. She always talks to me like I'm a person, not a little kid. Not all adults know how to do that.

"Hmm. You don't sound so sure," Joanne said.

"It was fine," I told her.

I really didn't feel like talking about it. Not just now, anyway. Sydney had put me in a really bad mood.

Joanne seemed to understand.

"Cool," she said. "Your mom's been talking about you all day. She can't wait to see you."

When we got to the office, my mom was busy with a patient. Joanne set me up in my mom's personal office, where she has a desk and a phone and all of her books about dentist stuff.

"Gotta go," Joanne said. "Yell if you need me. But not too loud. Don't want to scare the patients."

"Thanks!" I told her.

Then I took out my cell phone and called Callie. The phone rang three times before she picked up.

"Hello?"

"Cal, it's Katie. Can you talk?" I asked.

"Of course," Callie answered, and for a second I wondered if the whole day had been some kind of weird dream. Callie sounded like she always did.

"Why didn't you tell me we weren't taking the bus together?" I blurted out.

"Listen, Katie, I'm sorry," Callie said, and she sounded like she meant it. "I became good friends with Sydney, Maggie, and Bella at camp. And they asked me to join their club. I wanted to tell you, but we never got together."

"Okay, but—wait, Bella? I thought her name was Brenda?" I asked.

"It was, but she changed it to Bella," Callie explained.

"Oh," I said. I'd never known anyone who actually changed his or her name before. But that wasn't important right now. "You could have called me. Or texted me," I said.

"I know, I know, but I was really busy when I got back. Honest," Callie said. "Please don't be upset."

"Are we still friends?" I asked. There was a lump in my throat when I said the word.

"Of course!" Callie assured me. "You're my best friend."

"But you won't walk to school with me or have lunch with me," I pointed out. I knew I sounded like a baby, and I really was about to cry. I was just so confused.

"It's not like that," Callie protested. "Katie, we're

in middle school now. Middle school is bigger than just the two of us. We're going to make lots of new friends. Both of us."

I thought briefly about Mia, Alexis, and Emma. Callie had a point—but I was too angry and hurt to admit it.

"Sure—right," I said lamely.

"And I'll see you this weekend," Callie said. "For the annual Labor Day barbecue."

"Okay," I said with a sigh.

"Hey, did you notice I got contact lenses?" Callie asked. "No more glasses for me!" So that explained why she wasn't wearing glasses today.

"Well, I already have homework to do. Plus I need to figure out what I'm going to wear tomorrow!" Callie said, and then we hung up.

I felt better after the call—not much, but just a little. I was glad Callie was still my friend. But the whole thing was weird. Callie was basically saying, "I'm sorry, but I'm still going to ignore you at lunch tomorrow."

I've heard "I'm sorry—but . . ." a lot in my life. Mostly from my dad. As in, "I'm sorry, Katie, but I can't come visit you this summer. . . ."

It doesn't feel good.

I took out my math assignment—my only homework assignment for tonight—and started working on the problems. Just as I was finishing, Mom opened the door.

"There you are!" she said, crushing me in a hug. She smelled like mint toothpaste. "I'll be ready to go in just a few minutes, okay?"

As you can probably guess, Mom was full of questions on the car ride home.

"Are your teachers nice?"

"Did you get any homework?"

"Did you find the bus stop okay?"

"Did you like your cupcake?"

"Is Callie in any of your classes?"

That one was the hardest to answer. I couldn't bring myself to tell Mom everything that had happened with Callie. How could I, when *I* wasn't even sure what was happening?

"We only have lunch together," I replied.

"Oh, that's too bad!" Mom said with a frown. "At least you get to sit together."

I just nodded and looked out the window.

"You must be tired," Mom said. "You've had a big day today. Try to relax when we get home. I'll call you when it's time to set the table."

Because it was the first day of school, Mom made my favorite food for dinner: Chinese-style chicken and broccoli with rice. (Yes, I'm a weirdo who likes broccoli.) It smelled so good!

"Would you like to do anything after dinner?" Mom asked. "It's nice out. We could walk over to Callie's."

Not a good idea! But I didn't tell Mom that.

"I was thinking," I said. "Can we make some pineapple upside-down cupcakes?"

Mom got a knowing look on her face. "Ah. So you need a cupcake cure?"

Once, when I was seven, I fell off of my bike and messed up my knee really bad. Mom made me pineapple upside-down cupcakes and gave them to me with a note: "Turn your frown upside down." Hey, I've been telling you she's corny. Since then, we make pineapple upside-down cupcakes together whenever one of us is feeling sad. We call it the "cupcake cure." It's hard to not feel better when you eat a cupcake.

I nodded. As we took out the ingredients and started measuring, I started talking—not about Callie, but about everything else. My evil locker. Being late for class all the time. Scary Mrs. Moore.

Mom listened while I talked. When I was done, she had a bunch of suggestions for how to make things better. Mom lives to solve all of my problems. Unfortunately, I didn't tell her about my biggest problem.

Pineapple upside-down cupcakes are not that hard to make. The trick is that you don't use cupcake liners. You spray the cupcake tins with that nonstick stuff. Then you fill the bottom of each cup with a mix of canned pineapple and some spices. You pour the batter on top and then you bake them.

When the cupcakes are done, you take them out of the pan and turn them upside down. Each cupcake has a beautiful golden pineapple on the top. To make them extra nice you can add a candied cherry on top like we do.

Mom and I each ate one with a glass of milk. They were still warm. So yummy!

As Mom packed one for me in my cupcake holder, I remembered what I'd told the girls at lunch.

"Can I bring in three more?" I asked. "For the girls at my lunch table."

"Of course," Mom said. "I have a small box we can use."

I found myself looking forward to tomorrow's lunch—even without Callie.

CHAPTER 6

The Perfect Plan . . . Almost

By lunchtime the next day, I was sure of one thing.

My locker is an evil robot in disguise, sent here to Earth to prevent me from finishing middle school. Or maybe it's from the future; I'm not sure.

But I'm sure its mission is to ruin my middle school career. Maybe one day I'll become president of the United States and save the Earth from the alien or robot invasion. But if I never finish middle school, I can't become president, and the robots will rule forever.

My mom had written my combination on an orange rubber band for me to wear around my wrist so I wouldn't forget. But even with the right combination the locker wouldn't open on the first try, or even the second try! How could that be?

I was late for science again, but Ms. Biddle didn't care. I knew that Mrs. Moore was another story, though. So I devised a plan: I would take my math book with me to lunch. Then I would walk to class with Alexis, who seemed to know her way around. That way, I'd be on time.

When I finally got my locker open before lunch, I spotted the white box of cupcakes on my top shelf. I couldn't forget those! I carefully picked them up by the string, eager to show them off to the girls.

I was a little nervous, of course. What if they all decided to sit somewhere else? But when I got to the table in the back of the room, Mia was already there.

Mia's eyes got big when she saw the white box.

"Ooh, are those cupcakes?" she asked.

"My mom and I ended up making some last night," I explained.

"That's really nice of you," Mia said.

Alexis and Emma came over and dropped their books on the table.

"We've got to get in line before it gets too long," Alexis said.

"Hurry back," Mia said. "Katie brought cupcakes."

43

Emma flashed me a grateful smile as she and Alexis headed off to the lunch line.

Soon we were all eating lunch together. Mom had packed me some leftover chicken and broccoli, which tastes even better cold.

"I can't believe it's Friday already!" Alexis said. "It's weird, starting school and then having three days off."

"I think they're trying to ease us into it—you know, like how you stick only your foot in a pool when it's really cold, and then slowly put the rest of your body in," I guessed.

"I always jump right in," Emma said. "Cold or not."

Mia shuddered. "You're brave!"

"I think we're going to the beach this weekend," Alexis said. "Last swim of the summer."

"I'm going to the city this weekend, to see my dad," Mia chimed in.

"Are your parents divorced?" Alexis asked, like it was no big deal.

Mia nodded. "Four years ago."

I didn't say anything about my own parents being divorced. To be honest, I was a little jealous that Mia was going to see her dad. I hadn't seen mine in years.

"We're going to my grandma's house for a picnic," Emma spoke up.

"We're going to a barbecue," I said. "Over at . . . Callie's."

I glanced over at the PGC table.

"Isn't that the friend who dumped you?" Alexis asked.

"She didn't dump me," I protested. "We're still friends. Best friends."

"Emma is my best friend," Alexis said. "If she sat at a table with other girls, I'd sit next to her."

"But I wouldn't sit at a table with other girls," Emma said, and then she gave me an apologetic look, like she was worried she'd hurt my feelings.

"Exactly," said Alexis. They both looked at me.

"Look, it's kind of complicated," I said. "They formed this club. The Popular Girls Club. And you can't sit at the table unless you're a member. It's a rule."

"Are you serious? They actually named themselves the Popular Girls Club?" Alexis asked. "If you're popular, do you really have to advertise it like that? Plus, what did everyone do—take a vote or something?"

Mia had an amused smile on her face. "It does seem a little desperate," she admitted. "But I have all of those girls in a lot of my classes. They seem nice."

"Callie is nice," I said. "Really. I'm just not so sure about the others."

There was a weird silence.

"So, Katie." Mia nodded to the white box. "When do we get to try those cupcakes?"

"Right now," I answered. I slipped off the string and opened up the top of the box. The cupcakes looked perfect.

"They're so pretty!" Emma cooed.

"What is that golden stuff?" Alexis asked.

"It's pineapple," I explained. "These are like pineapple upside-down cake, except they're cup-cakes."

Mia shook her head. "Where do you get all these amazing cupcake ideas?"

"It's my mom, mostly," I admitted. "She's cup-cake crazy."

Mia laughed. "My mom is shopping crazy."

"You're lucky," said Alexis. "My mom is cleaning crazy."

Emma shrugged. "My mom says me and my brothers make *her* crazy."

"She has three brothers," Alexis told us. "They're all monsters. Emma is the only normal one."

Emma blushed.

"Less talking, more cupcakes," I joked, and each of us picked one up.

It was quiet for a second as we took a bite of golden goodness.

"These are absolutely delicious," Mia said.

Alexis nodded. "The pineapple is supergood."

"I love the cherry on top," Emma said.

I was happy that everyone liked them.

"I'll bring in cupcakes every day if I can," I offered.

"That might be cupcake overload," Alexis pointed out. "Even for your cupcake crazy mother. How about one day a week? Like every Friday?"

"Cupcake Friday," I said. "I like it."

I liked it for a bunch of reasons. Making cupcakes is fun. But it also meant my new friends wanted to sit with me—for at least another week.

The bell rang, and I turned to Alexis. "Can I follow you to math? I don't want to be late."

"Of course!" Alexis replied.

We got to math in plenty of time. Mrs. Moore was already there.

"How nice to see you on time, Miss Brown," Mrs. Moore told me.

I felt fantastic. My plan had worked.

When the bell rang, Mrs. Moore asked us all to

take out our math books. I looked down at my desk. I had my notebook with me, but not my math book! Had I left it at lunch?

Then I remembered. I had grabbed the cupcake box instead of my math book! It was still in my locker.

With a sigh, I raised my hand. "Excuse me, Mrs. Moore . . ."

She gave me *two* worksheets that night!

CHAPTER 7

Just Like Old Times . . . Almost

The morning of Labor Day I woke up with a huge knot in my stomach. I didn't know what it would be like with Callie at the barbecue. And this year I wanted everything to be especially perfect.

Unfortunately, my need for perfection made me argue with my mom about what kind of decorations to put on the cupcakes we were bringing. The night before, we made vanilla cupcakes with vanilla icing, which are Callie's dad's favorite. That's a pretty boring cupcake, so we always add some decoration on the top. Sometimes it's candy. But lately, Mom's been into using this stuff called fondant. It's like a kind of dough, but it's mostly made out of sugar. You can color it, roll it out, and cut shapes out of it just like cookie dough. But you don't have to cook it. Then you can put the shapes on top of your cupcakes and they look amazing. It's a little hard to make, but as I said, Mom is like Martha Stewart. She could make a house out of fondant if she had to.

Mom and I were looking through the tin of mini cookie cutters for shapes to use. I wanted to use a sun and color the fondant yellow. Mom wanted to use a leaf shape and color the fondant orange.

"But it's still summer," I whined. "It's, like, a hundred degrees out there."

"Eighty-five," Mom corrected me. "And summer is over. School's started."

"But the first day of autumn isn't until September twenty-third," I said. "That's a fact. A scientific fact."

"Technically," Mom agreed. "But as soon as I see school buses driving around, I think of fall."

I frowned. I didn't want summer to end just yet. Mom looked at me. She knew something was wrong and I didn't want to tell her what it was. I sighed and gave in.

"How about half suns and half leaves?" I suggested.

Mom smiled. "Perfect! The orange and yellow will look nice together."

By noon we were pulling into the driveway of

Callie's house. It's easy to find because it's the only house on the block painted light blue. From the sidewalk you can tell which room is Callie's—it's the window on the second floor on the left with the unicorn decal on it. I have one just like it on my bedroom window.

We walked through the white wood gate and headed right for the backyard. Callie's dad was standing by the grill on the deck.

"Hey, Katie-did!" he called out. He wiggled his eyebrows when he saw the cupcake holder in my arms. "I hope that is filled with lots of vanilla cupcakes!"

"Of course!" I replied. "With vanilla icing."

Mr. Wilson gave me and my mom a hug. He's got kind of a big belly, so his hugs are always squishy.

"It's Barbara's fault. All that good cooking," he'll say, patting his stomach, and everybody always laughs.

I've known Mr. Wilson—and Callie's whole family—since even before I was born. My mom and Callie's mom met in a cooking class while they were pregnant. In a way, the Wilsons are like my second family. Mrs. Wilson is like my second mom. Callie's like a sister. And Mr. Wilson's like a dad. And since I never see my dad, he's the closest thing to one that I've got.

Then it hit me as I was standing there on the deck. If Callie and I stopped being friends, what would happen to my whole second family?

I didn't have much time to think about it because Callie and her mom came out onto the deck. Callie's mom and my mom gave each other a big hug. Callie and I nodded to each other. Things definitely felt a little weird between us.

"Where's Jenna today?" Mom asked. Jenna is Callie's older sister. She's a junior in high school. Callie has an older brother, too, named Stephen. He just started college this year.

"She's with her *friends*," Mrs. Wilson said, rolling her eyes. "When you're sixteen, a family barbecue is apparently a horrible punishment."

Mom looked at me and Callie. "Well, we've got a few more years left with these two, don't we?"

I hate when parents talk like that. Like when we're teenagers we're going to turn into hideous mutants or something. It kind of made me nervous, in a way. What if they were right?

"So how do you like middle school, Katie?" Callie's mom asked me.

I shrugged. "It's only been two days. It's kind of hard to tell."

"I'm so glad the girls are on the same bus route,"

my mom said. "Middle school can be pretty scary. It's nice that they have each other to navigate through it."

Mrs. Wilson looked confused. "Callie told me she's been walking to school. Aren't you two walking together?"

Callie looked down at her flip-flops.

"It's no big deal," I said quickly. "I like to take the bus. Callie likes to walk."

I just didn't want to get into a whole big discussion about it. Not in front of our mothers, anyway. I saw Mom biting her bottom lip. She looked at Callie's mom and raised her eyebrows.

"Callie, why didn't you mention this?" her mom asked.

Before Callie could answer, Mr. Wilson stepped into our circle.

"Hey, it's going to be about a half hour before the food is ready," he said. "I inflated the volleyball this morning. How about a game of moms against kids?"

That sounded good to me. I'm terrible at volleyball, but I still think it's fun. Besides, anything would be better than standing around talking about why Callie and I weren't taking the bus together.

"Kids serve first!" I yelled, and I ran into the yard

and grabbed the ball. I tossed it to Callie. "You'd better start. You know I usually can't get it over the net."

Callie laughed, and we launched into the game. Let me explain what happens when I play volleyball: I will chase after any ball that comes over the net. I will hit it with everything I've got. The problem is I have no idea how to aim it. Sometimes the ball goes way off to the side. Sometimes it goes behind me, over my head. If I'm lucky, it'll go right over the net. But that doesn't happen a lot.

Pretty soon Callie and I were cracking up laughing. We kept bumping into each other, and once we both tumbled onto the grass. It was really hilarious. And the funniest thing is that even though I am terrible at the game, we still beat the moms!

"That's game! Katie and Callie win!" Mr. Wilson called up from the deck.

"Woo-hoo!" Callie and I cried, high-fiving each other.

"And that's perfect timing," Callie's dad added. "Lunch is ready!"

Mr. Wilson might blame Callie's mom for his big stomach, but he is a great cook too. After I drank two big glasses of lemonade (volleyball makes me thirsty) I dug in to the food on the table. There were hamburgers, hot dogs, potato salad, juicy tomatoes from the garden, and of course, corn on the cob. I put a piece of corn on my plate before anything else.

"Katie, remember the time you ate six pieces of corn on the cob?" Callie asked, giggling.

"I was only six!" I cried.

"I can't believe we weren't paying attention," my mom said, shaking her head. "Six pieces. Can you imagine that?"

"And I didn't even get a stomachache," I said proudly.

"I love corn on the cob, but I could never eat six pieces," Callie added.

The rest of lunch was like that. We told funny stories, and we laughed a lot. It was just like last year's Labor Day barbecue. Like nothing at all had changed.

"Want to go to my room?" Callie asked when we were done.

"Sure," I said.

"I might eat all the cupcakes while you're gone!" Mr. Wilson warned.

I hadn't been in Callie's room in more than a month. Some things were the same, like the unicorn decal and her purple walls and carpet. And the picture of me and Callie from when we went to an amusement park and had our faces painted like tigers. Callie with her blond hair and blue eyes, me with my brown hair and brown eyes. Totally different—but the tiger paint made us look like sisters.

Other stuff was new. Like now she had lots of posters on her walls—lots of posters of boys. Most of them were from those vampire movies.

When did she start liking those? I wondered.

"You've got to see my pictures from camp," Callie said. "I have so much to tell you."

"I know," I said. "This is, like, the first time we've been together."

Callie held up her cell phone so I could see it and started scrolling through the photos. As they whizzed by, I saw lots of pictures of her and Sydney and the others. She stopped at a photo of a boy on a diving board.

"That's Matt," she said. "Isn't he cute? He was a lifeguard at camp."

I squinted at the photo. Matt had short brown hair and he was wearing a red bathing suit. He looked like a regular boy to me. But he didn't have tentacles or antennae or a tail or anything, so I guessed that was a good sign.

"He's in eighth grade," Callie said. "I pass him in the hallway every day between fifth and sixth period. The other day he actually said, 'Hi, Callie.' Isn't that amazing?"

Wow, he can put two words together, I thought. But out loud I said, "Yeah, amazing."

Callie's cell phone made a sound like fairy bells. The photo faded and a text message popped up on the screen.

"No way!" she cried. "*Teen Style* magazine has posted the best and worst fashion from the music awards last night. You have got to check this out!"

It was easy to guess who the text message was from—Sydney. It had to be.

Callie grabbed her laptop and started typing away. A page popped up on the screen.

"That's hilarious," she said. "They divided the page into 'Killer Looks' and 'Looks That Should Be Killed.' Ha!"

I briefly wondered what kind of weapon would be used to kill an ugly dress. Maybe some robo-scissors?

"Oh my gosh, that is *awful*!" Callie squealed. She grabbed her cell phone and started texting.

Any fuzzy feelings I'd had before were evaporating. Callie was supposed to be hanging out with me today. It was like I wasn't even in the room.

"Hey, Callie," I said.

"Yeah?" She looked up from her phone.

"I know we're still friends," I said. "But the other day you said we were still best friends. I'm just wondering about that. I mean . . . *best* friends sit together at lunch. They talk to each other during school."

"I know," Callie said. "But it's complicated. I still wish we could be best friends, but . . ." She sighed and looked away.

That's the moment I knew there was no going back. Callie had changed over the summer.

"But what?" I asked.

"You're still my friend, Katie. You'll always be my friend."

"Just not best friends," I said quietly.

Callie didn't answer, but she didn't have to.

"I don't under—"

Then I heard my mom's voice in the doorway. "Girls, it's cupcake time."

Mom had a kind of sad look on her face. I wondered how long she'd been standing there.

I figured Mom would be full of questions on the ride home. But for once, she wasn't. I stared out the window, thinking.

Tomorrow I'd start my first full week of school. There would be no more barbecues. No more swimming. Just day after day of middle school.

Maybe Mom was right. It wasn't September twenty-third yet, but summer was officially over.

CHAPTER 8

Just Call Me "Silly Arms"

Tuesday wasn't just the start of my first real week of school. It was also the first day of gym.

I knew gym was going to be different from how it was in elementary school. For one thing, we have to wear a gym uniform: blue shorts and a blue T-shirt that says PARK STREET MIDDLE SCHOOL in yellow writing on it. I wasn't too worried about the changing-into-the-uniform thing. I just put my favorite unicorn underwear in a different drawer so I won't accidentally wear it during the week. Nobody needs to know about my unicorn underwear.

I also knew that the gym would be bigger, and the teachers would be different. But what I didn't count on was that the kids in gym would be different too. I'm not just talking about the kids from other schools. Kids I've known all my life had completely changed. Like Eddie Rossi, for example. Somehow he grew a mustache over the summer. An actual mustache! And Ken Watanabe—he must have grown a whole foot taller.

The boys were all rowdier, too. Before class started they were running around, wrestling, and slamming into one another like they were Ultimate Fighting Champs or something. I moved closer to Emma for safety.

"They're gonna hurt somebody," I said, worried.

Emma shrugged. I guess having three brothers, she's used to it.

Our gym teacher's name is Kelly Chen. She looks like someone you'd see in a commercial for a sports drink. Her shiny black hair is always in a perfect ponytail, and she wears a neat blue sweat suit with yellow stripes down the sides.

She blew a whistle to start the class.

"Line up in rows for me, people!" she called out. "We don't do anything in this class without warming up."

We did a bunch of stretches and things to get started. That was easy enough. Then Ms. Chen divided us into four teams to play volleyball.

You can probably see what's coming. I didn't—not right away. We always played volleyball in elementary school. Everybody had fun, and most kids were pretty terrible at it, just like me. So I wasn't too worried.

My first warning should have been when I got my team assignment. Ms. Chen put me on a team with Sydney and Maggie! Ken Watanabe was on our team too, along with two boys I didn't know named Wes and Aziz.

On the other team were a bunch of kids I didn't know and George Martinez from my old school. Emma was on a team playing on the other side of the gym, so George was the only friendly face in sight.

"All right, take your places!" Ms. Chen called out.

Everyone scrambled to get in line. For some reason, I was in place to serve the first ball. Ken tossed it to me.

My hands were starting to sweat a little.

"What are you waiting for?" Sydney called out.

I took a deep breath and punched the ball with my right hand.

It soared up . . . up . . . and wildly to the right, slamming into the bleachers. It bounced off and then bounced into the basketball pole, ricocheting like a pinball in a machine. Then it rolled to Ms. Chen's feet. She tossed it to the other team.

"Nice serve," Sydney said snidely, and Maggie giggled next to her.

My face flushed red. The only good thing about messing up the serve was that I got to move out of serving position. I wouldn't have to serve again for a while.

I was safe while I was in the back row. Ken was in front, and he was so tall that no ball could get past him. The other kids were all hitting the ball pretty well too. It was like everyone had suddenly become volleyball experts over the summer. Why hadn't I acquired this amazing skill?

But then it was time for us to switch positions, and I was in front of the net. My hands started to sweat again.

Sydney served the ball, and George volleyed it back. It was one of those balls that kisses the top of the net and then slowly drops over, like a gift. It should have been easy to hit.

Not for me. I swung my arm underhand to get to it, and the ball went flying behind me. Aziz tried to get it but it bounced out of bounds.

George was grinning. "Katie, you look like that

sprinkler in my backyard, you know, Silly Arms? The one with all those arms and they wave around and sprinkle water everywhere?"

George started spinning around and waving his arms in a weird, wiggly way. Everyone started laughing.

I was laughing too. George and I have been teasing each other since kindergarten. I knew he wasn't trying to hurt my feelings.

But then Sydney and Maggie had to take the fun out of it.

"Do you guys want Silly Arms on your team? We'll trade you," Sydney called out.

"Yeah, we'll never win with this one on our team," Maggie added.

I couldn't wait for gym to be over. For the rest of the game, George wiggled his arms like the Silly Arms sprinkler every time the ball came to him. If I wasn't so mad at Sydney and Maggie, I would have thought it was funny. Instead, I was miserable. As soon as I got back to the locker room I changed fast and ran out.

I had English class next. It's the one class I have with Mia, Emma, and Alexis. George Martinez is in that class too. He walked past me on the way to his seat.

"Hey, Silly Arms," he said with a grin.

"What's that about?" Mia asked.

"Gym class," I said with a sigh. "We were playing volleyball, and George said my arms look like the Silly Arms sprinkler."

"That's so mean!" Mia said.

"But it's true," I told her. "I think I hate gym now."

"Tell me about it." Mia rolled her eyes. "Gym was so much better in my old school. We got to bring in our iPods and dance to the music we brought in."

I noticed that Mia was wearing another model-worthy outfit: a belted gray sweater vest over a blue-and-black striped T-shirt dress, tights, and short black boots with heels. That gave me an idea.

"Hey, do you know anything about the *Teen Style* website?" I asked her.

Mia's eyes lit up. "Of course! They are the best with all the new fashion trends. Why?"

"Just wondering," I said. Honestly, though, I was thinking that if I knew more about it, maybe Callie and I would have something to talk about some-time.

"I know," Mia said. "Why don't you take the bus home with me today? We can check out the web-site at my house."

The bell rang. "I'll text my mom and let you know," I whispered as Mrs. Castillo took her place in front of the room to begin today's class.

I know what you're thinking, but I did *not* text my mom in class. I had learned my lesson in homeroom. I waited until the bell rang and texted her before my next class.

Can I go to my friend Mia's after school?

The answer came back quickly. My mom may be an adult, but she is a superfast texter.

Not until I talk to Mia's parents. And what are you doing texting during school? I will take your cell phone privileges away next time.

See? Even when I try to do the right thing, I get in trouble.

I knew there was no point in replying, or I'd lose my phone. Mom is pretty strict that way.

It's not fair. I fumed as I stomped down the hall. I lost my best friend. How was I supposed to make new ones if my mom wouldn't let me?

CHAPTER 9

Teen Style and Two Tiny Dogs

I was embarrassed to tell Mia that I couldn't go until our mothers met, but she was cool about it. She quickly took my phone from me.

"Hey, why fight it?" She laughed. "My mom is the same way. I'll enter my number in your address book," she said. "Your mom can call me tonight, and I'll put my mom on the phone. Maybe we can do it tomorrow. Don't stress it."

I really admire the way Mia handles things. She's pretty cool about everything. *And* she's down to earth, too. She's totally not snobby or anything. I realized how much I liked Mia. I was starting to feel really glad that her mom had moved to our town.

So that night, I decided to play it cool, like Mia would. I gave Mia's number to Mom and told her I wanted to go the next day after school. I didn't give her a hard time about not letting me go. I couldn't resist arguing about the cell phone, though.

"You know, texting between classes doesn't count," I said.

"It's still in school," Mom countered. "And your cell phone is for emergencies *only* while you're in school, whether you're between classes or not."

It's very hard to win an argument with Mom.

But the good news is that she talked to Mia's mom, Ms. Vélaz, and they both said it was okay for me to take the bus to Mia's house after school. My mom agreed to pick me up on her way home from work. She was laughing on the phone with Mia's mom, so I figured she liked her. That was a good sign.

I was pretty excited to go to Mia's house the next day. Even gym couldn't bring me down. Ms. Chen mixed up our teams, so I didn't get stuck with Sydney and Maggie again. Even better. But I did get stuck with George, who kept calling me Silly Arms even though I was on *his* team this time. Go figure.

Mia's house was one of the last houses on the bus stop route. That's because it's in the part of town where the houses are really big and far apart. The bus stopped in front of a white house with a perfect green lawn in front. The lawn at our house is usually filled with dandelions, but Mom and I think they're pretty so we let them grow.

Mia let us in through the front door, and the first thing I noticed was the noise. Loud heavy-metal music was blasting through the whole house. Two tiny white dogs were barking on top of it. They ran up to Mia and me and started sniffing my sneakers.

"That's Milkshake and Tiki," Mia told me. "If you don't like dogs, I can put them in their crate."

"No, I love dogs!" I said. "I want one so bad, but Mom's allergic. Can I pet them?"

"Sure," she replied. I reached down to touch them, but the skittish dogs wouldn't stand still. I could barely feel the fur under my fingers.

"Follow me," Mia instructed. We went down a hallway and through one of the doors there.

A woman with black hair like Mia's and headphones on was sitting at a desk, typing on a computer.

"Mom, can you please tell Dan to turn down the music?!" Mia yelled.

But Ms. Vélaz didn't see or hear us. Mia walked over and took the headphones off her mother's ears. Ms. Vélaz smiled.

"Oh hello, Mia." She nodded to me. "And this must be Katie."

"Nice to meet you," I said.

"Mom, can you *please* tell Dan to turn down the music?" Mia pleaded.

"Would you mind asking him yourself?" her mom asked. "I'm IM'ing a potential client, and I can't leave the computer right now."

Mia sighed. "All right. But I bet he won't do it."

"Please get a snack for Katie too!" Ms. Vélaz called out to us.

We left the office, and Mia grabbed a bag of cookies before we headed up the gleaming wood staircase. Mia told me her story as best as she could over the loud music.

"Mom used to work at a fashion magazine in New York, but then she met Eddie, who already had a house out here," she explained. "So now she works out of the house. She's starting her own consulting business."

We stopped in front of a door on the second floor.

"This is Dan's room," Mia shouted. "He'll be my stepbrother when Mom and Eddie get married in a few months."

Mia pounded on the door. It slowly opened, and

a teenage boy with dark hair hanging over his eyes stood behind it.

"Too loud?" he asked.

"What do you think?" Mia shouted back.

Dan closed the door and a few seconds later the music was much quieter. Mia shook her head as we walked to her room.

"He's a junior in high school," she said. "Two more years and he's out of here. I hope."

I wondered if he knew Callie's sister, Jenna. Callie was always popping up in my head.

We stepped into Mia's room. I was kind of expecting it to be as neat and stylish as Mia. The rest of her house looked like something from a magazine. But her room was a little messy, which was fine, just kind of a surprise.

"My old room in Manhattan was *so* much nicer," she said, pointing to the wallpaper. "Can you believe those flowers? I think some old lady must have lived in here before. Eddie keeps promising that we'll paint it, but he and Mom are always so busy."

I forgot who Eddie was for a minute until I realized Mia was talking about her almost-stepdad. I have never called an adult by their first name before, except for Joanne at my mom's office, but she's not like a real adult anyway. I tried to imagine calling my mom by her first name, Sharon. Weird!

Mia pushed aside some clothes on the bed and opened up her laptop. "You want to check out *Teen Style*?" she asked.

"Sure."

"It's pretty fun," Mia said as she typed away. "They have a whole section of celebrities, and you can rate the outfits they're wearing."

She clicked a few times, and a photo of a thin, blond actress came on the screen. She was wearing a red dress with feathers on the bottom.

"What do you think?" Mia asked me.

I shrugged. "It's nice, I guess. I mean, if she likes it, then what's the difference?"

"I think it's too long," Mia said. "Take a few inches off of it and it would be perfect." She clicked on the number "7" and then a new picture popped up.

I really didn't get it. I had no idea why one outfit was better than another. But Mia had a definite opinion about everything.

We did that for a while, and then Mia clicked on another page. "This is *really* fun," she said. "You create an avatar of yourself and then you get to try on different outfits to see how they would look."

Mia made my avatar: skinny, medium height,

wavy brown hair, brown eyes. Then she started clicking on clothes, and they appeared on my avatar's body.

I couldn't tell what was wrong with other people's clothes, but it was cool to experiment and see what different stuff looked good on computer me. I had to admit that part was pretty fun. Well, for a while. Then it got a little boring. After I tried on a leather skirt, flowered dress, and five different pairs of boots, Mia looked at me.

"Want to play with the dogs?" she asked.

"Yes!" I answered gratefully.

The dogs were completely adorable. Mia said they were Maltese dogs. They could both roll over and sit. Then Mia did this trick where she sneezed and the one called Tiki ran to the tissue box and took a tissue out of it.

"That is truly amazing," I said.

Before I knew it, Mom came to pick me up. On the drive home, she asked me the usual questions about how things went. Then she sneezed.

"That's odd," she said. "My allergies usually don't bug me this time of year."

I knew the dog hair on my clothes was probably making her sneeze, but I didn't say anything.

I wanted to be sure I could go back to Mia's.

CHAPTER 10

The Best Club Ever

$\mathscr{T}$he next night I made a batch of cupcakes for Cupcake Friday. I remembered that I hadn't made chocolate cupcakes in a while. They're one of my favorites, and I don't even need Mom to help me make them.

I thought I knew the recipe by heart, but while I was adding the ingredients to the big mixing bowl, I realized that I didn't know how much baking powder to add. So I took the big binder of cupcake recipes from the kitchen shelf and looked up the chocolate cupcakes.

Recipes amaze me. If you follow the directions exactly, you can make something completely awesome.

There should be a recipe for middle school, I thought.

Follow the steps, one by one, and you'd have a perfect middle school experience.

So far, my middle school experience had been kind of a mess. If I had been following a recipe, it probably would look something like this:

Mix together:
1 evil locker
1 confusing best friend
3 mean girls
1 strict math teacher
2 silly arms
Bake until it hardens. If you overbake, go directly to detention.

Luckily, the recipe for the chocolate cupcakes is much better. Soon the whole house smelled like chocolate. After the cupcakes baked and cooled, I spread chocolate icing on them. Then I used a white icing tube to write a name on each cupcake: Katie, Mia, Emma, and Alexis.

Mom came into the kitchen as I was icing.

"Are these the girls you eat lunch with?" she asked.

I nodded.

"You forgot one," Mom said.

I counted again. "No," I said, and then I realized where she was headed.

I froze. Was she going to start asking me about Callie again?

Mom picked up the icing tube and started writing on one of the cupcakes: M-O-M. I relaxed.

"This is going in my lunch bag tomorrow," she said. "Hey, would it be okay if I decorated some for everyone who works in the office?"

"Sure," I said. "I'll help. We can both do Cupcake Fridays."

That's one of the best things about cupcakes. When you make them, there's always a lot to share.

At lunch the next day, I hadn't even sat down yet when everyone started asking about cupcakes.

"So, did you bring them?" Mia asked.

"What kind are they?" asked Alexis.

"I bet they're delicious," added Emma.

"I went for the classic chocolate today," I announced. I opened the lid, and everyone started to ooh and aah.

"We should save them for after lunch," Alexis said.

"Are you kidding? I can't wait!" Mia took hers out of the box.

"I'll wait," Emma said. "I like to save the best

for last—especially in this case. They smell delicious though."

Mia bit into her cupcake. A slow smile came across her face. "You don't know what you're missing."

Alexis and Emma headed to the lunch line. When they got back, Alexis looked agitated.

"You will not believe what those so-called popular girls just did!" she said, fuming. "Emma and I were waiting in line, and Marcus Ridgely was standing in front of us, and that girl Sydney came up with those other girls, and Sydney was like, 'Hey, Marcus, we're behind you, okay?' and then they cut right in front of us!"

"Right in front of us," Emma echoed.

"Did you say anything?" Mia asked.

"Well, no," Alexis admitted. "But what's the point? It's not like they were going to move. They think because they're in some club, that gives them special privileges or something. It's annoying. I can't stand them!"

I looked down at my sandwich. I totally understood why Alexis was upset. But still—she was talking about Callie.

"Alexis, Katie's friend is one of them," Emma said quietly.

Alexis's face turned red. "I know. I'm sorry. I mean, I'm sure your friend is nice. Maybe you get brainwashed or something when you join the Popular Girls Club."

"Not all clubs are bad," Mia said. "At my old school we had a Fashion Club. And a club for kids who like movies. Stuff like that."

"Well, that makes sense," Alexis said. "Those clubs are about something *real*. Not something made-up, like being popular."

I picked up my cupcake. "You know what would be the coolest club ever? A Cupcake Club!" I was mostly kidding around. "You don't have to be popular to join. You just have to like cupcakes."

Alexis grinned. "Now *that* is a club I could like!"

"The Cupcake Club," Emma repeated. "It sounds like fun."

"We should totally do it," Mia said.

"Really?" I asked.

She nodded. "Why not? This school needs more clubs."

I was getting into the idea. "We could have our meetings every Friday at lunch. That's when I bring cupcakes in anyway."

"I like to make cupcakes too," said Emma. "I could bring them in sometimes."

78

"Maybe we should take turns," Alexis suggested. "I could make up a schedule for all of us."

"Good idea, except I've never made a cupcake before in my life," Mia told us.

"Not even from a mix?" I asked.

Mia shook her head. "We always got them from the bakery down the street. They were soooo good."

"But ours will be better," Alexis said confidently. "Although I don't have a lot of cupcake-making experience either. I know mine won't be as good as yours, Katie."

"It's easy," I assured her. "You just have to follow a recipe."

Then I thought about the first few times I made cupcakes by myself. Mom was always there to help me. She taught me some tricks that weren't in any recipe. "You guys should come to my house this weekend," I blurted out. "We can have a cupcake-making session."

"A cupcake lesson," said Mia. "That sounds like fun."

"I just need to ask my mom," I said. "I'll call everyone tonight, okay?"

I was really excited about the Cupcake Club. Still, I found myself looking over at Callie. Callie loved to make cupcakes as much as I did. It was weird to think of being in a Cupcake Club without Callie.

Would Callie leave the Popular Girls Club to become a member of the Cupcake Club?

Somehow, I didn't think so.

CHAPTER 11

It's Time to Make Some Cupcakes!

So, how many girls are in the club?" my mom asked me as we ate our pizza that night.

"Four," I said. "Me, Mia, Emma, and Alexis."

Mom nodded. "Did you invite Callie to join?"

"I was thinking about it," I said honestly. "I just don't . . . I don't know if she wants to. She kind of made other friends this year."

There, I said it. It was the first time I'd told my mom about what happened with Callie. I felt relieved.

"That happens sometimes," Mom said gently. "People grow up, and they change sometimes. It happened to me in fifth grade. A new girl came to our school, and my best friend, Sally, suddenly became best friends with the new girl instead. I was really, really sad. But then I met new friends."

It was hard to imagine my mom as a little girl. I pictured her going to school in her dentist coat. But I knew what she meant.

"Callie and I said we'd still hang out sometimes," I told my mom. "I think I'm going to text her."

I sent the text after dinner.

Hey Cal. Making cupcakes tomorrow at 2. Wanna come?

Callie texted me back.

Sounds like fun! Wish I could go but I'm going to the mall. Maybe next time?

I texted back.

Sure.

I was a little disappointed, but not too much. I knew tomorrow was going to be fun, even without Callie.

"Callie's not coming," I told my mom. "Can we call the other girls now?"

"Of course," Mom replied. "I was thinking we could do simple cupcakes—vanilla with chocolate icing. I think we're out of sugar, but we can shop in the morning."

"Let's do something different on top," I suggested. "What about those little chocolate candies covered with white candy dots? That would be cool with a vanilla and chocolate cupcake."

Mom grinned. "Perfect!"

"And, um, Mom?" I said. "We might, you know, need some help, but I'm thinking that if we're going to be a Cupcake Club, we should learn to make them on our own."

"Oh!" Mom said, and I was afraid I hurt her feelings. "Well, I'll have to be home, of course, but that sounds right to me. You can just yell if you need me."

Sometimes Mom surprises me. For someone so corny, she can sometimes be very cool.

By two o'clock the next day, we were ready for the first official meeting of the Cupcake Club to begin. I helped Mom wash the yellow tiles on the floor and scrub the kitchen table until there wasn't a crumb on it. We got out our cupcake tins, the flour sifter, Mom's big red mixer, the glass measuring cup, and the little cup with the bird on it that holds the measuring spoons.

Finally, the doorbell rang. Mia was standing there.

"Hi," she said when I opened the door.

Then a blue minivan pulled up in front of the house, and Emma and Alexis got out, along with the woman driving the van. She was short, with blond hair that she wore in a ponytail. She was wearing a sweatshirt with a hummingbird on it, jeans, and sneakers.

"You must be Katie," she said, holding out her hand to shake mine. "I'm Wendy Taylor, Emma's mom. I was hoping I could meet your mom."

My mom magically appeared in the doorway. "Wendy, nice to meet you in person. I'm Sharon. Please come inside."

The moms walked in ahead of us, and Emma gave me an apologetic look.

"Sorry," she whispered. "My mom is really over-protective."

I smiled. "I know how you feel. My mom's the same way."

I led the girls into the kitchen.

"Whoa. It's like cupcake central," Mia remarked.

"We bake a lot of cupcakes," I admitted. "So we've got all the stuff."

We have a big closet in our kitchen that Mom calls the pantry. One whole shelf has all the stuff we need to bake cupcakes, cakes, and cookies: icing tubes, sprinkles, plastic decorations like balloons and flowers that you can stick into the top of a cupcake—stuff like that.

I opened the door to show the girls. "Everything we need is in here," I said. I started grabbing things and handing them to everyone. "Flour. Baking powder. Sugar. Vanilla."

"Don't you use a mix?" Alexis asked.

"Mom says it's just as easy to do it from scratch, and at least you know what's going in it," I said.

I got two eggs out of the refrigerator and picked up the butter that had been softening on the counter.

"That should do it for now." I nodded to the sink. "Before we start, we should all wash our hands."

"Wow, you are a strict teacher," Mia joked.

I laughed. "Can you imagine if Mrs. Moore taught us how to make cupcakes?" I did my best to imitate her voice, which was kind of deep and a little bit musical. "Concentration is the key to succeeding in this class, students! Without concentration, you won't be able to make your cupcakes."

Alexis and Emma started giggling like crazy.

"That is too perfect," Alexis said. "Can you do Ms. Biddle?"

I thought for a minute. Ms. Biddle had an upbeat

voice, like a cheerleader. And she always made everything about science.

"Who wants to make a hypothesis about how these cupcakes will taste?" I asked.

Mia raised her hand. "Delicious!"

"Wait, I can do Ms. Chen," Alexis said. She made her back really straight. "Look alive, people! It's time to make some cupcakes!"

By then I was cracking up so hard, my stomach hurt. That's when Mom walked in.

"I never knew cupcakes were so funny," she said.

I went back into my Mrs. Moore voice. "You are late, Mrs. Brown! Detention!"

That just made everyone laugh even harder. Mom shook her head and smiled.

"Emma, your mom will be back for you and Alexis at four," she told us. "So, girls, get started. I'll be in the den if you need me."

I kind of led the cupcake demonstration. First we mixed the eggs, butter, and sugar together in the mixer. We added the vanilla. Then we sifted the dry ingredients together in another bowl: the flour, baking powder, and salt. Everybody took turns measuring. When it was Alexis's turn to sift the flour, it puffed up like a cloud and settled on her face like powder.

"No flour in this classroom! Detention!" I cried out in my Mrs. Moore voice, and we all laughed again.

Then we slowly mixed the dry ingredients and wet ingredients together using the mixer. When it was all done, Mom popped in to check on us and showed us how to use an ice-cream scoop to put the perfect amount of batter into each cupcake cup, which is good because I always forget that part and they kind of get big and explode. Then we had to wait while the cupcakes baked. That was okay, because we had to clean up the whole mess we made. When the cupcakes were cooling, we used the mixer again to make chocolate icing.

I've always thought that icing the cupcakes is the hardest part. Mom got us special flat knives to use, but it's still kind of hard.

Alexis and Emma were struggling with the icing, just like me. But when Mia put it on, it was smooth and perfect.

"I thought you never did this before?" I asked.

"I haven't," Mia said. She looked really happy. "I guess I have a hidden talent for icing cupcakes."

"Mine looks like a very sad cupcake," Emma said, holding hers up.

"I know what will make it happy," I told her. I

took out the bag of chocolate candies Mom and I had bought and put one right in the middle. "See? Perfect!"

"It does look better," Emma agreed.

Everyone dug into the bag and we decorated the top of each cupcake. Emma, Alexis, and I put a single candy in the middle of each one. Mia got really creative. On one, she put the candies all around the edge of the cupcake. It looked really cool. She also made some look like flowers.

"You're a natural," I told her.

Mia beamed. "Can I try making the cupcakes for lunch next Friday? I really think I can do it."

"Sure," I said. "You can always call if you need help."

Before we knew it, it was four o'clock. Mom had small boxes for everyone so they could take some cupcakes home. Emma took home the most: one for each of her parents and her brothers.

There was some stuff to clean up after the girls left, but I didn't mind. Mom helped.

"It looks like the Cupcake Club got off to a good start," she remarked.

I smiled at her. "I think you're right!"

CHAPTER 12

Middle School Roller Coaster

Something happened after we formed the Cupcake Club: Middle school got a little bit easier.

Honest! For example, my locker started opening up on the first try. Coincidence? I don't think so. Alexis says I probably just loosened up the insides of the lock so it opens more easily, but I don't believe it. I'd rather think that the superpowers of the Cupcake Club defeated my evil alien locker.

Now, take math class. I wish I could say that Mrs. Moore was suddenly nicer, but I can't. What happens now is that every time Mrs. Moore says something serious, or threatens to give us all detention, I write down what she says so I can use it the next time I do an impression of her. She's not so scary anymore.

Not that everything is perfect. Take gym class. On Tuesday we were picking teams for flag football, and Sydney said, "Don't pick Katie unless you want to lose!" She said it really loudly, and a bunch of kids laughed. Sometimes I feel like saying something, but I don't. I keep waiting for the time when we have races outside on the track. I've been a faster runner than Sydney ever since third grade.

Then something happened in English class on Wednesday. It didn't happen to me, exactly, but to another member of the Cupcake Club: Alexis.

Here's what happened. At the beginning of class Mrs. Castillo told us she was giving us a vocabulary worksheet for homework. But she didn't hand it out. Then, right before the bell rang, Alexis raised her hand.

"Mrs. Castillo, what about the vocab worksheet?" she asked.

Everyone groaned. Everyone except for me, Mia, and Emma.

We know that Alexis is just like that. She likes to do things exactly the way you're supposed to. She especially likes to make teachers happy.

As you can guess, nobody was happy with Alexis.

"Thanks a lot, Alexis," Eddie Rossi said from the back of the room.

"Yeah, what, are you in love with homework?" added Devin Jaworski.

"Please settle down," ordered Mrs. Castillo. "You're lucky Alexis reminded me. Otherwise you'd have double homework tomorrow night."

But of course that didn't make anyone feel better. When the bell rang and we poured into the hallway, a lot of the boys were still giving Alexis a hard time.

"Teacher's pet!"

"Thanks for the homework!"

Alexis started to look like she might cry. I felt bad for her.

"Leave her alone," Mia said bravely, and we all hurried off to our lockers.

That was pretty much the worst thing that happened all week—until Cupcake Friday.

Mia came into the cafeteria carrying a really pretty pink bakery box. She opened the lid to reveal four perfect cupcakes with chocolate icing dotted with chocolate candies.

"They're so pretty," Emma said.

"I hope they taste good," Mia said with a small frown. "We didn't have any vanilla. And I lost count when I was putting in the teaspoons of salt. I might have put in an extra amount."

91

Alexis pounded her fist on the table. "Let the second meeting of the Cupcake Club begin!"

That's when Sydney and Brenda—I mean, Bella—walked by. Sydney stopped cold.

"Cupcake Club?" she asked. "Are you serious? What is this, third grade?"

"Yeah, that's so lame!" Bella added, making a big deal out of rolling her eyes.

"Not as lame as a Popular Girls Club," Alexis said under her breath.

Sydney raised an eyebrow. "Excuse me? Did you say something?"

Alexis, Emma, and I were all kind of afraid of Sydney. But not Mia.

"Maybe I'll bring some next time for you to try," she said coolly.

Sydney snorted. "No thanks," she said, and then she and Bella walked away.

"Well, that was fun," I said.

"Who wants a cupcake?" Mia asked.

We all reached for one, but I had a little knot in my stomach. I watched Bella and Sydney slide into their table with Callie. They were all reading some magazine. I tried not to look.

The cupcakes were good. They tasted a tiny bit weird because of the extra salt, but not too weird.

Plus the icing was especially delicious.

"Nice job," I told Mia, and she smiled at me. I could tell she was proud.

That same day, when the eighth-period bell rang, I was walking to my locker and I saw Mia talking to a bunch of girls from her class. They were all laughing.

For a second I got a strange feeling. Then it hit me. Not that I care about how "cool" people are or anything, but Mia is a lot cooler than me. What if she got bored with the Cupcake Club? What if she found other friends, like Callie had?

"There's no use in worrying about what might happen," Mom always says. "Concentrate on how things are right now."

I remember a lot of stuff Mom tells me, usually because she says it over and over again. Also, it's just me and her most of the time, so I guess she's a pretty big part of my life.

Anyway, I'm glad I remembered that. Because right now, Mia was my friend. She rode the bus with me every day and ate lunch with me every day. She invited me to her house and baked cupcakes for the Cupcake Club.

Maybe in the future that would change, just like things had changed with Callie over the summer.

But for now, everything with Mia was all right.

Mia saw me standing there and waved.

"Hey, Katie! See you on the bus!"

See? Sometimes Mom is right.

CHAPTER 13

Alexis Has an Idea

I did see Callie a few times over the next few weeks. One night my mom invited the Wilsons over for Italian food night. It's kind of a tradition between our families, like the Labor Day barbecue. My mom makes tons of pasta and salad. She lights candles on our dining-room table, puts out a red-and-white-checkered tablecloth, and goes all out, of course. But it's actually usually a pretty fun night.

Then another night Callie called and invited me to come over and watch the first episode of *Singing Stars* on TV. It's our favorite show. I had a good time, even though Callie kept getting texts on her cell phone the whole time.

Mostly I hung out with the Cupcake Club. Everyone came over one Saturday, and Mom showed us how she makes her P-B-and-J cupcakes. And one night Mia invited me over for dinner. Her mom got takeout food from an Indian restaurant. I'd never eaten Indian food before, and it was good—and spicy. Mia's mom and stepdad were nice, and her stepbrother, Dan, seemed nice too. Which was kind of a surprise, because Mia is always saying what a beast he is.

Oh, and I got detention from Mrs. Moore. Twice. But the whole class had it, so it wasn't so bad.

And the best thing was that I could talk to Mia, Emma, and Alexis about it. That's mostly what the Cupcake Club did. We baked cupcakes; we ate cupcakes; and we talked about stuff.

Things were not perfect, but they were good.

One Monday we were eating lunch, and everyone was talking about the announcement that Principal LaCosta had made that morning after the Pledge of Allegiance.

"This morning your homeroom teacher will be distributing permission slips for the first dance of the year," she said. "Please hand them in by next Monday if you're going to attend. This year's dance will be bigger than ever. That afternoon, we'll be holding a special fund-raising event for the school. Check your flyer for details."

Now we were sitting around the lunch table, looking at the flyers.

"I always heard we had dances in middle school," Alexis said. "I just didn't think it would be so soon."

"Do you think we actually have to *dance* at the dance?" I asked. My mom loves the movie *Grease*, and in that movie the high school kids twirl and throw one another in the air and stuff like that. I didn't think I could do that in a million years.

"We had dances at my old school," Mia informed us. "Sometimes people danced. Mostly everyone just hung around and talked."

"Did boys and girls dance together?" Emma asked. She sounded a little worried.

"Sometimes," Mia replied.

We were quiet for a minute. I think all of us except for Mia were feeling nervous about the dance.

"Did you see the part about the fund-raiser?" I asked. "It's going to be in the parking lot of the school. If you have an idea to make money for the school, you can set up a booth. The booth that makes the most money will get a prize."

"I heard the basketball team is doing a dunking booth with all of the gym teachers," Alexis reported. "I bet that will make a lot of money."

"Maybe we could have a dunking booth for math teachers," I joked.

Over at the PGC table, Sydney was talking in a loud voice on purpose.

"Our club is going to have the best booth at the fund-raiser," Sydney bragged. "That's why we have to keep it top secret."

Alexis rolled her eyes. "This is supposed to be for the whole school, not just the Popular Girls Club," she said. "Only Sydney can turn a good cause into something about herself."

"I wonder what their top secret idea is?" Emma asked.

Alexis had that look on her face where you know the wheels of her brain are spinning faster than a car's.

"You know, I bet we can raise a lot of money just by selling cupcakes," she said. "Who could say no to a cupcake for a good cause?"

"That's not a bad idea," Mia agreed. "But we'd have to make a lot of cupcakes, wouldn't we?"

Alexis took out her notebook and started scribbling numbers.

"There are about four hundred kids in the school," she said. "Let's say half of them go to the dance. That's two hundred. Then there are teachers. And parents, and younger brothers and sisters. So let's say that's another two hundred people, for a total of four hundred. Now let's say that half of those people buy cupcakes—"

"We'd need two hundred cupcakes," I said, and then gasped. "Oh no! I did math. Mrs. Moore must be getting through to me."

"That sounds like a lot of cupcakes," Emma said.

"Not really," Alexis said. "It's about seventeen dozen. We could bake a few dozen at a time over four or five days. Since it's for the school, I bet we can ask our parents to donate the ingredients. If we sell each cupcake for fifty cents, we'd make a hundred dollars."

"Fifty cents?" Mia asked. "At the cupcake shop in Manhattan, they charge five dollars a cupcake. Katie's cupcakes are just as good as theirs."

Alexis's eyes were wide. "Who would pay five dollars for one cupcake?"

"Maybe we could charge two dollars a cupcake," Emma suggested.

"That could work," I chimed in. "If we sold all of the cupcakes, we'd make four hundred dollars. We might even win the contest."

"We should definitely do this," Mia said, her eyes shining with excitement.

"I'm sure this is better than whatever Sydney is planning," Alexis said smugly.

I looked over at the PGC table. I wasn't really thinking about beating Sydney. I was thinking about Callie. She wasn't too interested in the Cupcake Club when I talked about it. But if we won the fund-raising contest . . . maybe Callie would be convinced she was in the wrong club.

"I'm in," I said. "So how exactly are we going to make two hundred cupcakes?"

CHAPTER 14

The Mixed-up Cupcakes

We should have a meeting so we can figure this out," Alexis suggested. "We could do it at my house this time. How about Saturday?"

"I'm going to my dad's this weekend," Mia said.

"Next weekend should be fine," Emma said. "It's a month until the dance, anyway."

"We need to figure out what kind of cupcake to make," I reminded everyone.

"We can do that next week," Alexis said. "We'll work out a schedule, too."

So the following Saturday I showed up at Alexis's front door with a whole bunch of recipes and enough ingredients for a couple dozen. If we were going to decide on a cupcake, we would have to do some research.

Alexis lives in a brick house with a very neat front lawn. The bushes on either side of the white front steps are the kind that are trimmed into a perfect globe shape.

Alexis looked surprised when she answered the door.

"Hi, Katie," she said. "What's all that?"

"It's for our meeting," I explained. "So we can experiment with cupcake flavors."

"Oh," she said. "I thought we were just going to talk about it."

"Why just talk when we can taste?" I asked.

Alexis led me into the kitchen. I've been in her house a few times so far, and I'm always amazed how clean it is in there. For example, there is nothing on the kitchen counter, not even a toaster. Our counter has a toaster, the big red mixer, a cookie jar shaped like an apple, Mom's spice rack, and usually a bowl of fruit.

Alexis's mom was at the kitchen table, setting up a pitcher of water and glasses for our meeting, along with a bowl of grapes. I noticed there was a piece of paper and pencil at each of the four places around the table.

Mrs. Becker was wearing a button-down light blue shirt and dark blue dress pants. I've never seen her wear jeans, not even on a Saturday. Her hair is auburn like Alexis's, but it's cut short.

"Hello, Katie," she said when she saw me. She noticed the bag I was carrying. "Did you bring snacks? How nice."

"It's actually supplies, so we can make test cupcakes," I told her.

"You mean you'll be baking?" she asked. "Oh dear. I didn't know you'd be baking today, Alexis."

"We'll clean up when we're done, Mom," Alexis said. "Promise."

"It's true. We clean up all the time when we bake at my house," I added.

Mrs. Becker gave a little sigh. "All right. But let me know when you are ready to turn on the oven!"

She hurried out of the kitchen.

"Mom doesn't like it when the plan changes," Alexis explained. "Especially when there's a mess involved."

"I promise we won't make a mess," I said. Then I remembered what my kitchen usually looks like when I bake cupcakes. "Well, not too much of a mess, anyway."

Emma and Mia arrived next, at the same time. Alexis neatly piled up the pencils and paper, and

I took all of the ingredients I'd brought out of my bag. Besides the basic cupcake-making stuff, I had mini marshmallows, chocolate chips, nuts, sprinkles, red-hot candies, tubes of icing and food coloring, and a jar of cherries—just about everything I could grab from the pantry.

"Mmm, everything looks so yummy," Mia said.

"Well, I was thinking that we have to make a really *incredible* cupcake if we're going to sell a lot," I said. "Something we've never done before."

"How do we do that?" Emma asked.

"We experiment," I said. "Mom and I do it all the time. That's how we came up with our famous banana split cupcake. Only I didn't have any bananas, so we'll have to come up with something else."

I turned to Alexis. "Do you have a mixer?" I asked.

"Not the kind you have," she replied. "It's the one you hold in your hand."

"That's fine," I said. "First we need to make a regular vanilla batter."

I had made so many vanilla cupcakes over the last few weeks that I didn't need a recipe at all. Pretty soon we had a perfect bowl of batter ready.

"Now we just have to figure out what to add in," I said.

"Everyone loves chocolate chips," Mia suggested. We stirred some in.

"Marshmallows go well with chocolate," said Alexis.

Emma nodded. "Definitely."

We added some mini marshmallows to the batter.

"What about nuts?" Emma asked. "It might be good to have something crunchy in there."

"Some people are allergic to nuts," Alexis pointed out.

"That's true," I said. "But sprinkles are crunchy too. Maybe we could put sprinkles in."

Alexis wrinkled her nose. "You mean put them *in* a cupcake instead of on top?"

"Why not?" I asked.

Nobody had a good argument. I dumped in half a bottle of rainbow sprinkles.

"They look good," Mia said. "And I don't think there's room in the bowl for anything else."

We scooped all of the batter into the cupcake tins Alexis put out for us. Because of all the stuff we mixed in, there was a lot of batter left over.

"I don't have any more pans," Alexis said.

"No problem," I told her. "We can always bake more when the first batch cools."

Mrs. Becker came in to preheat the oven for us.

She raised her eyebrow when she saw our cupcakes.

"My, those look interesting," she said.

"Wait till you taste it, Mom," Alexis told her. "You're going to love it!"

While the cupcakes baked, we whipped up some plain vanilla icing.

"Should we add anything into the icing?" I asked.

"I think the cupcakes have enough inside them," Mia said.

"Good point," I said.

We cleaned up our mess while we waited for the cupcakes to bake. When the timer rang, Mrs. Becker helped us with the oven.

"Do you take them out now?" she asked.

"We need to test them first," I said.

Mom had taught me how to stick a toothpick into the middle of a cupcake. If it came out clean, it was done. But if it had batter on it, the cupcake needed to cook more.

I stuck a toothpick into the middle of one of our mixed-up cupcakes. When I took it out, it wasn't clean. But it didn't have batter on it. It had gooey marshmallow, chocolate, and a sprinkle stuck to it.

I frowned. "I'm not sure if it's done or not," I said.

Alexis looked over my shoulder. "They look

done. They're a little brown on top, see?"

I realized there would be no sure way to tell if the cupcakes were done. We might as well take them out. Besides, I was dying to try one! The delicious smell of baking cupcakes was taking over my brain.

We put the cupcakes on a rack to cool. Normally, we talk a lot when we're waiting for cupcakes to cool off. But that day we stared at our cupcakes, like we were going to cool them off with the amazing power of our minds alone.

Finally Mia blurted out, "Maybe we should try them without icing. You know, to get a true sense of how they taste."

"That sounds very logical to me," I said.

We each picked up a cupcake. They were warm, but cool enough to handle. I unwrapped the paper and took a bite. A hot, gooey mess of chocolate and marshmallow exploded in my mouth.

"Mmmmmm," was all I could say.

Alexis had a weird look on her face. "It's too sweet!"

"There's no such thing as too sweet," I told her, and Emma nodded in agreement.

Mia had another complaint. "They're kind of messy," she said, wiping her hand on a napkin.

"Let's see what my mom thinks," Alexis said.

She left the kitchen and returned with both parents. Mr. Becker was tall and skinny with curly hair and glasses like his wife.

"I think you girls have a great fund-raising idea," he said. "Everybody loves cupcakes!"

Alexis handed one to each parent. "They're not iced yet," she said. "They might taste different when they're iced."

We held our breath as Mr. and Mrs. Becker bit into their cupcakes. Mrs. Becker made the same weird face that Alexis had.

"My, they're very sweet!" she said.

"They're tasty," said Mr. Becker. "But I'll tell you something. I'm not a big fan of marshmallows. Never liked them. You know what makes me happy? A plain vanilla cupcake. Mmm."

I thought of Callie's dad. "I think that's a parent thing. Parents like vanilla cupcakes."

"And don't forget, parents are a big part of our sales," Alexis reminded us.

I was starting to feel discouraged. "But plain vanilla cupcakes are boring! We need our cupcakes to be extra special so everyone wants them."

"Well, maybe they could *look* special," Mia said.

"What do you mean?" I asked.

"Well, this is a school fund-raiser, right? Maybe

they could be in the school colors or something," she said.

I immediately knew what she was talking about. "Mrs. Becker, can we have another bowl, please?"

I scooped half of the vanilla frosting we had made into the new bowl. Then I put a few drops of blue food coloring into one bowl, and a few drops of yellow into the other. Emma helped me stir them up.

"Make that one bluer," Mia said, pointing.

After a couple of more drops, we had the perfect blue and yellow—the official colors of Park Street Middle School.

"Mia, do your magic," I told her.

Mia expertly iced one cupcake with blue frosting and another cupcake with yellow frosting. Then she used an icing tube to write "PS" in yellow on the blue cupcake, and "PS" in blue on the yellow cupcake.

"Just imagine there are plain vanilla cupcakes inside," Mia said, holding them out to us.

"They're just right!" said Mrs. Becker.

"I bet you'll sell a hundred of those," agreed Mr. Becker.

"*Two* hundred," Alexis cheered.

"We will," I said confidently. "We are definitely

going to win this contest. We just have to do one thing."

"What?" Alexis asked.

"We have to *bake* two hundred cupcakes!"

CHAPTER 15

How to Bake
Two Hundred Cupcakes

Even though I was disappointed that we were making plain vanilla cupcakes, I loved Mia's cupcake design. And the next Cupcake Friday, Emma brought in cupcakes for us that she made herself.

When I bit into one, I tasted chocolate chips and sprinkles!

"I left out the marshmallows, so they wouldn't be too sweet or too sticky," she said. "What do you think?"

"I think they're amazing," I said.

Emma blushed a little. "Well, I really did like our mixed-up cupcakes."

That made me feel better. At least Emma liked them!

As we ate our cupcakes, we went over our plan

for the next week. Our parents had agreed to let us bake cupcakes once a day for four days before the contest. We would start baking on Tuesday and finish baking on Friday night. Then Saturday morning, we would ice and decorate every single one. We had to promise to get all of our homework done right after school.

Mom said we could do all the baking at our house. Each one of us would take turns bringing the ingredients and cupcake liners.

Alexis had the whole thing mapped out on a chart.

"Tuesday night, Katie will provide the supplies," she said, reading out loud. "I'll bring them Wednesday, Emma can bring them Thursday, and Mia will do Friday. Then Saturday, we'll all chip in for the icing. We'll have to make four dozen cupcakes every night, and do an extra dozen on Friday. Then we'll have four left over."

I leaned across the table to get a better look at the chart. Alexis had worked out a whole system with stickers. One cupcake-shaped sticker equaled a dozen cupcakes. It all looked very complicated.

"It looks a lot harder to bake two hundred cupcakes than I thought," I said.

I heard a laugh. When I turned around, I saw

Sydney and Maggie standing by the table.

"I saw the sign-up sheets for the fund-raiser," Sydney said. "You're doing a bake sale? Now *that's* really original."

"Bake sales are so boring!" Maggie added.

You know what's boring and unoriginal? I thought. *Following Sydney around and repeating everything she says like a parrot.*

I thought it, but I wasn't brave enough to say it. As usual, though, Mia wasn't afraid to speak up at all.

"Everybody likes cupcakes," Mia said. "So, what are you guys doing? On the fund-raising sheet it just says 'Popular Girls Club.'"

"It's top secret," Sydney said. "Nobody has ever done what we're planning. We're going to blow everyone away."

"Not everyone," said Alexis under her breath.

But Sydney and Maggie didn't hear her and walked away.

"I wonder what they're planning?" Emma asked worriedly. "I bet it's really good."

"I bet they haven't even thought of it yet," I said. "Otherwise, they wouldn't be bragging about their idea to everyone."

Alexis laughed. "You're probably right."

113

After Sydney's comments, I wanted to win that contest more than ever. We had a recipe. We had a plan.

Now we just had to make it happen.

Our first baking night was the Tuesday night before the fund-raiser. I could tell Mom was really excited too. She even bought extra cupcake pans for us to use.

Mia, Alexis, and Emma all got to my house right at seven o'clock. Mom gave us a little pep talk—and some instructions.

"There are enough pans here for four dozen cupcakes," she said. "But I wouldn't make a double batch of batter. Baking is tricky. Make one batch first, put it in the oven, and then start the second batch. Then you'll end up with perfect cupcakes."

"Thanks, Mrs. Brown," Mia said.

"Now, how about a huddle?" Mom asked.

Oh, Mom. . . . To make her happy, we all put our hands on top of one another's. Mom led the cheer.

"Goooooooo Cupcake Club!"

Then we got to work. By then, we were getting into a cupcake groove. Emma liked sifting the flour, Alexis liked measuring things, Mia liked mixing things, and I liked cracking the eggs. We had the first batch of two dozen cupcakes done in record time, and then the phone rang.

I wiped off my hands and picked it up. "Hey, Katie." It was Callie. "I tried texting you. Are you watching *Singing Stars*? Ryan just advanced to the finals. Can you believe it?"

I realized that I totally forgot it was time for *Singing Stars*. "Uh, I'm not watching it," I said. "We're making cupcakes for the fund-raiser."

"Hey, Katie, how many eggs is it again?" Mia called out.

"Oh," Callie said. "You have company. Sorry to bother you." There was a little silence. "Well, I'll talk to you tomorrow."

"Text me with the results, okay?" I asked.

"Sure," she said, and then she hung up.

I felt a little sad for a minute. Callie belonged in the Cupcake Club. She could be having so much fun with us if she wanted to.

"Earth to Katie. How many eggs?" Mia asked.

"Oh, sorry. Two," I replied.

By the time Alexis's dad came by to pick up everyone, we had four dozen cupcakes in boxes stored safely in our freezer.

"Forty-eight down, one hundred and fifty-two to go," Mia said as they were leaving.

"Actually, it's one hundred and fifty-six, since we're making two hundred and four cupcakes," Alexis pointed out.

"One hundred and fifty-six?" I cried. We had worked really hard tonight. Yet it didn't seem like we'd done much, after all.

After my friends left I flopped on the couch—for about five seconds.

"Time to jump in the shower, Katie," Mom told me. "I don't want you getting to bed late."

I rolled over onto the floor. "You'll have to drag me."

"Hmm," Mom said. "Maybe all this cupcake baking is too much for you."

I jumped to my feet. Mom always knows how to get me.

"Nope. I'm fine!" I told her. Then I ran to the bathroom.

As I drifted off to sleep that night, I thought about what the instructions would look like for someone making two hundred cupcakes.

How to Make 200 Cupcakes:
1. Do homework in a dentist office.
2. Eat dinner.
3. Clean up after dinner.

4. *Make four dozen cupcakes.*

5. *Clean up after making four dozen cupcakes.*

6. *Shower.*

7. *Rinse.*

8. *Sleep.*

9. *Repeat.*

10. *Repeat.*

11. *Repeat.*

CHAPTER 16

The Purple Dress

"Two hundred one, two hundred two, two hundred three, two hundred four!"

We counted together as the last cupcake—the last of seventeen dozen exactly—went into its box.

"We did it! Woo-hoo!" I cheered. Everyone kind of jumped around.

"You know, it's funny that there are exactly four cupcakes left over," Alexis pointed out. "One for each of us."

"I think that's a sign," Mia said. "We need to eat those four to make it an even two hundred."

"But four cupcakes equals eight dollars," Alexis reminded us.

"I know," I chimed in. "But maybe it's, like, a good luck thing."

That satisfied Alexis. "Good point. We should probably taste them anyway, to make sure they're okay."

The vanilla cupcakes were delicious, even without the icing.

"So we'll meet here tomorrow at eight to ice them," I reminded everyone. "The fund-raiser starts at noon."

The doorbell rang, and Alexis's mom came to pick up her and Emma. Then Mia's stepbrother beeped his horn outside.

"Mom and I will pick you up after dinner," Mia told me.

"Okay. I'll be ready," I said.

I forgot to mention that on Friday we baked the cupcakes right after school because we didn't have to do our homework right away. The night before, Mia had had an idea about how we should spend Friday night.

"What is everybody wearing to the dance?" she wanted to know.

Alexis shrugged. "I don't know. What I always wear."

"I was thinking about wearing my favorite dress," Emma said. "The one with the pink flowers."

"I didn't even think about it," I admitted. "Do

we have to get dressed up to go to the dance?"

"Well, no," Mia admitted. "You don't *have* to. But it's fun. I was thinking that tomorrow night we should all go to the mall and look for dresses to wear."

"I can't," Alexis said. "We're going to my aunt's for dinner."

"I'll probably just wear the dress I have," Emma said.

Mia looked at me. "Come on, Katie. What do you say?"

"I have to ask my mom," I said. Honestly, I don't like shopping at all. But I think Mia could make anything fun. "But yeah, why not?"

My mom agreed (after talking to Mia's mom, of course), and so Ms. Vélaz and Mia picked me up at seven.

The Westgrove Mall is really big, with a lot of buildings all connected together. It reminds me of a big maze. When we walked through the doors, Ms. Vélaz turned to us.

"What store are we going to first?" she asked.

Mia looked horrified. "Mom, seriously?"

"Of course! This is a big mall," her mom pointed out. "Besides, I promised Mrs. Brown that I'd stick with you girls."

I felt like sinking into the floor. My mom sticks to me like glue when we go to the mall. She used to make me wear one of those kid leashes until I was five. Here I was, in middle school, and I could still feel the invisible leash tugging at me.

Ms. Vélaz must have seen the look on my face. "You know, you girls are lucky to have an expert fashion consultant accompanying you!"

Mia grabbed me by the arm. "Come on. There's a supercute store right around the corner."

Mia's mom walked slowly behind us as we raced into the store. Loud dance music blared through the speakers. The store was pretty crowded with girls looking through racks of dresses, shirts, skirts, and jeans.

Mia skidded to a stop in front of a black dress with a zipper down the front.

"This is so cute," she said. "Katie, you should try it on."

"I don't know," I said. "It's black. Black clothes remind me of vampires."

Mia looked me up and down. I was wearing a pair of old jeans with a rip in the knee and a red T-shirt with a peace sign on it.

"So you like bright colors," she said. "What else do you like?"

I shrugged. "I don't know. I don't know what's in style and what's not. When I go shopping with my mom, we get some jeans and then I pick out whatever shirts I like."

"So you can do that with a dress, too," Mia said. "Just look around and see what you like."

That sounded easy enough. I started looking through the racks of clothes with Mia. At first I was just confused. There were so many dresses! And even though they were different colors and different styles, they kind of all looked the same to me.

Then a splash of purple caught my eye. I walked over to a display with a headless mannequin wearing a purple dress. It was *really* purple. Grape jelly purple. But I liked it. It had short sleeves and a straight skirt with a black belt around the middle.

I took one off the rack. "I kind of like this," I told Mia. "It looks good on the mannequin. But she doesn't have a head, so anything would look good on her, I guess."

"No, I like it!" Mia said. I could tell she was excited. "Try it on!"

The dressing rooms were lined up on the side wall. A salesperson used a key to open up one of the silver doors for me. I stepped inside and tried on the dress.

I looked at myself in the mirror. "Not bad," I had to admit.

Then I heard Mia's voice outside. "Katie, come out! I am dying to see how you look!"

I cautiously stepped outside the dressing room. Mia's eyes got wide when she saw me.

"Ooh, it's perfect! Turn around!" she ordered.

I felt like the world's worst fashion model as I turned in a circle for Mia's inspection.

"You have got to get it," she said. "Wear it with some short black boots and it'll be fabulous."

"What if I don't have short black boots?" I asked.

"Then you can borrow mine!"

I looked at the price tag. It cost less than the money Mom had given me to spend. "I think I'll get it," I said. "That was easy!"

Then I heard a familiar loud voice nearby. "That dress is gross, Mags. I wouldn't wear that to gym class."

Sydney! I had to get inside that dressing room before she saw me. I turned to run, but it was too late.

"Isn't it a little too early for Halloween, Katie?"

There she goes, I thought. If I couldn't escape, I might as well face her.

I spun around. "What do you mean, Sydney?"

"Well, that's a grape costume, isn't it?" she asked. "No, wait—you're that purple dinosaur."

She made me so angry! I wished I had some great comeback to give her. But as usual, she left me tongue-tied.

"You know, Sydney, violet was a hot runway color this fall," Mia said in that supercool tone of hers. "I was just reading about it in the color trends column in *Fashion Weekly*."

Now it was Sydney's turn to get tongue-tied. But she managed to recover. "Violet or not, it's an ugly dress."

For the first time ever, I thought of something to say to Sydney. And I wasn't afraid to say it, either. Maybe Mia was rubbing off on me a little.

"I don't care if *you* think it's ugly," I said. "I like it."

Then I marched back into my dressing room and out of the corner of my eye I saw Mia smirk. My heart was pounding. Something about that dress made me feel good. Good enough to tell stupid old Sydney to shut up.

And that's why my purple dress is still my favorite dress to this day. And as it turns out—it's my lucky one, too.

CHAPTER 17

PGC's Secret Is Revealed!

Saturday morning was, as the skateboarding dudes in my school say, intense. Mom and I got up super-early and started mixing batches and batches of icing. The girls came over, and Emma's mom came over to help too.

It took hours, but we got everything done. My mom and Emma's mom iced the cupcakes with me. Mia wrote the letters on them with her perfect handwriting. Alexis and Emma made a big cardboard sign for the table that said CUPCAKES $2.00. Then they helped us with the icing.

By eleven o'clock we had two hundred perfect cupcakes. We carefully transferred them to Emma's mom's minivan, and she drove them to the school. My mom and I brought the sign, a cash box, one blue and one yellow tablecloth, and plastic trays for the cupcakes.

The day was perfect for a fund-raiser—sunny but not too hot. When we got to the school, the big parking lot was roped off with police tape. There were a bunch of canopies set up in a square all around the lot. Blue and yellow balloons tied to the canopies waved and wiggled in the air. We searched around until we found a table with a note that said CUPCAKE CLUB on it.

We started setting up. We spread out the blue tablecloth and then draped the yellow one over it in another direction so you could see both colors. Alexis and Emma taped up their sign. We put about half the cupcakes on platters. Then we stood back and checked out our table.

"Not bad," I said.

"It's a little flat," Mia said, turning her head sideways. "Maybe next time we could put the platters on pillars or something so that some are high and some are low."

Mom walked up behind us and put her arm around me.

"Well, *I* think it looks perfect!" she said. "Why don't you girls go stand in front of the table? I'll take a picture."

We quickly lined up: me, Mia, Alexis, and then Emma.

"Say 'cupcake'!" Mom called out.

"Cupcake!" we shouted.

Alexis glanced at her watch. "We still have fifteen minutes. Let's check out the competition."

"Good idea," I agreed.

We walked around. There must have been about a dozen tables besides ours. The basketball team was still setting up their dunking booth at the end of the parking lot. The girls' soccer team had a booth where they would take your picture, print it out, and put it in a frame. Then you could decorate the frame with shapes like stars and soccer balls. Then we walked past the Chess Club's table.

"Oh, no!" Emma cried. "A bake sale!"

The table was covered with paper plates topped with cookies, brownies, and yes—cupcakes.

"I think our table stands out more," Mia whispered to us. "And they don't have special Park Street Middle School cupcakes, either."

"Besides, they have mostly cookies," Alexis pointed out. "And they're only charging fifty cents each for those."

Mia and Alexis made me feel better. I think Emma felt better too.

Then we heard loud music coming from the other side of the parking lot. It was dance music, just like I'd heard in the clothing store the night before. We all turned our heads at the same time.

The PGC had set up their booth!

"Let's get a closer look," Mia suggested.

We walked across the parking lot. I hated to admit it, but the PGC booth looked really cool. The table was covered with a black cloth with silver stars dangling from it. There were glittery makeup cases all over the table. They had a banner (the printed kind you order from the store) tied to the canopy up above. It read PGC'S MAKEOVER MAGIC.

"What exactly are they doing?" I wondered out loud.

We walked even closer. Sydney and Bella were busy spreading out makeup and brushes and stuff on the table. Bella had a small sign on the table in front of her that said, GOTH MAKEOVERS ARE MY SPECIALITY. She was wearing a black dress with a poufy skirt. Her reddish-brown hair was pulled back in a sleek ponytail, and her face looked kind of pale. Smudgy dark makeup ringed her eyes.

Next to her, Sydney wore her long blond hair straight and sleek. She was wearing a long white T-shirt over a gray tank with black leggings and boots. It reminded me of an outfit that Mia might wear.

Callie was sitting at a tiny round table set up next to them with a cash box behind her. I noticed that she was dressed exactly the same as Sydney.

So was Maggie. She looked as perfect as Sydney and Callie, except that a long lock of frizzy brown hair was hanging over her eyes. She darted through the crowd, handing out "Makeover Magic" flyers.

"Flyers! Why didn't we think of that?" Alexis said with a frown.

"We don't need flyers to sell cupcakes," Mia said. "Cupcakes sell themselves."

The PGC booth worried me. I mean, it looked really good, a lot better than our table with its cardboard sign. Maybe Sydney had been right all along—they were going to win the contest with their secret weapon.

"Speaking of selling cupcakes, we should get back to the booth," Alexis said.

That's when Maggie bumped into us.

"Oh, hi," she said, shoving a flyer into my hand. "When things get slow at your cupcake stand, stop by for a makeover."

"We'll try, but I don't think things are going to get slow," I said.

We walked away, determined more than ever to sell every last one of our cupcakes.

"The PGC might have music and flyers and glitter, but we have delicious cupcakes!" I cheered. "Let's go win this contest!"

We ran back to our cupcake booth just as the fund-raiser officially opened. A bunch of people came in all at once. We were right by the front entrance, which was a good thing. Almost everybody stopped to check us out. They said nice things like "Wow, it's the school colors!" and "What nice cupcakes!"

But for the first few minutes, nobody bought one.

Then Mrs. Moore, my math teacher, came to the table.

I almost didn't recognize her. When she's teaching us, she wears skirts and blouses and dark colors. Her hair is mostly gray and she always has it pulled back.

But today she was wearing a sweatshirt with a teddy bear on it and jeans. Her hair was loose and went down to the top of her shoulders. I thought it looked nice that way.

"Hello, Miss Brown," she said. She looked at the table. "It must have been a lot of work to make all of these cupcakes."

"There are more in boxes," I told her. "We made two hundred. Well, two hundred and four, actually. That's seventeen dozen."

I was hoping my math would impress her, and maybe it did.

"I'll take one, please," she said, and handed me two dollars in exchange for a cupcake. She took a bite right in front of me.

"Vanilla!" she said. "My favorite."

Then she walked away.

I couldn't believe it. "It's our first sale!" I cried. Everyone let out a cheer. I turned over the money to Alexis, who was in charge of the cash box.

Mrs. Moore must have brought us good luck, because we started selling cupcakes like crazy after that. Some people asked for blue, some people asked for yellow, but most people didn't care which ones they got.

We were so busy selling cupcakes that I forgot about the PGC booth—until a friend of Mia's came to our table. I recognized her as one of the girls Mia talks to in the hallway.

"Hi, Sophie," Mia said. Then she gave a little gasp.

I turned away from the cupcakes to see what had startled Mia. Then I noticed—Sophie's face looked really strange. Her skin had so much white makeup on it that she looked like a clown. The dark makeup around her eyes was smudged everywhere.

"I know," Sophie said, noticing Mia's face. "It's terrible, isn't it? And it cost me five dollars!"

That's when I realized—Sophie was a victim of the Makeover Magic booth!

"It's not so bad," Mia said.

"I was hoping to look pale and mysterious, but this is too much." Sophie sighed. "You should see what's going on over there. It's more like Makeover *Tragic* than Makeover Magic."

Mia and I looked at each other. Then I turned to Emma.

"Can you and Alexis handle things for a minute?" I asked.

Emma nodded. "No problem."

We quickly made our way to the PGC booth. A big crowd had gathered around.

"Maybe Sophie just got unlucky," I said. "It looks like they're doing great."

We inched our way closer so we could get a better view. I realized that most of the crowd wasn't in line to get a makeover. Instead they were watching the action at the booth.

Sydney swiped a brush across the face of a girl sitting across from her.

"There," she said. "You're ready for the runway!"

The girl turned around, and a few people giggled. I tried not to laugh myself. Sydney had put so much fake tanner on the girl that her face looked like a tangerine. Glittery blue eye shadow covered her eyelids.

"I don't know much about fashion, but that doesn't look right to me," I said to Mia.

"That shouldn't look right to *anybody*," Mia whispered back.

"Okay!" Sydney called out. "Who's next?"

Nobody stirred. Then the girl with the orange face nudged her friend. "You promised you would get one if I got one."

The friend looked terrified, but she knew she had to go through with it. She slowly walked up to Callie and handed her five dollars.

"Thanks," Callie said with a smile. But I know Callie really well, and behind that smile I knew she wasn't really happy. I felt just a little bad for her.

The crowd thinned out, and Callie noticed me and Mia standing there.

"Hey, Katie," she called out. "Do you want a makeover?"

"Um, you know I don't wear makeup," I said. "Sorry. You should come check out our cupcake table. I bet your dad would like one. They're vanilla."

A woman I didn't know tapped me on the shoulder. She wore sunglasses and her brown hair was swept back in a tan scarf with designs on it.

"Did you make the cupcakes with the school colors?" she asked.

"Yes—I mean, we did," I said. "We have a club. The Cupcake Club."

"They were beautiful *and* delicious," she said. "Made from scratch, I could tell. I would love to have you make some for the PTA luncheon this spring. We'd pay you, of course."

Mia and I exchanged glances. Someone wanted to pay us to make cupcakes. Just like professionals. How awesome was that?

Maggie flew up to the woman. "Mom! The Cupcake Club is a *rival* booth! You're consorting with the enemy."

"Calm down, Maggie," her mom said. "It's all for the school. I was just coming to get my makeover."

Maggie glared at us, but I didn't care. I was feeling pretty good.

Then Callie stood up. "Maggie, can you work the cash box for a minute? I'm going to get a cupcake."

Sydney dropped the makeup brush she was holding. "Callie, you absolutely *cannot* buy a cupcake. Do you want to win this contest or not?"

"It's just a cupcake," Callie said quietly.

Callie walked over. We smiled at each other.

Maybe Callie was right. Maybe it was just a cupcake.

But to me, it felt like so much more.

CHAPTER 18

The Icing on the Cupcake

The fund-raiser ended at three o'clock, and by then we had sold almost every single cupcake. Then Mia's stepdad, Eddie, came to pick her up.

"Hey, girls," he said, smiling big. "How did the cupcake sales go?"

"Great," Mia told him.

Alexis counted the remaining cupcakes. "We sold one hundred and eighty-three," she reported.

"So that means you have seventeen left?" he asked.

Alexis nodded.

"Tell you what," Eddie said. He took his wallet from his pocket. "I've got a big meeting on Monday. I bet everyone at work would like some cupcakes. I'll take everything you have left."

"Wow, thanks!" I said.

"That will be thirty-four dollars, please," Alexis said matter-of-factly.

Mia smiled. "Thanks, Eddie," she said, and she looked really happy. "You didn't have to do that."

"I did," said Eddie. "I'm making them all work late, but they don't know it yet!" He laughed. I still couldn't tell how Mia felt about Eddie, but he seemed nice enough to me. I wondered what it would be like if Mom got married again. That would be weird. Too weird to think about.

Thanks to Eddie, we sold every single one of our cupcakes. We turned over our four hundred dollars to Principal LaCosta. Then we headed home to get ready for the dance that night.

I put on my new purple dress and Mia's black boots. I checked out my reflection in the mirror. I still didn't feel like I could be in a magazine or anything. But I thought I looked pretty good.

Mom got teary-eyed when I came downstairs.

"My baby's first dance," she said, gripping me in a hug. "Oh, you look so glamorous!"

"Mo-om," I said in a complaining voice. (But to be honest, I kind of liked it.)

We picked up Mia, who of course looked great, and then Mom dropped us off. The gym was decorated just like you see in the movies or on TV. There were more blue and yellow balloons and streamers, and a DJ was set up over by the basketball hoop. I was happy to see that Alexis and Emma were there already, over by the food table.

"Wow, you look nice," Emma said.

"So do you guys," I replied. "So, what's to eat?"

"There's punch, some vegetable platters, and cupcakes," Alexis reported.

Emma groaned. "I don't think I can look at another cupcake today."

"I can *always* look at a cupcake," I said, examining the trays. They looked normal—chocolate with chocolate icing, and I could tell the icing came from a can.

"Speaking of cupcakes," Alexis said. "I talked to my parents at dinner about our PTA cupcake order. You know, they're accountants, so they can help us figure out what to charge so we make a profit. They said they could even set us up as a business if we want."

"Our own business?" I asked. I hadn't thought about our little Cupcake Club as anything more than . . . well, making and eating cupcakes. But making money, too? That couldn't be bad. "I like it!"

"I could design the logo!" said Mia.

"I bet I could make more than I do babysitting my brother!" said Emma excitedly. "I'm in!"

"Then," proclaimed Alexis, "we are officially the Cupcake Club. Open for business!"

"Yay!" We all laughed and went in for a group hug. It felt good. For the first time in a while I wasn't really worrying about anything. Not Callie. Not middle school. Not even math.

Then some girls I didn't know came up to us.

"Those cupcakes you made were sooo good," one of the girls said.

"Yeah," said her friend. "How did you make them?"

"It's easy," I said. "You just follow the recipe."

Then a funky beat blared through the gym. "Hey, I love this song!" Mia said. Before I could say no, she grabbed my arm and dragged me onto the dance floor. Alexis and Emma followed us. We danced to the whole song, and then the next one.

George Martinez was dancing by himself. He pointed at me.

"Hey, Silly Arms!"

I started waving my arms around like the Silly Arms sprinkler. George cracked up. Then Mia started doing it too.

"Hey, that's pretty fun!" she said.

139

Then the gym got quiet. Principal LaCosta walked up to the DJ and took the microphone from him.

"Students, welcome to Park Street's first dance of the year!" she cried, and a bunch of people cheered and whistled. "Now it's time to announce the winners of our first contest. The winning table today raised four hundred dollars for our school."

Alexis gasped. It still wasn't sinking in with me, though. Not until Principal LaCosta called our name.

"Let's hear it for the Cupcake Club!"

Emma let out a loud squeal. Then I realized I was squealing too. We won! We actually won! It was like the sweet icing on top of a delicious cupcake.

The four of us ran up to the DJ booth and Principal LaCosta handed us our prize. "Congratulations, girls! You've each won a Park Street Middle School sweatshirt!"

Everyone clapped. I still couldn't believe it. Then the DJ started to blast the song, "Celebrate!"

Mia draped the sweatshirt over her shoulders. "Victory dance!" she yelled.

Just then Callie ran up to me and gave me a big hug.

"Katie, that's so awesome!" she said.

Then we both stopped, stared at each other, and

140

started to laugh. We were both wearing the same dress! I had forgotten that purple was Callie's favorite color.

"You look great!" she said.

"You do too!" I laughed. I wondered if Sydney told Callie she thought the dress was ugly.

Mia, Alexis, and Emma were running out to the dance floor. I didn't know I was doing it, but I must have been following them with my eyes. A kind of sad smile crossed Callie's face.

"Go dance with your friends," she said.

Callie was the one who said we should make new friends in middle school. When she first said that, I was hurt. But she was right. It felt good to have new friends, but it felt good to have old friends, too.

"Come dance with us," I said.

Callie shook her head. "No, you go. I'll call you tomorrow, okay?"

"Okay," I told her, moving toward the club. Then I looked back. I saw her walking toward Sydney, Maggie, and Bella. Sydney did not look happy.

"Hey, Callie!" I called. She turned around. "I'm glad we're friends!" I yelled. I said it loud, so she could hear it over the music. But I also said it so Sydney could hear me.

"Me too!" Callie called back, and then walked toward the PGC.

I ran off to dance with the Cupcake Club. As I waved my silly arms in the air, I realized something.

The first day of middle school had been awful. Callie had let me down. I got into trouble. Things did not go the way I planned at all.

But the weird thing was that middle school was not a total disaster. Everything had worked out, somehow.

Maybe it was time for a new recipe.

Mix together:
One purple dress.
One corny mom.
Two hundred and four cupcakes.
Three new friends.
One old friend.
Stir gently until they're all blended together.
Then dance.

If you're not an expert baker like Katie, that's okay—here is a quick and easy-to-follow recipe that's just as sweet! (Ask an adult for assistance before you start baking since you might need help with the oven or mixer.)

Pineapple "Upside-Down" Cupcakes

• Makes 18 •

BATTER:
1 box of yellow cake mix
1 cup sour cream
½ cup of pineapple juice (use juice from canned pineapples; see topping)
⅓ cup vegetable oil
4 large eggs, room temperature
1 teaspoon pure vanilla extract

TOPPING:
8 tablespoons unsalted butter, melted
¾ cup firmly packed light brown sugar
1 can (20 ounces) crushed pineapple, drained (set aside ½ cup of the pineapple juice for batter)
maraschino cherries (optional)

Center baking rack in oven and preheat to 350°F. Grease cupcake tins well with butter or cooking spray.

CUPCAKES: In a large mixing bowl combine all of the batter ingredients. With an electric mixer on medium speed, mix the ingredients together until there are no lumps in the batter. Spoon the batter into the cupcake tins so that each tin is about halfway full.

TOPPING: Mix the melted butter and brown sugar together with a spoon. Sprinkle about a teaspoon of the mixture on top of the cupcake batter in the tins. Now add a layer of about a tablespoon of pineapple. If you'd like, put one cherry on top, pressing it into the pineapple layer so it's level.

Bake the cupcakes about 18 to 20 minutes or until a toothpick inserted into the center of a cupcake comes out clean. Remove from oven and place on a wire rack to cool for about 5 minutes. Carefully run a dinner knife around the edges of the cupcakes and invert the cupcake pan onto the wire rack. Let the cupcakes cool for about 20 minutes.

Yummy! :‿

Want another sweet cupcake?

Here's a sneak peek

of the second book in the

CUPCaKe 🧁 DIaRIeS

series:

Mia
in the mix

An *Interesting* Remark

$\mathcal{M}$y name is Mia Vélaz-Cruz, and I hate Mondays.

I know, everybody says that, right? But I think I have some very compelling reasons for hating Mondays.

For example, every other weekend I go to Manhattan to see my dad. My parents are divorced, and my mom and I moved out to a town in the suburbs, an hour outside the city. I really like living with my mom, but I miss my dad a lot. I miss Manhattan, too, and all of my friends there. On the weekends I visit my dad, he drives me back to my mom's house late on Sunday nights. So it's weird when I wake up on Monday and I realize I'm not in New York anymore. Every two weeks I wake up all confused, which is not a good way to start a Monday.

Another reason I don't like Mondays is that it's the first day of the school week. That means five days of school until I get a day off. Five days of Mrs. Moore's hard math quizzes. And I have to wait all the way till the end of the week for Cupcake Friday. That's the day that either I or one of my friends brings in cupcakes to eat at lunch. That's how we formed the Cupcake Club. But I'll tell you more about that in a minute.

Lately I've been looking over a bunch of journal entries, and I've realized that when annoying things happen, they usually happen on a Monday. Back in May, my mom told me on a Monday night that we were moving out of New York. When I ruined my new suede boots because of a sudden rainstorm, it was on a Monday. And the last time I lost my cell phone, it was Monday. And when did I find it? Friday, of course. Because Friday is an awesome day.

Then there was that bad Monday I had a few weeks ago. It should have been a good Monday. A *great* Monday, even, because that was my first day back at school after the Cupcake Club won the contest.

Remember when I mentioned Cupcake Club? I'm in the club with my friends Katie, Alexis, and Emma. It started because we all eat lunch together, and on the first day of school Katie brought in this amazing peanut-butter-and-jelly cupcake that her mom made. Katie is a fabulous cupcake baker too, and she and her mom taught us all how to make them, so we decided to form our own club and make them together. Fun, right?

A little while after we formed the club, Principal LaCosta announced there was going to be a contest the day of the first school dance. There would be a big fund-raising fair in the school parking lot, and the group that raised the most funds would win a prize at the dance.

We hadn't really planned on participating in the fund-raiser, but then this other group in our class, the Popular Girls Club, kept telling everyone they were going to win. The leader of the group, Sydney, bragged that they had some "top-secret" idea that was going to blow everyone away. It's not like we're rivals or anything, but once we heard that, we decided to enter the contest too. Our idea was to sell cupcakes decorated with the school colors (that part was my idea).

The PGC's big secret ended up being a makeover booth, which would have been a cool idea except they weren't very good at doing makeovers. In fact, they were terrible at it. But we were very good at baking cupcakes. We sold two hundred cupcakes and won the contest. At the dance that night, Principal LaCosta gave us our prizes: four Park Street Middle School sweatshirts.

I know it's not a huge deal or anything, but it felt really good to win. Back at my old school, things were really competitive. Just about every kid took singing lessons or art lessons or violin lessons or French lessons. Everyone was good at something. It was hard to stand out there, and I never won a prize before. I was really happy that we won. It made me think maybe it wasn't bad that we moved out here.

Just before my mom picked me up the night of our big win, Alexis had an idea.

"We should all wear our sweatshirts to school on Monday," she said.

"Isn't that kind of like bragging?" Emma asked.

"We should do it," Katie said. "All the football guys wear their jerseys when they win a game. We won. We should be proud."

"Yes, definitely," I agreed. I mean, Katie was right. We should be proud. Making two hundred cupcakes is a lot of work!

Except for one problem. I don't do sweatshirts. I'm sorry, but the last time I wore one I was five, and it made me look like a steamed dumpling. They are all lumpy and the sleeves are always too long.

Even though I wanted to show how proud I was of winning, I also knew there was no way I could wear that sweatshirt on Monday. I really care about what I wear, probably because my mom used to work for a big fashion magazine. So fashion is in my blood. But I also think clothes are a fun way to express yourself. You can seriously tell a lot about a person by what they choose to wear, like their mood for instance. And so to *me* a sweatshirt just says "I'm in the mood to sweat!"

I told Mom about my sweatshirt issue on the drive home.

"Mia, I'm surprised by you," she said. "You're great at transforming your old clothes into new and amazing creations. Think of your old school uniform. You made that look great and like you every day. If you *had* to wear a sweatshirt, I'd bet you could come up with something really cool and great."

Mom was right, to be honest, and I was a little surprised I hadn't thought of it first. Our old school uniform was terrible: ugly plaid skirts with plain white, itchy tops. But you could wear a sweater or a jacket and any shoes, so you could get pretty creative with it and not look gross on a daily basis. That's one of the good things about my new school—you can wear whatever you want. Inspired, I sat at my sewing table the next day and cut up the sweatshirt. I turned it into a cool hobo bag, the kind with a big pouch and a long strap. I added a few cool studs to the strap and around the school logo to funk it up a little. I was really proud of how it looked.

On Monday morning I picked out an outfit to go with the bag: a denim skirt, a blue knit shirt with a brown leather belt around the waist, and a dark-gray-and-white-striped-blazer. I rolled up the sleeves of the blazer, then put the bag over my shoulder and checked out my reflection in the long mirror attached to my closet.

Too much blue, I decided. I changed the blue shirt to a white one, then changed the belt to a braided silver belt and checked again.

Better, I thought. I pulled my long black hair back into a ponytail. *Maybe a headband . . . or maybe braid it to the side . . .*

"Mia! You'll be late for your bus!" Mom called from downstairs.

I sighed. I'm almost always late for the bus, no matter how early I wake up. I decided to leave my hair down and hurried downstairs.

Taking a bus to school is something I still need

to get used to. When I went to my school in New York, I took the subway. A lot of people don't like the subway because of how crowded it is, but I love it. I like to study the people and see what they're wearing. Everyone has their own distinct style and things that they're into. And there are all kinds of people on a subway—old people, moms with little kids, kids going to school like me, people from the suburbs going to work. Also, on the subway, nobody whispers about you behind your back like they do on the bus. Nobody makes loud burping noises either, like Wes Kinney does every single day in the back of the school bus, which is extremely disgusting.

The best thing about the bus, though, is that my friend Katie takes it with me. That's how we met, on the first day of school. Her best friend was supposed to ride with her, but she walked to school instead, so I asked Katie to sit with me. I felt bad for Katie, but it was lucky for me. Katie is really cool.

When Katie got on the bus that morning she was wearing her Park Street sweatshirt with lightly ripped jeans and her favorite blue canvas sneakers. Her wavy brown hair was down. She has natural highlights, as if she hung out every day at the beach.

If I didn't know Katie, I would have guessed she was from California.

"Hey!" Katie said, sliding into the seat next to me. She pointed to her sweatshirt. "I still can't believe we won!"

"Me either," I said. "But we did make some really fabulous cupcakes."

"Totally," Katie agreed. Then she frowned. "Did you forget to wear your shirt?"

"I'm wearing it," I told her. I showed her the bag. "What do you think?"

"No way!" Katie grabbed it to get a closer look. "Did your mom do this?"

"I did," I replied.

"That is awesome," Katie said. "I didn't know you could sew. That's got to be harder than making cupcakes."

I shrugged. "I don't know. It just takes practice."

Braaap! Wes Kinney made a big fake burp just then. His friends all started laughing.

"That is so gross," Katie said, shaking her head.

"Seriously!" I agreed.

This Monday was starting out okay (except for the part when I didn't get to wear my headband). But it got annoying pretty fast in homeroom.

None of my Cupcake Club friends are in my

homeroom, but I do know some kids. There's George Martinez, who's kind of cute and really funny. He's in my science and social studies classes too. There's Sophie, who I like a lot. But she sits next to her best friend, Lucy, and in homeroom they're always in a huddle, whispering to each other.

Then there is Sydney Whitman and Callie Wilson. Sydney is the one who started the Popular Girls Club. Callie is in the club too, and she's also the girl who used to be Katie's best friend. I can see why, because she's nice, like Katie.

Katie, Alexis, and Emma all think Sydney is horrible. They say she's always making mean comments to them. She's never said anything really mean to me. And to be honest, I like the way she dresses. She has a really good sense of fashion, which is something we have in common. Like today, she was wearing a scoop-neck T-shirt with a floral chiffon skirt, black leggings, and an awesome wraparound belt that had a large pewter flower as the buckle. So sometimes I think, you know, that maybe we could be friends. Don't get me wrong—the girls in the Cupcake Club are my BFFs, and I love them. But none of them are into fashion the way I am.

Sydney and Callie sit right across from me. Callie gave me a smile when I sat down.

"Those were great cupcakes you guys made on Saturday," Callie told me.

"Thanks," I said.

I thought I saw Sydney give Callie a glare. But when she turned to me, she was smiling too.

"That was a really *interesting* dress you wore to the dance, Mia," Sydney said.

Hmm. I wasn't sure what "interesting" meant. I had worn a minidress with black, purple, and turquoise panels, a black sequined jacket, and black patent leather peep toe flats. "Perfectly chic," my mom had said.

"Thanks."

"Very . . . red carpet maybe?" Sydney went on. "Although, I was reading this really *interesting* article in *Fashionista* magazine all about choosing the right outfit for the right event. You know, like how being *overdressed* can be just as bad as being underdressed."

I knew exactly what Sydney was doing. She was insulting me, but in a "nice" way. Sort of. I know my outfit might have been a little too sophisticated for a middle school dance, but so what? I liked it.

"There's no such thing as being overdressed," I replied calmly. "That's what my mom taught me. She used to be an editor at *Flair* magazine." Then

I opened up my notebook and began to sketch. I don't normally brag about my mother's job like that, but I didn't know what to say to Sydney.

"Wow!" said Callie. "*Flair*? That's so cool! Isn't that cool?" She turned to Sydney, who looked uninterested. "We read that all the time at Sydney's house. Her mom gets it."

Sydney opened her math book and pretended to start reading.

"You looked really great!" said Callie, like she was trying to make up for Sydney. I honestly didn't really care if they liked it or not. I thought I looked good and that outfit made me feel great.

I wasn't mad at Sydney—just annoyed. Which is not a fabulous way to start the day.

But what can you expect from a Monday?

SUNDAY
SUNDAES

CHAPTER ONE
PLOT TWIST

A hot August wind lifted my brown hair and cooled the back of my neck as I waited for the bus to take me to my new school. I hoped I was standing in the right spot. I hoped I was wearing the right thing. I wished I were anywhere else.

My toes curled in my new shoes as I reached into my messenger bag and ran my thumb along the worn spine of my favorite book. I'd packed *Anne of Green Gables* as a good-luck charm for my first day at my new school. The heroine, Anne Shirley, had always cracked me up and given me courage. To me, having a book around was like having an old friend for company. And, boy, did I need a friend right about now.

Ten days before, I'd returned from summer camp

to find my home life completely rearranged. It hadn't been obvious at first, which was almost worse. The changes had come out in drips, and then all at once, leaving me standing in a puddle in the end.

My mom and dad picked me up after seven glorious weeks of camp up north, where the temperature is cool and the air is sweet and fresh. I was excited to get home, but as soon as I arrived, I missed camp. Camp was fun, and freedom, and not really worrying about anything. There was no homework, no parents, and no little brothers changing the ringtone on your phone so that it plays only fart noises. At camp this year I swam the mile for the first time, and all my camp besties were there. My parents wrote often: cheerful e-mails, mostly about my eight-year-old brother, Tanner, and the funny things he was doing. When they visited on Parents' Weekend, I was never really alone with them, so the conversation was light and breezy, just like the weather.

The ride home was normal at first, but I noticed my parents exchanging glances a couple of times, almost like they were nervous. They looked different too. My dad seemed more muscular and was tan, and my mom had let her hair—dark brown and wavy, like mine—grow longer, and it made her look younger. The minute I got home, I grabbed my sweet cat, Diana (named after Anne Shirley's best friend, naturally), and scrambled into my room. Sharing a bunkhouse with eleven other girls for a summer was great, but I was really glad to be back in my own quiet room. I texted **SHE'S BAAAACK!** to my best friends, Tamiko Sato and Sierra Perez, and then took a really long, hot shower.

It wasn't until dinnertime that things officially got weird.

"You must've really missed me," I said as I sat down at the kitchen table. They'd made all of my favorites: meat lasagna, garlic bread, and green salad with Italian dressing and cracked pepper. It was the meal we always had the night before I left for camp and the night I got back. My mouth started watering.

I grinned as I put my napkin onto my lap.

"We *did* miss you, Allie!" said my mom brightly.

"They talked about you all the time," said Tanner, rolling his eyes and talking with his mouth full of garlic bread, his dinner napkin still sitting prominently on the table.

"Napkin on lapkin!" I scolded him.

"Boys don't use napkins. That's what sleeves are

for," said Tanner, smearing his buttery chin across the shoulder of his T-shirt.

"Gross!" Coming out of the all-girl bubble of camp, I had forgotten the rougher parts of the boy world. I looked to my parents to reprimand him, but they both seemed lost in thought. "Mom? Dad? Hello? Are you okay with this?" I asked, looking to both of them for backup.

"Hmm? Oh, Tanner, don't be disgusting. Use a napkin," said my mom, but without much feeling behind it.

He smirked at me, and when she looked away, he quickly wiped his chin on his sleeve again. It was like all the rules had flown out the window since I'd been gone!

My dad cleared his throat in the way he usually did when he was nervous, like when he had to practice for a big sales presentation. I looked up at him; he was looking at my mom with his eyebrows raised. His dark brown eyes—identical to mine—were *definitely* nervous.

"What's up?" I asked, the hair on my neck prickling a little. When there's tension around, or sadness, I can always feel it. It's not like I'm psychic or anything.

I can just feel people's feelings coming off them in waves. Maybe my parents' fighting as I was growing up had made me sensitive to stuff, or maybe it was from reading so many books and feeling the characters' feelings along with them. Whatever it was, my mom said I had a lot of empathy. And right now my empathy meter was registering *high alert*.

My mom swallowed hard and put on a sunny smile that was a little too bright. Now I was really suspicious. I glanced at Tanner, but he was busy dragging a slab of garlic bread through the sauce from his second helping of lasagna.

"Allie, there's something Dad and I would like to tell you. We've made some new plans, and we're pretty excited about them."

I looked back and forth between the two of them. What she was saying didn't match up with the anxious expressions on their faces.

"They're getting divorced," said Tanner through a mouthful of lasagna and bread.

"What?" I said, shocked, but also . . . kind of not. I felt a huge sinking in my stomach, and tears pricked my eyes. I knew there had been more fighting than usual before I'd left for camp, but I hadn't really seen

this coming. Or maybe I had; it was like divorce had been there for a while, just slightly to the side of everything, riding shotgun all along. Automatically my brain raced through the list of book characters whose parents were divorced: Mia in the Cupcake Diaries, Leigh Botts in *Dear Mr. Henshaw*, Karen Newman in *It's Not the End of the World*. . . .

My mother sighed in exasperation at Tanner.

"Wait, Tanner knew this whole time and I didn't?" I asked.

"Sweetheart," said my dad, looking at me kindly. "This has been happening this summer, and since Tanner was home with us, he found out about it first." Tanner smirked at me, but Dad gave him a look. "I know this is hard, but it's actually really happy news for me and your mom. We love each other very much and will stay close as a family."

"We're just tired of all the arguing. And we're sure you two are too. We feel that if we live apart, we'll be happier. All of us."

My mind raced with questions, but all that came out was, "What about me and Tanner? And Diana? Where are we going to live?"

"Well, I found a great apartment right next to the

playground," said my dad, suddenly looking happy for real. "You know that new converted factory building over in Maple Grove, with the rooftop pool that we always talk about when we pass by?"

"And I've found a really great little vintage house in Bayville. And you won't believe it, but it's right near the beach!"

I stared at them.

Mom swallowed hard and kept talking. "It's just been totally redone, and the room that will be yours has built-in bookcases all around it and a window seat," she said.

"And it has a hot tub," added my dad.

"Right," laughed my mom. "And there are plant-ings in the flower beds around the house, so we can have fresh flowers all spring, summer, and fall!" My mom loved flowers, but my dad grew up doing so much yard work for his parents that he refused to ever let her plant anything here. The house did sound nice, but then something occurred to me.

"Wait, Bayville and Maple Grove? So what about school?" Bayville was ten minutes away!

"Well." My parents shared a pleased look as my mom spoke. "Since my new house is in Bayville, you qualify for seventh grade at the Vista Green School! It's the top-rated school in the district, and it's gorgeous! Everything was newly built just last year. Tan will go to MacBride Elementary."

"Isn't that great?" said my dad.

"Um, *what*? We're changing *schools*?" The lasagna was growing cold on my plate, but how could I eat? I looked at Tanner to see how he was reacting to all this news, but he was nearly finished with his second helping of lasagna and showed no sign of stopping. The shoulder of his T-shirt now had red sauce stains smeared across it. I looked back at my mom.

"Yes, sweetheart. I know it will be a big transition at first. Everything is going to be new for us all! A fresh start!" said my mom enthusiastically.

Divorce. Moving. A new school.

"Is there any *more* news?" I asked, picking at a crispy corner of my garlic bread.

"Actually," my mom began, looking to my dad, "I have some really great news. Dad and I decided it probably wasn't a good idea for me to go on being the chief financial officer of his company. So I've rented a space in our new neighborhood, and . . . I'm opening an ice cream store, just like I've always dreamed!

Ta-da!" She threw her arms wide and grinned.

My jaw dropped as I lifted my head in surprise. "Really?" My mom made the best—I mean the absolute *best*—homemade ice cream in the world. She made a really thick, creamy ice cream base, and then she was willing to throw in anything for flavor: lemon and blueberries, crumbled coffee cake, crushed candy canes, you name it. She was known for her ice cream. I mean, people came to our house and actually asked if she had any in the freezer.

My mom was nodding vigorously, the smile huge on her face. She looked happier and younger than I'd seen her in years. And my dad looked happier than he had in a long time.

"And you two can be the taste testers!" said my mom.

"Yessss!" said Tanner, pumping his fist out and back against his chest. "And our friends, too?" he asked.

"Yes. All of your friends can test flavors too," said my mom.

"Okay, wait." I couldn't take this all in at once. It felt like someone had removed my life and replaced it with a completely new version.

Who were these people? What was my family? *Who was I?*

"Eat your dinner, honey," urged my dad. "It's your favorite. There's plenty of time to talk through all of this."

My eyes suddenly brimmed with tears; I just couldn't help it. Even if—and this was a big "if" for me—this would be a good move for our family, there was still a new house and a new *school*. What about my friends? What about Book Fest, the reading celebration at my school that I helped organize and was set to run this year?

I wiped my eyes with my sleeve. "What about Book Fest?" I said meekly.

My mom stood and came around to hug me. "Oh, Allie, I'm sure they'll still let you come."

I pulled away. "Come? I *run* it! Who's going to run it now? And what will I do instead?"

I scraped my chair away from the table, pulled away from my mom, and raced to my room. Diana was curled up on my bed, and she jumped when I closed the door hard behind me. (It wasn't a slam, but almost.) I grabbed Diana, flopped onto the bed, and had a good cry. Certainly Anne Shirley would have thrown herself onto her bed and cried, at least at first. But what would Hermione Granger have done? Violet Baudelaire? Katniss Everdeen? My favorite characters encountered a lot of troubles, but they usually got through them okay, and it wasn't by lying around crying about them. I sniffed and reached for a tissue, and slid up against my headboard into a sitting position so that I could have a good think, like a plot analysis.

My parents had been unhappy for a long time. I kind of knew that. I mean, I guess we were all unhappy because Mom and Dad fought a lot.

They both worked hard at their jobs, and I knew they were tired, so I always thought a lot of it was just crankiness. Plus Mom was the business manager and my dad ran the marketing group at their company, so I figured since they worked together all day, they just got on each other's nerves after work. But if I really thought about it, I realized that they were like that on the weekends, and even on holidays and vacations. They snapped at each other. They rolled their eyes. And sometimes one of them stomped out of the room. And the more I thought about it, I realized they hadn't spent a lot of time together over the past year. Either Mom would be taking me to soccer and Dad would be staying home with Tanner, or Dad would be doing carpool and errands while Mom went with Tanner to his music lessons. We always ate dinner together, but starting last winter and right up to when I'd left for camp, there had been a lot of pretty quiet meals, with each of us lost in our own thoughts. Mom would talk to me or to Tanner, and Dad would always ask about our days, but they never actually spoke to each other.

I squeezed my eyes shut and tried to think of the last time we'd all been happy together. The night before I left for camp, maybe? We had my favorite dinner, and Dad was teasing that it would be the last great meal before I ate camp food for the summer. Mom joked that we should sneak some lasagna into my shoes, which Tanner thought was a really good idea. Dad ran and picked up one of my sneakers, and Mom pretended to spoon some in. We were being silly and laughing, and I felt warm and snug and cozy. I loved camp and couldn't wait to go every year, but I remembered thinking right then that I'd miss being at the table with my family around me.

Later that night, though, I heard Mom and Dad

fighting about something in their room, like they seemed to do almost every night. Then for seven weeks I went to sleep hearing crickets and giggles instead of angry whispers, along with a few warnings of "Girls, it's time to go to bed!" from my counselors.

Now I heard whispers from Mom and Dad on the other side of the door. They weren't angry, but they didn't sound happy, either. Then I heard the whispers fade as they went downstairs.

I guess I fell asleep, because when I woke up, Dad was sitting on my bed and Mom was standing next to him, looking worried. The lights were out, but my room was bright from the moon.

"Allie," Dad said gently. "You need to brush your teeth and get ready for bed."

"Do you want to talk about anything?" Mom asked as I sat up.

Suddenly I was really annoyed. "Oh, you mean like how you decided to get a divorce and not tell me? Or sell our house and not tell me? Or that I would need to move schools and totally start over again? Nope, nothing to discuss at all." I crossed my arms over my chest.

"Allie," Mom said, and her voice broke. I could

tell she was upset, but I didn't care. "We are divorcing because we think it will make us happier. All of us."

"Speak for yourself," I said. I knew I was being mean, and on any usual day one of them would tell me to watch my tone.

"It is going to be hard," said Dad slowly. "It's going to be an adjustment, and it's going to take a lot of patience from all of us. We are not sugar-coating that part. But it's going to be better. You and Tanner mean everything to us, and Mom and I are going to do what will make you happiest. This separation will make us stronger as a family. Things will be better, and we need you to believe that."

"And what if I don't?" I said. I knew I was on thin ice. Even I could tell that I sounded a little bratty. "What will make me happiest is to stay in this house and go to the same school with my friends and . . ." I thought about it for a second. "Wait, if I'm moving to Bayville, when will I ever see Dad?"

"A lot still needs to be worked out," said Mom. "For now you and Tanner and Diana will live with me at the house in Bayville during the week. Dad will come over every Wednesday, and every other weekend you'll be at Dad's apartment in Maple Grove."

I looked at Dad. "So every other week I'll only see you on Wednesdays?" I felt my eyes filling with tears again.

"We can work things out, Allie," said Dad quickly. "I am still here and I am still your dad and I will always be around."

"I promise you, Allie, we're going to do everything we can to make this better for all of us," Mom said. I couldn't see her face clearly, but I could see that she was trying hard not to cry.

Dad reached over and gave Mom's arm a little squeeze. I sat there looking at them, not being able to remember the last time I'd seen Mom give Dad a kiss hello, or Dad hug Mom. Now here they were, but even that didn't seem right.

"I'm not brushing my teeth," I said. I don't really know why I said that. I guess I just wanted to feel like I was still in control of something, anything. Then I turned away from them and pulled up the covers. All I wanted to do was go to sleep, because I was really hoping I would wake up and this would all be a bad dream.

I woke up and blinked a few times, remembering that I was back in my room at home and not still at camp. Well, home for now.

I slowly got up and listened at the door. I could hear Mom talking and the *clink* of a spoon in a bowl, which meant Tanner was slurping his cereal. I didn't want to stay in my room, but I didn't want to go downstairs either. I grabbed my phone. With all of the drama the night before, I had completely forgotten to check it. I looked at the screen, and there were eighteen messages, ranging from did a big scary monster eat you???? to OMG she came back and now she's gone again! from my best friends, Tamiko and Sierra. I sent a couple of quick texts to them, and within seconds my phone was buzzing, as I'd known it would be.

Just then Mom knocked at my door and opened it. "Good morning, sweetie!" she said with her new Sally Sunshine voice that I was already not liking. "I'm so glad to have my girl home!"

I looked at her. Was she just going to pretend nothing had happened?

Mom came in and sat down on my bed. "Dad

left for work, but I took this week off. The movers are coming in a couple of days, and we'll need time to settle into our new house." She looked at me. I stared at the wall. The wall of my room, where I had lived since I was a baby. I looked at the spot behind the door, and Mom followed my eyes. She sighed. Since I had been tiny, Dad had measured me on the wall on my birthday and had made a little mark at the top of my head. He'd even done it last year, even though I'd told him I was way too old. "I'm going to miss this house," she said softly. "It has a lot of memories."

It was quiet for a second. Mom looked like she was far away.

"You took your first steps in the kitchen," she said, really smiling this time. "And remember your seventh birthday party that we had in the backyard?" I did. It was a fairy tea party, and each kid got fairy wings and a magic wand. There had been so many birthdays and holidays in this house.

I had never lived in another house. All I knew was this one. I knew that there were thirty-eight steps between the front porch and the bus stop. I could run up the stairs to the second floor in eight seconds

(Tanner and I had timed each other), and I knew that the cabinet door in the kitchen where we kept the cookies creaked when you opened it.

"I think you'll like the new house," said Mom. "Houses. You'll have two homes."

I looked straight ahead.

"Your new room has bookcases all around it. I thought of you when I saw it and knew you would love it." Mom looked at me. "And there's a really great backyard to hang out in. I'm thinking about getting a hammock maybe, and definitely some comfy rocking chairs."

"What about my new other house?" I asked.

"Well," Mom said, "Dad's house is an apartment, actually, and it has really cool views. It's modern, and my house is more old-fashioned. It's the best of both worlds!"

I sighed.

Mom sighed. "Honey, I know this is tough."

I still didn't answer. Mom stood up.

"Well, kiddo, we have a lot to do. I'm guessing Tamiko and Sierra are coming over soon?"

I looked at my phone lighting up. "Maybe," I said.

Mom nodded. "Okay. Well, let me know what

you want to do today. It's your first day back. Tomorrow, though, we do need to pack up your room. Dad and I have been packing things up for the past few weeks, but there's still a lot to do."

I looked into the hall. I must have missed the fact that there were some boxes stacked there. One was marked "Mom" and one was marked "Dad."

Mom followed my gaze. "We're trying to make sure there are familiar things in each house. You can split up your room or . . . I was thinking maybe you'd like to get a new bedroom set?" There was that fake bright happy voice again.

I looked around the room. I liked my room. If the house couldn't stay the same, at least my room could. "No," I said. "I want this stuff."

"We should also talk about your new school," Mom said.

I looked down at my feet. My toenails were painted in my camp colors, blue and yellow. I wiggled them.

"You're already enrolled, but I talked to the principal about having you come over to take a tour and maybe meet some of your new teachers."

I shrugged.

"I think it might be good to take a ride over, just

so you are familiar with it before your first day," she said. "It's a bigger school, so you could get the lay of the land. And I've been asking around the new neighborhood, and there are a few girls who will be in your grade."

I nodded.

"Okay," she said brightly. "Well, we have this week to do that, so we'll just find a good time to go."

I swallowed hard.

Mom stood in the doorway and waited a minute, then stepped back into the room quickly, gathered me up in her arms, and hugged me tightly. "It's going to be better, baby girl," she said, kissing the top of my head like she used to when I was little. She was using her normal voice again. "I promise you, it might be hard, but it's definitely going to be better."

I tried really, really hard not to cry. A few tears spilled out, and Mom wiped them away. She took my face in her hands and looked at me. "Now," she said, "first things first, because I think there's a griddle that's calling our names."

I knew the tradition, so I had to smile.

"Welcome-back pancakes!" we said at the same time. Mom's blueberry pancakes were my welcome-home-from-camp tradition. She always put ice cream on them to make them into smiley faces and wrote "XO" in syrup on my plate. I could already taste them. I stood up and followed Mom downstairs. Maybe she was right about things. This day was already getting a little bit better.

The next couple of days were a blur. On our last night in the house, we sat on the grass in the backyard. We had been packing and hauling boxes, and we were all sweaty and dirty and tired. Mom and Dad had emptied out the refrigerator and cabinets, so we had kind of a mishmash to eat. Tanner was eating cereal, peanut butter, crackers, and a hot dog that Dad had made on the grill. For dessert Mom pulled out the last carton of ice cream from the freezer, and since we had packed the bowls up, we all stuck spoons in and shared. "Hey!" I yelped as Tanner's spoon jabbed mine.

"I want those chocolate chips!" he said, digging in. Mom laughed. "In about a week we're going to have so much ice cream, we won't even know what to do with it!" Mom's store was opening soon, and since she was so busy with all the details, the packing at home hadn't exactly gone smoothly. Since Mom kept having to go to the store for things like the freezer delivery or to meet with people about things like what kind of spoons to order, we actually got Dad's apartment set up first. It was nice, but it was . . . well, weird. Tanner and I each had our own rooms, but they were kind of small. And Dad's house felt like Dad's, not really like our house. Dad had always loved modern things, so everything was glass and leather. It looked like it should be in a catalog. I was kind of afraid to mess anything up. There were a lot of pictures of me and of Tanner, but the first thing I noticed was that there were no pictures of the four of us.

"Where's the one from New Year's?" I asked, standing in front of a bookcase. We always took a family picture on New Year's Day.

Dad looked around. "Oh," he said, a little flustered. "I guess Mom took those shots. She has more room in the house."

I looked at him. *So this is how it's going to be,* I thought. *The three of us here and the three of us there.*

"We can take some new shots!" Dad said.

"Better," I kept whispering to myself. They'd both promised it was going to be better. But it wasn't really better. It was just downright weird.

The night before moving day, Tanner and I went to bed late. We had been packing all day, and we were beat, but I still couldn't sleep. I heard the back door open. I looked out my window and saw a shadow on the lawn. I almost freaked out, but then I realized that it was Mom, sitting on one of the rocking chairs that we'd bought for the new house but that had accidentally gotten delivered here. She was facing the house, and she looked like she was trying to memorize exactly the way it looked right then. I wondered if she could see me looking out at her. Then I saw Dad walk toward her. It was kind of weird that he was still here, since he had his apartment already, but they had decided that we would all move at the same time. Dad sat down on the grass next to Mom, and I could see them talking but couldn't hear what they were saying. I heard Mom laugh, and then I heard Dad laughing too. It was a nice sound. It was the last night we'd all be sleeping in this house together. I knew we were still a family—they kept telling us that—but it was the last time we'd all live together, and tomorrow morning everything was going to really change. I looked at

Mom and Dad laughing, but all it did was make my throat thick. Some things were too sad to see, so I flung myself into bed, hoping I'd fall asleep fast.

When the movers rolled up to the house early the next morning, Mom and Dad had already been up for hours, cleaning and sweeping and taking care of a lot of last-minute stuff. The house already didn't look like ours anymore.

When everything was loaded up, Mom locked the front door and handed Dad the key. We all stood there on the porch for a minute, looking up at the house. *Home.* I started to cry, and so did Mom. I buried my head in Dad's chest, and I could tell he was crying too. Only Tanner, who was sitting on the step playing a game on Dad's phone, seemed unmoved. "Tanner!" I yelled. "Say good-bye to your house!"

Tanner looked up, confused. "Uh, bye, house," he said, and we all laughed.

"Okay, troops," Mom said. "Onward." Tanner and I got into Mom's car, and we pulled out of the driveway. I looked back down our street as long as I could, saying good-bye to everything as it was.

We turned onto the main road, and Mom took a

deep breath. "Okay, gang," she said. "On to our next adventure! Here we go."

"To where?" Tanner asked.

"To our new house," Mom said, turning around to look at Tanner. "And to better things ahead."

"Oh," said Tanner. "I thought maybe we were going someplace fun." Mom looked at Tanner like he had ten heads. Then she looked at me, and we both cracked up. Some things, it seemed, weren't going to change at all.

CHAPTER TWO
THE PLOT THICKENS

I hadn't taken a bus to school in years. And even then, I'd had Tamiko and Sierra, and sometimes Sierra's twin sister, Isabel, to sit with. But here I was on the first day of my new school, stepping onto a big yellow bus. Mom had asked if I wanted to be driven to school, but I thought that might be more embarrassing. Mom had taken me to the new school the week before, and I met the principal and we walked around a little bit. I'd really wanted to meet the librarian, but she wasn't there that day. The school seemed fine but big. I was a little nervous about finding my way around, but the principal had given me a map, and Mom and Dad and I had looked at it together the night before.

Mom had started a kind of annoying ritual of after-dinner walks in the new neighborhood. I didn't mind the walking part, but Mom kept stopping to introduce herself to people and talk to them, which was really embarrassing. If she saw that they had a kid who looked remotely like they were my age or Tanner's, she practically marched up their front lawn. One night she spotted three girls my age getting out of a car. She called out "Hello!" before I could beg her not to.

"Hi! I'm Meg!" she said, smiling at the woman who got out of the driver's seat. "We just moved in on Bayberry Lane!"

"Oh, hi!" said the woman. "I'm Jill. This is my daughter Blair and her friends Maria and Palmer."

Blair gave me the once-over. Mom and I had been arranging furniture all day, so I was just wearing an old tank top and shorts. Blair and her friends were wearing cute outfits. Blair nodded at me, then said loudly, "We'll be inside. Bye!" She wiggled her fingers, and then her friends followed her to the house.

I hadn't exactly been expecting an invitation or anything, but Blair's mom said, "Oh my goodness. Well, Allie just moved here and would probably love to hang out too. Allie, would you like to come in? The girls are going to watch a movie."

"Oh, no," I said quickly.

Mom looked confused. "I can come pick you up later," she said.

"Or I can just run you home," Jill said.

"Maybe another time," I said, smiling. "Thank you."

"You are always welcome to drop by," said Jill. She looked behind her and seemed surprised to see that Blair had already gone inside.

Mom chattered on for a few more minutes while I looked down at my feet. "Mooom," whined Tanner. "I want to go hooome."

Jill laughed. "So sorry to keep you. We'll see you again soon!"

She and Mom exchanged phone numbers, and then Mom bounced down the driveway. "Isn't that great?" Mom said. "We just met three girls who will be with you at your new school!"

Yeah, I thought. *Absolutely wonderful.*

Now as I walked down the bus aisle, looking at all the unfamiliar faces staring up at me, I could feel my heart thudding and my face reddening. There weren't any empty seats in the front, and anyway, all the kids there looked younger than me. Toward the back, Blair, Maria, and Palmer were in two rows, one behind the other, all chatting with their heads bent together. They reminded me of me, Tamiko, and Sierra, and seeing them felt like a stab to the heart, but I headed toward them, seeking familiar territory.

They were pretty but not overly done up. Maybe they'd be my new friends? Maybe we'd all just gotten off on the wrong foot? As I drew closer, the bus lurched into motion and I was thrown toward the empty spot beside Blair. In a split-second decision, I started to sit down there, but all three girls looked up at me with such cold, withering stares that I gulped and turned to the closest seat. It was next to a boy who sat looking steadfastly out the window. He didn't even look at me as I sat down, but the girls turned to see where I'd landed and then put their heads back together, whispering and laughing. I'd never experienced "mean girls" in real life, only in books and movies, and I couldn't believe this was really happening to me.

My face flamed again, and I was momentarily filled with a surge of pure, white-hot anger at my parents. This new-school thing was not going to be easy, and it was all their fault!

Right then my phone buzzed, and I pulled it out to see that I had a new SuperSnap from Tamiko. Relief spread through my veins; I *did* have friends. In my old school I'd been popular, so take *that*, mean girls!

I opened the snap and studied the photo of Tamiko and Sierra in Mr. Sato's car on their way to school. It said Miss ya, Sistah! and had a big lipstick-kiss emoji on it. I knew they meant well, but it actually made me feel worse. Quickly I silenced the notifications, locked my phone, and slid it back into my bag. My fingers grazed *Anne of Green Gables* again. I wished I could pull out the comforting and familiar book, but to read something on the bus on the first day would probably just be asking for a snicker. I closed my eyes and took a deep breath, then let it out slowly like I'd learned in our mindfulness unit last year. I did it two more times, and then I let my eyes flutter open.

Yup. Still on the bus.

It was going to be a long day.

Okay, my mom was right about one thing: my new school was *super*-beautiful. I had gotten a small taste of it when I took the school tour, but now I couldn't help admiring all the swooping open spaces and comfy lounge areas—skylights, and terraces with seating, and plants everywhere. The lockers were all newish and smelled good, and the halls were carpeted so that it wasn't a total racket when kids were milling around on their way to class. I had to admit that Vista Green was waaaaay nicer than my old school.

The only problem was that it was really hard to find your way around. I mean, there were no straight hallways. Nothing lined up, nothing made sense, and from minute one, I was lost. I stood in the hall, my bag slung over my shoulder, slowly turning in a circle as I tried to orient myself using the map that the principal had given me. The locker combo they'd given me had worked fine, the schedule they'd given me was very clear, and the office ladies had been pretty nice. But I could not figure out where I needed to go. I tried walking one way, and the room numbers went in the opposite direction of what I'd expected. So I tried walking the other way, but those rooms had letters and not numbers on them. And with each step I took, fewer and fewer kids were walking on the soft sage-green carpeting. I was going to be late.

Just as I was about to give up and walk back to the office, I spied Blair. My stomach clenched as I looked around for someone—*anyone*—else to ask for directions from. I clutched the now-damp corners of the map and stared intently at it, hoping she would just pass me by, but she didn't.

"Hey, new girl, are you lost?" she asked.

I looked up. She was looking at me curiously but not meanly. Maybe this was one of those things where the girls were nice when they were apart but not so nice when they were together; I'd read books where that was what happened. There was no way to avoid speaking to her, and anyway she was my last hope, so I took a deep breath and said, "Do you know how to get to the science lab, room C243, by any chance?"

She hesitated for a split second, and I braced myself for a mean comment. But instead she grinned widely and said, "Sure! It's easy. Head down to the lower level—that's two flights down—and it's right past the pool on your right! You can't miss it." She flounced off.

"Okay, thanks!" I called after her, and I set off down the stairs in relief.

I was wandering the lowest level, peeking in

through the doorway of what turned out to be an empty English classroom, when a series of quiet chimes rang out. I guessed that was Vista Green's version of the earsplitting jangle that signaled the start and end of classes at my old school—also an improvement.

I was just pulling open the door of what might have been a laboratory, or a library—through the window I could see rows of desks with computers—when I heard a stern voice.

"Are you meant to be in class, young lady?"

I turned quickly and found myself face-to-face with a tiny, middle-aged woman, her dark hair long and wavy, a pair of funky rectangular glasses perched on her nose. She was dressed in a chic batik dress with a wide braided leather belt.

"I—I—" I stammered, holding the map out toward her. "I'm lost."

Her expression softened, just slightly. "Oh, you're new. Where are you meant to be? Let's see." In relief I held out the schedule to her.

"Tsk, tsk!" she tutted. "You're way off. The science labs are all the way on the third floor. How on earth did you end up down here?" She sighed heavily. "I'd better take you up in the elevator." She began walking briskly up the hall, her slingback heels scuffing the carpet, as she talked a mile a minute. "I'm Mrs. K. I'm the librarian; that was the library; lowest level is library and English. Reading is very important here at Vista Green; all students must have an independent reading book at all times so that you can Drop Everything and Read. You know, *D-E-A-R*? If you don't have a book, come see me. . . ."

We hopped into the elevator, and she continued her chatter. I tried to answer what seemed like questions (yes, I had an independent reading book; no, I didn't have English class until tomorrow), but it was as if she didn't really need the answers. She was on a roll.

The elevator pinged on the third floor and the doors opened.

"Take a left, then a right; it's on your right. Off you go now. No dillydallying!"

"Thank you. I'm Allie Shear," I said as I backed away down the hall.

"I know!" she said as the elevator doors closed.

Huh? *That was weird. How did she know my name?* I didn't have time to think about that, though, as I hustled left, then right, and then to the science room.

When I finally flung open the door, the class was already in session, and who do you think was sitting right in the front row, center?

Yup. Blair, in all her glory. *Thanks for helping the new girl,* I thought.

She smirked as I sank into the nearest seat.

Lunchtime can be hard even when you're at a school with your best friends. If you come at the wrong moment, the line can be so long that your friends are finished by the time you sit down with your food. A bunch of dumb boys might nab the table you like by the window so that you have to sit with the younger kids somewhere. Sometimes the food can be awful. But nothing, nothing is worse than the feeling of standing with a full tray and having absolutely no one to sit with.

Standing with my iced tea, a steaming bowl of fresh ramen noodles, and a side of kimchi on my tray (the food options were way better here than at my old school), I surveyed the terrain. To my left were the younger kids: noisy, messy, not my speed. To my right were the older kids: cool, quiet, boys sitting with girls. Straight ahead, the kids seemed to be my age—boys still sat with boys, and girls with girls—but the tables were packed. The only possible spot was near Blair and a bunch of her friends, and there was no way I was making that mistake again.

Way in the back by the garbage bins was a half-empty table: social Siberia. I trudged toward it, not looking up; I didn't want to make eye contact with anyone, especially those girls. I set my tray down on the table and lifted my messenger bag off my shoulder, then sat and pulled out my phone. Never had I missed Tamiko and Sierra more than right then, not even when I'd been at camp for seven weeks.

I snapped a picture of my lunch tray and sent it to them, captioning it, Jealous? but what I really wanted to do was snap a pic of myself all alone at the table and send it to them with a caption saying, I miss you guys so much, it's taking all my willpower not to cry my eyes out right now.

I pressed send and began to eat, awaiting a reply. A minute passed, then two, and then I saw that they'd read it. I waited for a peppy reply, at least from Tamiko, who's super-quick on her phone, but nothing came. After another minute I felt worse than before. Were they also at lunch? Were they missing me too? Or had they already made a new friend to replace me?

The food was tasty, and without anyone to talk to, I finished quickly. I still had twenty-five minutes until my next class, and I couldn't sit there by myself and scroll through my phone the entire time; I'd be a sitting duck, just waiting to be picked on in some new way by the mean girls. So I gathered up my things, dealt with the unfamiliar trash/recycling/compost bins, and ditched my tray.

Back out in the hall, I didn't know where else to go, so I decided to head to my usual happy place: the library.

At least I knew where it was.

CHAPTER THREE
IRONY

The Vista Green library was a really beautiful space, and I knew I'd spend a lot of time there. I was looking forward to seeing Mrs. K. again—the only friendly (if somewhat odd) person I'd met so far that day. Back at my old school, Martin Luther King Middle, the librarian had been my favorite teacher, and she was the faculty member in charge of Book Fest, so we'd spent a lot of fun time together, planning and working on the event. Maybe Vista Green had something like Book Fest that I could get involved in; I'd ask Mrs. K.

The door swung open silently. There were a few students at computers at the desks, and even more spread around the back of the room, which opened out to a garden with lounge chairs. Around the room there were beanbag chairs and a few armchairs, and even a sofa, plus a rack of magazines and newspapers, and then rows and rows of books on the shelves beyond. There was a big desk area to my left, which was obviously Mrs. K.'s, and just to the right of it a massive fish tank was set into the wall. I let out a sigh of happiness. This could be my new happy place.

Mrs. K. emerged from the stacks and seemed utterly unsurprised to find me standing in front of her again. She strode across the open area to her desk and surveyed me quickly from head to toe.

"Allie. Allie Shear. A reader. Come. Shelve these books for me, please." She nudged a cart full of books toward me.

"I . . . uh . . . okay." It was so weird how she knew who I was. And how did she know I liked to read? I'd barely said two words to her. Did the school distribute the new kids' files to every staff member here?

Mrs. K. paused for a brief moment, tiny hands on tiny hips, and looked me in the eye. "You *do* know the Dewey decimal system, don't you?"

"Yes!" My brain suddenly sprang to life. I ditched my messenger back next to her desk and pushed the cart toward the bookshelves, grateful to have a place to be and something to do for the next twenty-two minutes.

I felt happy and safe as I shelved the books, confidently locating their homes, and saying hi to my favorite books as I passed them. It was like seeing old friends. Plus, I spotted lots of appealing new books as I worked. *Okay,* I thought. *So I won't have any human friends here, if today was any indication. At least I can have books as friends.*

Pretty soon the cart was empty and I had a few minutes left to get to my next class. I finally felt like myself as I wheeled the cart back to the front of the library and Mrs. K.'s desk, only to find my messenger bag splayed open on the floor and *Anne of Green Gables* lying out in the open on the sage carpet. Worse, Blair was standing over it, snickering.

My jaw dropped and my face flushed with heat as I tried to think of what to do or say. But suddenly Mrs. K. was there, taking the cart from me and giving a withering stare to the mean girls.

"Blair! Maria! Palmer! Don't just stand there. If you knock something over, you must pick it right up!"

Shockingly, they did just as she'd said, putting the book and my phone back into the bag and handing my bag to me sheepishly.

"Sorry," whispered Maria, with the long white-blond hair. She didn't look sorry, though.

I glanced around, and I could see all the kids in the area watching us. I nodded.

Mrs. K. continued. "Excellent choice of reading material, Allie. Nothing like a classic, and right on trend. I suppose you've seen all the film adaptations of the Anne series, including the latest, which is *very* stylish and, I must say, quite well done, though really for teens, not middle schoolers. You must have quite sophisticated taste. Okay. Now, girls, don't let me see you hanging around here again with nothing to do, or I'll put you to work. Now, Allie, where to next, you? Upstairs? Hmmm?"

The girls scuttled off while Mrs. K. yammered on, but I was still standing there in shock at how quickly she'd defused the situation and sent the mean girls packing. I let her give me directions to my math room, and then I stumbled out the door like a zombie from Tanner's new favorite show, *The Walking Zombie Toads* (which is totally gross and inappropriate, as usual).

On the stairs I had a bit of a delayed reaction to

the bag incident, and I felt tears well. Why were these girls so mean? But just as quickly I channeled Anne Shirley and made myself focus on the limitless possibilities of Mrs. K. and the library.

Mrs. K. was a little odd, but at least she seemed to know me, and she had already helped me twice today. Plus she obviously loved books, and her library was awesome.

I survived the first day and lived to tell the tale. It wasn't a good day, but I guess it wasn't a total disaster. At home Tanner was filled with rambling stories of his new school and how he had two best friends, and the teacher had said he was so smart, and their classroom had a pet guinea pig. My mom beamed in satisfaction at him. But whenever she looked at me, her face would cloud over. I was always the happy student in the family, and Tanner was always fighting against school. It was pretty funny to see him as the happy student now, and me as the miserable one. My old English teacher, Mr. Campbell, would have called that "ironic."

Finally my mom interrupted Tanner's story of the ketchup at lunch, saying, "Hey! Do you guys want to come see the progress we've made on the store?"

"Like, now?" asked Tanner.

Usually we went to buy the rest of our school supplies on the first day of school. I guess everything was changing.

"Sure," I said, though all I really wanted to do was go lie on my new bed with Diana and lose myself in a good book. I couldn't face calling Tamiko or Sierra yet to see how their first day had gone, and I really didn't want to tell them about mine.

We walked to the store—it was only five blocks from our new house, and close enough to the beach for us to hear seagulls and feel a cool breeze. My mood lifted as the temperature dropped a little, and soon we reached the store.

The last time I had seen the store, it had been just an empty white box. "Okay, are you ready? Close your eyes," my mom instructed as we rounded the corner. She reached for our hands, and though I felt stupid walking down the street with my eyes closed, my hand in my mom's, I let her lead me. She brought us to the front of the store and then said, "Open!"

I opened my eyes and gasped. It was beautiful!

Outside hung a pale-blue-and-cream striped

awning, and the big plate-glass window said MOLLY'S ICE CREAM in fat and swoopy gold lettering. Molly was the name of my mom's grandmother, who'd taught my mom how to make ice cream.

"Wow!" I said. "Does Grandma know?"

"Uh-huh," said my mom, grinning. "Now go in!"

Inside there was a tall, white-painted wooden counter to my left for the cash register, with a built-in organizer on the side for, I guessed, spoons and straws and things like that. Behind the counter hung a white painted sign that said MENU in fancy black script. There were slots where flavor names could slide in, and lists of drinks, some I'd never even heard of. (I knew what a root beer float was, but an egg cream? A lime rickey?)

Straight ahead were two long freezers with curved glass case tops and enough bins for twelve ice cream flavors. To the right of that were little buckets set into the counter for toppings, with a slab of marble behind it for creating mix-ins.

Behind the freezers was a wall of open shelves, and above that were vintage metal letters with light bulbs in them that spelled out ICE CREAM, like from an old-fashioned carnival. A counter ran along the back with electrical outlets in it (for milkshake blenders and hot fudge warmers?), and at the far right was a tall glass freezer with a door that swung open.

The store's floor was laid in tiny black and white square tiles with flecks of gold in them, and the wall to the far right was a giant mirror; past that was a little hall with a bathroom and a closet. Up in front was a high counter with stools looking out the window, and three white-marble-topped tables with fancy curved wire chairs around them. The puffy chair cushions were done in plastic fabric that was the same as the awning outside: blue and cream stripes.

The light fixtures hung from the ceiling at all different heights, and above the register was a cluster of individual light bulbs hanging from cords; the bulbs had been fitted with ceramic cones above them so that it looked like a cluster of ice cream cones hanging upside down.

I couldn't believe it.

"*Wow*, Mom! This is awesome! It's like one of those makeover shows on TV, where they do everything really fast!"

"Where's all the candy and ice cream?" asked Tanner, looking around anxiously.

My mom laughed. "Excellent question. I have a big shipment coming in tomorrow, and then I have some ice cream in deep freeze storage at the industrial kitchen where I rent space. There's actually a little kitchen in the back here, where I can hand-make small batches of ice cream, and also bake the mix-ins, like marshmallow treats and pie. I'll probably have one or two fresh flavors of the day at any time, and then make the standard flavors in big batches at the industrial kitchen and bring them in as needed."

I was really impressed. It seemed like she'd been working on this for years, not just months. Maybe she had, if only in her imagination. I looked at my mom closely; she was like a different person in here—confident, upbeat, happy! It was kind of hard to believe she used to sit behind a desk looking at numbers all day and now she was going to scoop ice cream. I reached over and gave her a sideways hug.

"I'm so happy for you, Mama," I said, using my baby name for her.

She put her arms around me and Tanner (Tanner tried to squirm out, of course) and sighed happily, saying, "It's going to be better than great." Then she kissed each of us on our heads and gave one more squeeze before releasing us.

I glanced out the window and saw a group of girls about my age walking by. I didn't want to know if any of them were the mean girls.

Quickly I turned back toward my mom.

"Yes. We're going to be better than great," I agreed. But I crossed my fingers for courage as I said it.

CHAPTER FOUR

BOOK CLUB

Tamiko, Sierra, and I had a lot to say that first evening
after school. My heart pinched as we video-chatted—
they were together after carpooling home—and I
missed them so much. Tamiko was wearing one of her
usual eclectic outfits: a painted T-shirt with a bedazzled
vest and a high ponytail sprouting out of the top of her
head. Sierra looked soft and pretty in a loose-fitting
romper. They were full of funny stories about kids we
knew. Like, Jim Beatty had grown a mustache over the
summer (it didn't look intentional), Lori Chambers
had grown nearly a foot taller, and Jamie Hansen was
dating a high schooler who might or might not ride a
motorcycle. There was a new head lunch lady, and the
food might have gotten marginally better.

I told them about the food at Vista Green, and how new and pretty the school was, and about kooky Mrs. K. If they noticed that I didn't mention any kids, they didn't let on, luckily. I tried to stay upbeat because I knew if I started to complain, I'd end up in tears, and I didn't want to go there just yet.

"We miss you, Allie Shear!" said Tamiko. "When are we going to see you?"

I sighed. "Maybe after school one day? Could we get together?"

Tamiko nodded. "I bet I could have my mom bring us over to your house one day this week."

My heart soared. "That would be so amazing."

As we were getting ready to hang up, Sierra smacked her forehead and said, "Oh, Allie, by the way, I'm going to need your help! Mrs. Olson was desperate for someone to help with Book Fest since you left, so I volunteered. I have no idea what I'm doing!"

My heart sank. Not only had my best friend taken over my old, beloved job, but she didn't even like to read! Plus she was always totally disorganized and overcommitted! Book Fest was in trouble, and there was not much I could do about it except grit my teeth and say, "Happy to help, anytime."

My second day of school was a little better than my first. For one thing, Tamiko and Sierra had texted our group chat to say they could come over after school. Knowing I was seeing my friends kept a little flame of happiness burning in my heart all day. For another thing, I knew my way around the building a little better, so I didn't feel like a total alien. And finally, I didn't waste any time at lunch but quickly ate my bánh mì sandwich and ran straight down to the library. Mrs. K. was at her desk and said, "Yes. Good. Okay. Mmm-hmm. Here they are, all ready for you," as I walked in.

I always felt like Mrs. K. was mid-conversation with me whenever I saw her—like we'd already established something, but I was never sure what. Being with Mrs. K. was like reading a book that took place entirely in the present, and you had to figure out the backstory as you went along—confusing but also kind of intriguing.

Today she handed me a stack of flyers to deliver to every teacher around the school, not really asking me to do it but proceeding as if I'd already agreed to whatever it was. I had to laugh a little, she was so funny with her run-on monologues and her chic outfits. (Today: a caramel-colored wrap dress with caramel-colored slingbacks—*click, click, click*—and a chunky necklace of smooth wooden links.) I scooped up the pile of flyers from her and began walking, classroom to classroom, to hand them to the teachers or leave them on their desks.

I wasn't sure if I should look at the flyers or not, since they were for the teachers, but after a few empty classrooms (all the teachers were at lunch), I decided that Mrs. K. wouldn't have given them to me to distribute if they'd been private. So I ducked into an alcove to read what the flyer said. It was a questionnaire, and Mrs. K. was looking for teachers to each fill one in and return it.

The questions were:

- Would you prefer an author visit or a book fair?
- Would you participate in an all-school read?
- Would you prefer that we emphasize fiction or nonfiction?
- Do the kids in your classes read independently? Do you?

My heart leapt at the words "book" and "fair" in the same sentence. Book Fest had been my absolute favorite thing at my old school. It was a three-day-long book fair with piles of books for sale on tables, where kids could stock up on their independent reading books for the year or learn about new books that their favorite authors had written. Sometimes authors or artists would come talk to us about writing or about the characters in the books. It would take over our lunchroom for the three days it ran, and we'd get to bring brown-bag lunches and eat at our desks. Each grade would get a shopping slot, and when it was our turn, we'd swarm the tables and make the tough decisions on how to spend the money we'd brought. Sometimes authors came and signed their books after we bought them. Best of all, we were allowed a free half hour of reading in our classroom every day during Book Fest.

My favorite times were once, in fifth grade, when my mom gave me the money to buy the *Anne of Green Gables* boxed set of beautiful flowered hardcovers and put it away for my birthday. The other was when I met a real live author of some books I'd read and she signed a book for me. She told me I could be an author too, but not in that kind of way adults sometimes do. She said it like I could really do it.

This year I was supposed to be in charge of all the student volunteers, and I was going to be the most senior student involved. I was also going to help the little kids make their book selections, which is something I would have loved. The librarian, Mrs. Olson, was going to let me have a lot of responsibility in running Book Fest this year, and I'd been looking forward to it all summer. Now I wouldn't even get to go.

But if we could have a book fair here at Vista Green, I could help, just like I had at my old school! I rushed to deliver the flyers all around, and if I met a teacher, I talked up the book fair idea. In about twenty minutes I had finished, and I raced back to the library to get my messenger bag. My next class was English—right next door to the library—and I was excited and nervous. English was always my favorite class.

I swooped into the library. Mrs. K. was at her desk. She was busy looking at something on her computer. It was funny how she never thanked me for my help, but I didn't mind. I struggled with whether or not to say something about a book fair—mentioning it would reveal that I'd read the flyers—but how could

I not, given my background and experience?

"Oh, Mrs. K.! I hope we get to have a book fair! It would be so wonderful! At my old school—"

"Pish-posh!" said Mrs. K., spinning in her chair to face me. "We don't need a book fair! Book fairs are crass and commercial. They have to do with shopping, not reading. Some schools sell *trinkets* at their book fairs. And *dolls*!" She shivered dramatically. "Give me a well-read, well-loved copy of an old book any day. I'd like an all-school read, but the teachers don't want the extra work. We'll see about that. Yes. Mmm-hmm. Okay." She spun her chair back around to her computer and was clearly finished with me for the day.

I stood there, stunned, for an extra second. I felt as if I'd been slapped in the face. All my enthusiasm drained out of me and I turned to slink out the door.

Was I wrong for loving Book Fest? So what if they sold trinkets and toys? They brought people in to look at the books. And wasn't that what Book Fest was all about?

I turned left toward the classroom for my first English class. I did not have high hopes. I felt totally out of sync with the only book lover I had met so far at my new school.

Ms. Healy was the name of my new English teacher, and I fervently hoped we would be in sync—*kindred spirits*, as Anne Shirley would have said. I entered Ms. Healy's classroom cautiously, but I hadn't needed to be nervous. The kids were all milling around, some sitting on Ms. Healy's desk, legs swinging happily as they chatted with her. Ms. Healy was young, with thick blond hair that fell to her shoulders, like a girl in a shampoo commercial, and with apple cheeks and sparkling blue eyes. She kind of looked like a kid herself, as she was wearing a cute pink-and-white dress I'd admired recently at the mall.

There were beanbag chairs in the back of the classroom, and there was a whole wall of low bookshelves packed with books. Along the top of the bookshelves were huge stacks of paper and colorful jars of pens of every kind. The bulletin boards on the two walls were papered in bright hues but blank, waiting for our work, I guessed. Along another wall was a display. It said: THE MUSEUM OF THE WRITTEN WORD: SOME OF ITS MANY USES. And there were a bunch of DVDs under a sign that said SCREENWRITING, then a bunch of grocery store products with a sign saying

MARKETING, ADVERTISING, PROMOTIONAL WRITING. Next was a stack of newspapers and magazines with a sign that said JOURNALISM, and finally there were some old cell phones in a pile under a sign that said SOCIAL MEDIA. All around the border of the classroom, next to the ceiling, were portraits of famous writers with their names underneath them, like a gallery. There was everyone from Gary Paulsen and Beverly Cleary to Jane Austen and Alice Walker.

Hmm, I thought, cautiously optimistic. *This is pretty cool.*

Suddenly Ms. Healy called, "Colin, the lights, please!" and a kid jumped up and turned off all the lights. *What on earth?* I thought. *Should I be scared?* I looked around. None of the other kids seemed nervous. It was like they knew what was coming.

Then Ms. Healy switched on a spotlight at her desk. The spotlight shone up onto a disco ball hanging from the ceiling, and loud pop music came blaring out of a speaker. I stood, speechless, as all the kids jumped up—onto desks, chairs, anything—and began dancing. Ms. Healy danced her way over to me and spoke loudly over the music. "Hi, Allie! Welcome to our class! We like to get our creative juices flowing with our disco minute at the start of every class." She led me to a desk in the middle of everyone. "Here's your seat. Enjoy!" Then she danced away, back to her desk.

I stood and looked around in wonder, bobbing a little to the beat, feeling self-conscious but liking what I saw. Sure enough, when the minute was over, Colin flipped the overhead lights back on, Ms. Healy silenced the music and switched off the spotlight, and everyone sat down, smiling.

I knew I had just found my favorite teacher at Vista Green.

"Okay, and then, the room has beanbags, and there was a disco minute, and Ms. Healy is much more fun than Mrs. K., who I'd *thought* was going to be my favorite. And maybe they're *both* my favorite, but . . ."

Tamiko and Sierra were over at my house, and I was filling them in on everything. It felt weird for them to not know who I was talking about, or be able to picture the layout of the school. I promised to snap some pics on my phone or take a little video of it and e-mail it to them.

"Do they give you a lot of homework?" Sierra asked, eyebrows knit together.

I smiled. Sierra absolutely hated homework, but I think it was because she always left it till the last minute and then forgot to bring home the reading, or softball practice would run late, or the star of the play would get sick and she'd be the understudy and have to learn all the lines. It was always some drama with her and homework. "I can't tell yet. I have a ton of reading—"

Tamiko waved her hand in the air and made a "Pffft!" noise. "Oh, please. Reading isn't work for you. It's like breathing. You're gonna do it anyway! Your whole life is like one long book club." She flicked her long, dark side ponytail over her shoulder and scoffed again.

I grinned and reached over for a hug, but Tamiko batted me away, as always. "Oh, stop with your fancy hugs. You know I hate that stuff!"

"And that's why we love you!" cried Sierra, which was our cue to dive onto Tamiko and grab her in a big group hug.

We spilled off my bed onto the floor, laughing. It was such a relief to be with my friends again, people who knew me and got me and liked me. I had felt like an alien on another planet these past two days—like an invisible person, or worse, depending on who was around. Tamiko and Sierra always made me feel better.

I hadn't yet told Sierra and Tamiko about the mean girls at Vista Green. Partly because it was so humiliating that I thought I might cry in the retelling, and partly because Tamiko would want immediate revenge, and I wasn't up for that negative energy right now.

"So do you guys want to come see the store, or what?" I asked, bouncing in place.

"Yes! Let's go! I'm dying to see it!" said Tamiko, hopping up. Tamiko was all about the *new*. She was always on these wild websites looking for new trends and following foreign fashion accounts that her cousins in Japan told her about, and building inspiration boards with clips of her latest obsessions. Everything was a blank slate for Tamiko, just waiting for her imagination to roar into gear and tweak, decorate, redo, enhance, and make it unique. I couldn't wait to see what she thought of Molly's Ice Cream. It was pretty great as it was, but she just might have some ideas on how to make it even better.

We walked to the store, the blocks whizzing past as we chatted a mile a minute. Being with them was like drinking a cool milkshake after a long, dry thirst. Sierra was filling us in on her twin sister Isabel's soccer triumphs, and Tamiko told us about her brother Kai's latest entrepreneurial scheme to sell hurricane survival packs door to door. (We got hit by bad hurricanes almost every year.) There wasn't much for me to tell about Tanner (who wants to hear about burps and stinky sneakers?), so we quickly ended up on the topic of my parents, which is where I think we were headed anyway.

I'd told them both the news by text after I had woken up and realized that it wasn't all a bad dream. Sierra had replied immediately, her text filled with emojis of sad faces and hearts and "I love you." Tamiko didn't respond for about half an hour, and when she did, it was with one bracingly simple word: Good.

It actually shocked me into laughter when I saw it, because for goodness' sake, she was right! It *was* good that they were getting divorced. My parents seemed so much happier already, and I felt so much gratitude to Tamiko in that moment for looking beyond the obvious reaction to the true reaction. But just because my parents were happier didn't necessarily mean *I* was happier.

218

"So, how's it going with, you know . . . ," began Sierra, gentle and considerate, as always.

"The big split," said Tamiko, always one to just rip off the bandage and take the pain as it came.

"It's weird," I said, relieved to talk about it. I'd been thinking in advance about what I'd tell them, because I knew they'd ask, and I wanted to answer as truthfully as possible. "I think with all the changes happening at once, it's sort of good because it's distracting. And then on top of it, they're both so crazy happy, like *relieved*, that it's kind of contagious. And then there's the store, which will be great," I added.

Tamiko looked at me and raised an eyebrow. "Okay. It's good for them. How about you?"

Sierra looked at me expectantly. I was trying to be brave, but these girls knew me too well. "It's hard," I said softly. "It's weird and hard and, well, just a lot to process."

Sierra gave me a squeeze.

"They keep telling us that this is going to be better," I said.

"Well, you just have to trust that it is," said Sierra.

"Well, it might not be," said Tamiko, and Sierra shot her a look. "I mean, new house, new school, you don't see your dad as much. That's a lot to deal with."

"Tamiko!" Sierra scolded.

"No," I said, laughing. "She's right. It's a lot. A whole lot."

"But your parents were really miserable together," said Tamiko. "So I do think it will be better."

"Well, I don't know about 'miserable,'" I said.

"Oh, yes," said Tamiko. "They were miserable. I mean, they fought all the time. They couldn't stand to be in the same room together!"

"TAMIKO!" shouted Sierra.

"What?" said Tamiko. "It's totally true! I can't believe you didn't see that, Allie."

"I saw it," I said. "But it's a different thing to process when it's your own parents."

Everyone was quiet as we rounded the corner.

"You're right," said Tamiko. "I'm sorry. It's not like it's just anyone's parents. They're your parents."

"It's okay," I said. "It's good to talk about it a little."

Sierra flung her arm around me. "Okay, now let's talk ice cream."

"Close your eyes and give me your hands," I directed, mimicking my mom.

I led them to the edge of the curb in front of the store. Then I said, "Voilà!"

CHAPTER FIVE
CHARACTER DEVELOPMENT

Sierra gasped and lifted her hands to her mouth. She clasped them there and shook her head slowly in wonder. Tamiko laughed out loud and turned to high-five me.

"Wow!" she said appreciatively. "Talk about curb appeal!"

"Pretty cool, huh? Do you like it?" I asked, but I couldn't hide my grin; I could already tell they loved it.

"Cool? I'm moving in. Now get out of my way!" Tamiko pushed me aside and entered the store, and a new little bell tinkled above the door.

My mom was inside, and she came out from the back at the sound of the bell, wiping her hands on her apron.

"Girls!" she cried, holding her arms wide. My mom loves my besties, which makes me so happy. She always tells me that if she were my age, she'd pick them as her friends too.

Tamiko and Sierra ran to embrace her, squealing and jumping up and down in excitement.

"Mrs. S.! This rocks!" said Tamiko, turning in place to take it all in.

"Are you so excited? It's your lifelong dream come true!" said Sierra.

My mom was beaming. "I *am* so excited. And thank you for your enthusiasm. Now come into the back and try my new flavor. It's cinnamon ice cream with crumbled lace butter cookies in it."

"Yum!" said Sierra.

We trailed my mom into the back, and she doled out samples of her new flavor while we chatted.

"Oh, Allie, Mrs. Olson says hi and she misses you," said Sierra. "We had a planning meeting for Book Fest, and she kept mentioning you."

My smile faded. "Bummer. Tell her I say hi back. I miss her, too."

"Yeah, well, we're really understaffed this year," said Sierra, shaking her head regretfully. "And I have so much going on, with the can drive for Thanks-giving, and student council, and dance, plus the newspaper. . . ."

I had to crack a smile at her laundry list of activi-ties. Sierra always overcommitted herself and then had a hard time delivering. Inside, I cringed a little to think of it being her instead of me helping Mrs. Olson with Book Fest.

"Hey! I know. You should ask MacKenzie to help you!" said Tamiko.

"Oh! That's a great idea!" Sierra turned to me. "MacKenzie is this new girl. She's super-nice. You'd really like her, Allie. We've told her all about you. You two definitely need to meet!" said Sierra, nodding enthusiastically.

Tamiko turned to me. "Yeah, she's in all our classes, so we've gotten to know her pretty fast. You'll love her."

"Great," I said weakly. I could feel my mom watching me, but I refused to meet her eye. I couldn't help but feel it was her fault that I didn't get to go to school with my best friends anymore, and her fault that I didn't know this new girl. No one had tried to be friends with me at the new school. There was only

Blair and her band of mean girls trying to send me to the nonexistent pool.

"Oh, Allie! Guess what else! I can't believe I forgot to tell you. I've already told everyone else I know, so I guess it feels like old news, but Maya Burns is coming to sign her books at Book Fest this year!"

My jaw dropped. "Maya Burns? Seriously? She's only my second-favorite author, after—"

"Lucy Maud Montgomery!" singsonged Tamiko and Sierra. They love to tease me about my *Anne of Green Gables* obsession.

"I know!" added Sierra. "Maybe I can get her to sign a book for you!"

"Yeah," I said, feeling deflated. My best friends would get to meet my second-favorite author, and I wouldn't, and they didn't really even care about books!

Tamiko's phone pinged. "Oh, that's MacKenzie now." She read the snap and laughed. "She sent a funny photo, but she just wants to know what the homework is for math." Tamiko consulted her notes, then typed back quickly, her thumbs a blur on the screen.

"Anyway," said Sierra, sensing that Tamiko's behavior was a little rude. "Tell me more about your plans for the store, Mrs. Shear. It's so amazing already."

I suddenly wondered if my mom would continue to go by "Mrs. Shear." It would be weird for my friends to call her anything else. I mean, they couldn't really call her "Meg" like *her* friends did, could they? Was she going to go back to her maiden name? There were so many things I just didn't know right now. I glanced at my mom. I'd have to ask her about all this later.

Mom chatted about the shop and led the girls back out to the front to point out a few things.

"You should get one of those customized photo frames, so people can hold it in front of them and snap pics to post on social media," suggested Tamiko. "Also, make sure to register your business name and GPS so people can tag it in posts. And you might want to consider purchasing a filter. You know, like the one where people's faces turn into dogs, but maybe instead of puppy ears, they get ice cream cone hats!"

"Good ideas!" said my mom admiringly. She pulled a small notebook out of her pocket and wrote down Tamiko's suggestions.

"Will you do mail order?" asked Tamiko. "And

what about flavor of the day or month? That's so big on social media."

While Tamiko and my mom were devising marketing strategies, Sierra and I sat down on stools at the window-front counter to chat.

"I miss you guys," I said.

"We miss you so much, *chica*!" said Sierra, her eyes misting. She reached over and hugged me hard. "But we can still see each other a lot, like this."

I shook my head. "I think it's going to be hard to fit in, once homework ramps up and the school year gets going. I wish we did some activity together, like soccer or ballet, where it was a guarantee that we'd see each other every week."

"Yeah," agreed Sierra, lost in thought.

Tamiko arrived at our side. "MacKenzie thinks it's so cool that your mom owns an ice cream store. I told her to come by."

"What, *now*?" I said. I had thought this was our time to be together—you know, the three of us, just like it used to be.

"Yeah! She's super-cool. You're going to love her. I can't wait—"

"Tamiko!" said Sierra sharply. "*No.* This is *our* time

with Allie. Tell MacKenzie maybe another day."

"What?" Tamiko looked confused. But then comprehension washed over her face. "Oh! Right. Oh, I'm sorry, Allie. I wasn't thinking. You're right. Hang on." Her fingers flew over her keyboard as her dark eyes narrowed in concentration. "Okay. Done. Sorry. That wasn't very sensitive of me." She patted me on the head. "Sorry, little one."

We all laughed, because I was about three inches taller than Tamiko.

One of the things I loved most about Tamiko was that there was never any drama, never any beating around the bush. She was so direct that little upsets didn't have time to fester and become big problems.

"Anyway, *someday* you'll meet MacKenzie, *if* we're even still friends with her, and then you *might* like her. That's all! Now, what are we going to do this weekend?" Tamiko grinned.

"Something fun," I said.

Soon we were planning what to do on Saturday—movies, mall, maybe lie out by the beach. By the time I got home that evening, I felt much better—reconnected to my friends, and with something to look forward to for the weekend.

On the bus the next morning, I headed straight to the back. But halfway down the aisle, Colin from my English class looked up from the newspaper he was reading. "Hey! Allie. Here." He patted the seat next to him as he scooted toward the window.

I had an urge to look over my shoulder to make sure it was me he was really talking to (as if there might be another Allie standing behind me), but I decided the better part of being cool was just *acting* cool, so I smiled and joined him.

"Hi," he said. "I'm Colin. From English class."

I nodded. "I know. You do a mean light switch."

He smiled. "Thanks. I was new last year too. Came in at the middle of the year. It stinks at first, but then it gets suddenly much better. I couldn't watch the girls torture you again this morning."

I grinned. "So you saw that?"

"I didn't even need to see. But don't worry, no one really pays attention to them. There are nice kids in the grade too. I'll introduce you."

"Cool," I said, and we chatted the whole rest of the way to school. Colin was the assistant editor of the school paper, hoping to run it next year, and he told me all about it on the ride. Like me, he loved to read and write, and English was his favorite subject. He confirmed my feelings about Ms. Healy (she was awesome, and everyone was desperate to be in her class), and Mrs. K. (a little kooky but smart and very nice and interesting).

As the bus pulled in and we shuffled off, Colin said, "See you in English!" and I knew I'd just made my first friend at Vista Green—a kindred spirit.

At lunch I sat with Colin, and he introduced me to two nice girls, as promised. Amanda and Eloise were both in my grade, and we connected well, even if they weren't immediate replacements for Sierra and Tamiko. It's hard for new friends to compete with friends you've had since you were a toddler.

I didn't want to overstay my welcome, so I ate pretty quickly and then excused myself. I was curious to see if Mrs. K. had gotten any results in from her survey, so I headed down to check in.

In the library Ms. Healy and Mrs. K. were chatting at Mrs. K.'s desk, and they both looked happy to see me.

I guess I must have looked a little anxious, because Ms. Healy jumped in immediately.

"We were just discussing some of the literacy initiatives for the year," said Ms. Healy. I knew that "literacy initiatives" meant "reading events and projects."

I looked at Mrs. K. "Any feedback on your surveys?" I privately hoped that there would be such an overwhelming vote for a book fair that she would have to cave. And then I could help her organize and run the whole thing! And we could call it Book Fest!

Mrs. K. hemmed and hawed and shuffled papers around on her desk as I waited for an answer.

"I'm a big fan of the all-school read," said Ms. Healy. "It would be wonderful to build some programming around the book's topic and have some guest speakers come in. My friend Ellen teaches over at Saint Joseph's High School and said her school read a nonfiction crime book. The school had the mayor and the chief of police read it, and then they came in and met with the students. Each teacher had to prepare two classes around the book, so Ellen, being a science teacher, did a class on forensics and evidence and crime scene contamination. She even had a teacher friend barge in and out during the class, and then she quizzed kids on their eyewitness descriptions of the woman, to see how observant they were."

"Cool!" I said. "Just like on TV!"

"Hmm, yes, very interesting," agreed Mrs. K., nodding her head enthusiastically.

"There are a million things you could do. I get excited just thinking about it!" I gushed.

Ms. Healy smiled at me. "Maybe we need to form a committee, with student advisors. . . ."

My heart leapt! This was just what I'd been hoping! Maybe I'd get to help run a book fair after all.

But she continued. "We might not be able to organize something for this year, but we could get ready for next year."

Inwardly I groaned. A whole year? Outwardly I continued to nod and said I'd love to help.

Mrs. K. was biting her lip thoughtfully as she gathered the stack of surveys and shook and tapped them into a neat pile. "The surveys are saying book fair." She rolled her eyes.

My heart leapt again, but I played it cool. "I'd help with that! I mean, if you did it. I love book fairs."

"Maybe we could do a book fair off-site on a

weekend?" suggested Ms. Healy. "Or join forces with another school, or even the town library. Make it a fund-raiser?"

Mrs. K. hammered away on her keyboard, finished with the conversation for now and ignoring us. Ms. Healy winked at me. "You're on our steering committee now, anyway. We'll figure something out. We've got a budget for something."

The chimes sounded, and Ms. Healy and I walked to her classroom together.

When I got home at dinnertime, I had a whole series of snaps from Tamiko with suggestions for the ice cream shop, and a few from Sierra, asking what she should wear to the grand opening of the store this Sunday. I also had friend requests from Colin, Amanda, and Eloise, all of which I accepted. Things were looking up!

Just before bed I got one last snap from Tamiko. It said, Can I bring MacKenzie to the opening on Sunday?

My heart sank. *This again?* As I was mulling over my reply, Tamiko pinged me once more.

Kidding! it said, and I laughed out loud.

CHAPTER SIX
SETTING

This weekend was my and Tanner's first weekend to spend with our dad, and it all went pretty well. He burned the hamburgers on Friday night because he wasn't used to cooking them on a stove instead of a grill, but it didn't matter because we cut them in half and scooped out and ate the middles dunked in ketchup. Then we ran upstairs to try the rooftop pool.

Let me tell you, when you are used to being at ground level, or maybe on a second or third floor, and suddenly you get the chance to be seven stories up, it is pretty eye-opening. The whole town was spread out before me, and it felt like I was looking at a map from the end pages of a book, like *The Boxcar Children*, which was my favorite book when I was little. Tanner and I even mapped out where our old house was. Even better, the pool was awesome! It was outdoors, open to the night sky, and encircled by brand-new cushy white lounge chairs. There were bright yellow foam floats that anyone could use, and Tanner and I had a pirate war with ours (me stooping to his level, I admit) while my dad read the newspaper on a lounge chair.

But the best part was that while Tanner and I were resting between pirate bouts, Amanda from my class showed up with her younger sister. It turned out that her mom lived in this building too. We spent the rest of our time playing Marco Polo, all four of us in the pool, until it was dark and my fingertips were like raisins.

As we got off the elevator at my dad's floor, I invited Amanda and her sister, Maddy, to the ice cream shop opening on Sunday. Then I winced as I realized that I was having a double standard, since I hadn't wanted Tamiko to invite MacKenzie. So when I got back to my new room, I raced to my phone and snapped Sierra and Tamiko to say that they should bring MacKenzie if she wanted to come, and anyone else. The more the merrier, anyway!

Being at Dad's was fun, but it was kind of like we were away on a vacation without Mom, which was weird. Plus I wasn't used to being in an apartment. I could hear doors opening and closing and someone upstairs walking around. It was comforting to know that I was surrounded by people. Then I heard my door swing open.

"Allie?" It was Tanner.

"What's wrong?" I asked.

"I can't sleep," he said softly. "My room is scary."

"Scary?" I asked. "You mean just because it's new and everything is unfamiliar?"

"Yeah," he said. "I keep hearing footsteps."

"Come here," I said, scooting over and making room for him. He climbed in next to me and put his head on my shoulder. He hadn't done that in a long time.

"I want to go home," he said.

"To Mom's house?" I asked.

"No, *home*," Tanner said emphatically. "Our old house."

I sighed. I knew what he meant.

The light flicked on in the hall, and Dad peeked in. He looked worried for a second, but then smiled.

"You guys okay?" he asked.

"It's weird in my room," said Tanner.

"What's weird?" asked Dad. "The lights? Is your bed not comfortable?"

"It's just weird," said Tanner.

Dad sat down on the bed. "Well, this is new for all of us. We all have new rooms and new beds and new houses. It's a lot to get used to."

"Times two!" said Tanner. "New at Mom's house and new at your house."

"I know," said Dad softly. "I know, buddy. It's really weird for me to be in the apartment by myself when you guys aren't here. I miss you so much. But we're going to get through this together."

We were all quiet for a while.

"I have an idea," Dad said. "Who wants a midnight snack?"

"I do!" yelled Tanner, sitting up.

We followed Dad out to the kitchen. He opened a cabinet and looked a little guilty. "I, uh, got a few snacks for the new place."

He took out some chips and dips, then a bag of marshmallows.

"Dad!" I said, laughing. "That's quite a stockpile!"

236

Dad put everything on a plate and carried it out to the living room. We put on one of our favorite movies and all settled in.

"We can have a slumber party!" Dad said.

Tanner fell asleep pretty quickly lying on Dad. Then Dad fell asleep too. I thought for a minute about going into my room, but I put my head on Dad's shoulder and just snuggled in.

Saturday morning Dad took us to the batting cages and miniature golf, which was kind of a family tradition. It was weird to be there without Mom, and I think we were all feeling it. Dad kept saying, "This is our *new normal*," like it was some kind of spell he wanted to come true. We were all a little sad afterward, so when Dad suggested we stop by to see Mom at the ice cream store, we were all in favor.

At Molly's, Mom was all aflutter: accepting a delivery, painting part of the counter that had gotten dinged up by the dishwasher installation, talking on her cell phone to the health inspector about where to post her certificate, and baking some Saint Louis butter cake to try in a new ice cream flavor. She waved happily when she saw us and gratefully doled out a few tasks. I think we were all relieved to experience

237

the "old normal" for an hour and a half before my dad said it was time for lunch for him and Tanner.

Tamiko and Sierra wanted us all to go to the mall in the afternoon. I had felt funny about ditching Dad on his first weekend alone with us, but Mom had assured me it would be okay. She said it wasn't my job to entertain my parents; I just needed to go on living my life, and things would start to feel normal. (There was that word again! Ms. Healy would be asking me for an alternative word choice by now.) So I agreed to the plan.

Mrs. Sato was picking me up at Dad's at twelve thirty, and I was ready and downstairs by twelve twenty-five. Sure enough, at twelve twenty-nine their white SUV cruised up, and Tamiko rolled down the window and gave me the peace sign. It was always so funny to see her short mom driving around in such a big car. She practically had to take a running start down the driveway to get into it.

I hopped in and submitted to Mrs. Sato's grilling me about my new school all the way to the mall. She was envious that I got to go to Vista Green and said she was always looking for a house to move to so Tamiko and Kai could rezone to that school district.

"Imagine if I got to come to your school!" said Tamiko.

"Nooooo!" wailed Sierra. "Who would help me with all my assignments if you were both gone?"

"Hmm," I said, turning to Tamiko. "Maybe you *should* move to my school, and maybe then Little Miss Forgetful would start to take care of herself a tiny bit better!" I teased.

Sierra folded her arms across her chest and fake-pouted. "I just have a lot on my plate!" she said.

"That's because you always take extra helpings!" joked Tamiko.

Sierra made a scoffing noise. "I can't help it if I like to be involved."

"I think you need to start sitting on your hands in meetings so that you don't volunteer for anything else," I said. I felt a little mean saying it, but secretly I wished she hadn't volunteered to run Book Fest.

"I'll sit on them for you!" shouted Tamiko, scooching over toward Sierra, who shrieked.

"Here we are, kiddos!" announced Mrs. Sato as she pulled up in front of the Commons, which was our town's answer to a mall. It wasn't like the old-fashioned malls where everything was on multiple

239

floors under one huge roof. Instead it was styled as a small village, and you had to be outdoors on these cool covered boardwalk-style sidewalks to go from store to store. We all loved it. There was one area that was all food trucks—this mall's version of a food court—and it had lots of seating under a huge shady tentlike canopy, and big outdoor air conditioners that blew mist over you to cool you off.

We hopped out of the car with promises to behave, and set a pickup time for four o'clock. Then we began the bargaining.

"Please, please—bookstore first!" I said.

"But you never even buy anything. All we do is go there for an hour and you visit the books you already own!" protested Sierra.

"That's not true! I buy a new book every month; I just like reading library books and eBooks, so I mix it up and don't spend all my money on one thing."

Tamiko said, "All I know is, I have to get to the arts and crafts store for some new sequins and yarn, and then the hardware store for a glue gun."

"I can only imagine what kind of project this is for. Are you customizing your toilet seat this week?" I teased.

"No, but *that* is a great idea! I need to search for ideas for that when I get home!" said Tamiko.

I groaned. "It was a joke!"

It felt great to be back with my besties doing one of our usual activities. We had a certain routine at the mall and certain things we liked to visit (the Wishing Fountain, the human-size chessboard, the Skee-Ball arcade, and the temporary-tattoo vending machine, to name a few), and of course, certain things we liked to eat, in certain orders. A lot of it was unspoken—we just settled into our usual pattern. The day was warm but not hot, and the sky was blue, and I was happier than I'd been since camp, practically skipping as we walked and joked.

We didn't do much before we were all starving and had to go to the Arepa Lady's truck. She made these delicious thick and chewy cornmeal pan-cakes filled with cheese that you could top with any kind of shredded meat (or not). We always started with her, and then went to the Belgian frites guy for french fries with sriracha mayo dipping sauce, and then the bubble tea guy for drinks. We'd finally completed gathering everything and were just turning to sit at a picnic table when there was a loud squeal from behind us. Everybody turned around.

"Niñas!" cried a voice.

"Niña!" Tamiko and Sierra called in excitement, hastily dropping all their things onto the table and turning quickly toward someone.

I carefully put my assorted things down onto the table and lifted a few of their things that had toppled over, then turned curiously to see who had called to us. I couldn't make out the person's face because the three of them were in a group hug, jumping up and down. But I could see that she had long, straight, bright red hair and wore very stylish white jeans with a thick white T-shirt, and on her feet, a pair of black sneakers with a shiny logo, which I knew were Tamiko's absolute favorite brand of sneaker. (Or at least they once were—her favorite seemed to change daily.) As they pulled apart from their little love fest, I looked at the girl's face and did not know her. My heart sank.

A new friend.

"Niñas," they called one another. The three of us always called ourselves *"chicas."*

The three of them stood chatting rapidly, and I wasn't sure what to do. I was standing there debating whether to say something and idly eating french fries from the paper cone they'd come in, when I looked around to see who else was there, and suddenly my stomach dropped. The "Mean Team" was at a table across the tent, their eyes bouncing back and forth between me and the threesome. Now I was really doomed.

Standing there alone, I looked like the loser they already thought me to be. I wanted to shout, *"Those are my best friends over there!"* but the girls would have just laughed at me, because, come on, it sure didn't look like it.

But if I walked over to Tamiko, Sierra, and the other girl and they ignored me, left me standing on the outside, it would look even worse. My face grew red and my heart thudded as Maria leaned in to Blair and Palmer and whispered something that made them all giggle.

That was it! I had to act!

Quickly I marched across the open pavilion to the bubble tea truck to get an extra straw. I already had one, but I needed something to do with myself while I waited for my friends. I needed to look busy!

I passed as close as possible to Tamiko, Sierra, and

"*niña* girl," but none of them acknowledged me; they were all chatting away excitedly. I couldn't help it. Tears welled in my eyes and I bypassed the bubble tea guy and headed straight for the bathroom at the far end of the food area.

The tears spilled over just as I reached the door, but I held my head up and didn't cave until I'd reached the stall and locked the door behind me. Then I gave in to the silent, racking sobs I'd been fighting for what felt like forever. What was happening to me and my friends? It was all too much.

I blew my nose and patted my wet cheeks with some tissue. I stepped out of the stall and went to wash my face, and just as I reached the sink, Sierra appeared.

"Allie! There you are!" she cried in relief. "We were worried about you!"

She saw that I had been crying and rushed over. "Oh, Allie! What's wrong?"

I felt huffy. "It sure didn't seem like you noticed me," I muttered.

"Allie, that was MacKenzie! We wanted you to meet her. But Tamiko was scared after the other day that you'd be mad if we dragged her over to you. So we were waiting for you to come say hello, but then you blew us off. What happened to you?"

"Wait, *I* blew *you* off? You guys didn't even look at me once MacKenzie showed up! It was like I was invisible! And what's worse, the Mean Team was there...."

Sierra paused. "Who?"

Uh-oh. I had deliberately not told Sierra and Tamiko about the mean girls because it was so embarrassing (and, as I mentioned before, I did not want Tamiko to start a rumble with them).

I sighed. "The three mean girls from my class who are always making fun of me. They were out there, and I got embarrassed at being left out, so I ran in here."

"Oh no!" said Sierra. "I'm so sorry! I didn't know there were mean girls in your class. Why didn't you tell us?"

I didn't want to cry again, so I said, "Can we just go eat? I'm sure all our food is cold by now, but I think I'd feel better if I ate. Then I can tell you everything, okay?"

Sierra looped her arm through mine. "Let's go, *chica*."

We walked back to the table, and I saw the Mean Team looking at us. I must have been looking in that direction, because Sierra whispered, "Is that them?" as we walked by. I nodded a little, and she squeezed my hand.

When we got back to the table, Tamiko was blustering about where I had been, and how I'd missed MacKenzie, but Sierra just put her palm out in Tamiko's face like a traffic cop and said, "Wait. She's starving," so Tamiko waited.

I stole a glance across the tent as I wolfed down my arepa, and saw that the mean girls were gone, thankfully. By the time my stomach was full and I had taken a few deep breaths, I did feel much better. I told Sierra and Tamiko everything, and it felt so good to come clean and be totally honest with them. I realized I'd been sugarcoating everything, not wanting to look like I couldn't handle the changes, not wanting to look like I was a loser in my new school, and most of all, not wanting to look like I couldn't make it without them. The funny thing was, it was *I* who hadn't been treating *them* like my best friends.

As expected, Tamiko's face tightened and her fists balled as I told them about the bus and the phony directions to the science lab, the book bag "accidentally" dumped onto the library floor, the giggles in the lunchroom and under the tent today. But I redirected her by saying it really wouldn't help me at all if my friend from my old school was mean to kids from my new school. By then we'd cleaned up our lunch wrappers, sorted all the recycling, and headed back down Market Street toward the bookstore.

"I am so sorry you've been having a hard time without us," said Sierra, and I could see that her eyes were tearing up a little.

"Thanks," I said.

"Don't let anyone push you around, Allie. You're too nice," warned Tamiko.

I laughed. "You say that like it's a bad thing."

"Humph," said Tamiko.

We entered the bookstore to cheer me up, and my heart began to sing.

"Well, look who's here!" said Mrs. O'Brien, who owns the bookstore. "It's my Book Fest friend!"

Upon which I burst into tears again.

CHAPTER SEVEN
PACING

Sunday was hot and hazy. "A perfect day for selling ice cream!" declared my dad when he woke us up practically at dawn. Tanner and I shuffled to the table in our pj's to eat the oatmeal my dad had prepared. I know oatmeal isn't everyone's cup of tea, but the way my dad makes it—with hot maple syrup and a puddle of warm cream on top—is delicious, and makes me feel like Laura Ingalls Wilder on the prairie every time I eat it.

"Your mother is going to be very nervous today, kids," Dad counseled us as he sipped at his coffee. "This is a lifelong dream, so she's feeling a lot of pressure to succeed. She may or may not want our help; we just have to be ready but not get in the way. Okay?"

I nodded sleepily, and Tanner just sat there licking

his oatmeal spoon. "Any more?" he asked. I hadn't realized he had already finished. He lifted his bowl to lick around the inside of it, like a dog.

"Tanner! Seriously? What's happened to your table manners?" I reprimanded him.

But my dad headed off the bickering before it could begin. "No fighting today. Just let her know you're there for her. Okay?"

I nodded at him, chastened.

I was excited and nervous for Mom. I wanted the store to be a huge success, and I hoped tons of people would come. But I was also nervous for her. I hoped it wouldn't be so many people that she couldn't handle it or that she'd run out of ice cream or something. And I didn't want it to be embarrassing, like if no one came. I just wanted it to be good. We had called her the night before, and she'd sounded a little lonely, I thought. I'd asked if she wanted us to come home, and she'd said she had a ton of paperwork to do and that we should have fun with Dad. It was really hard needing to be in two places at the same time and thinking you weren't in the right one.

My dad took us to the new house at eight o'clock,

and we picked up a load of things that Mom needed at the store. She was already there, cleaning and putting the finishing touches on everything. It was weird for me to see my dad in our new house; he was already out of place. He kind of just stood in the hallway, not even plunking himself down onto a chair or anything like he normally would when we came home. I think he felt it too, because he kind of hustled to get out of there, like he was spying on her and didn't want to get caught. It made me sad.

At the store Tanner and I did little tasks, and my parents did big tasks, and pretty soon it was opening time. A reporter from the local paper was the first arrival, and she asked my mom a ton of questions and took some photos to run with the article. My mom gave her all sorts of samples, and she really loved everything. When the reporter left, we congratulated Mom but were shocked when she was upset.

"No one was here! I looked like a failure!" she wailed.

My dad laughed in surprise. "You've been open for only ten minutes. And it's still morning! I think it was great that she came when she did. You had time to answer all her questions and give her samples.

What if she came during a rush and you didn't have time to get your message out there?"

"What message?" asked Tanner.

I sighed in exasperation. "'Molly's Ice Cream is handmade with love. It's thick and creamy and good for the soul.' Where have you been?" Tanner shrugged and helped himself to a small cup of mini M&M's.

"Don't eat all my profits!" scolded my mom, flicking a dishtowel at him as he shoved them into his mouth. "Okay, quick. Here come some customers. Act natural!"

I picked up a broom and swept some imaginary crumbs up from the floor, while Tanner turned his back and neatened up the already-neat row of ice cream scoopers on the back counter. My dad ducked into the kitchen to do something there, and my mom helped her very first customers ever.

After they left, we hugged her, and that was basically the last time we had a chance to speak to her for the rest of the day.

Families poured in, one after another, all on their way to the beach for the day. At some point my dad ran out and got a pizza, and we each took a turn scarfing down slices back in the kitchen, out

251

of view. The work was hard—physically demanding, and tiring because you had to be friendly and chatty with everyone—but I ended up being pretty good at it. Tanner lost interest quickly and got his friend Michael's mom to come pick him up. My dad had to run to the grocery store for more napkins, and there was a little bit of a lull around one o'clock, as people ate their lunches somewhere. My mom and I quickly wiped down tables, cleaned the countertops, swept straw wrappers from the floor, and grabbed more rolls of coins from the safe.

"Good job, Mama," I said as we raced past each other in our tasks.

"Thanks, sweetheart. You're an angel for helping me, and you're a natural at it."

"I think we've got this!" I said. But little did I know.

Right then, in walked Colin with a friend of his from school, and I was back on duty. We joked around while I gave them tons of samples and then made them each a sundae with my mom's trademark Kitchen Sink ice cream (crumbled pretzels and potato chips with fudge and caramel in a vanilla bean base). My mom was happy to see me with a friend from

Vista Green, and she smiled approvingly at Colin when I introduced them, which made me proud. I was really happy he had come. It made me feel like I had a real friend at my new school.

Right as Colin was leaving, in walked Tamiko and Sierra. I introduced them all in passing, and everyone was polite, but it wasn't like they had a chance to become great friends right in the doorway, so that was frustrating.

Tamiko and Sierra arrived at the counter super-excited and full of ideas, but my mom couldn't chat. If she wasn't helping a customer, she was refilling the paper goods or swapping out almost-empty tubs of ice cream. They wanted to talk to me, too, but my mom needed my help. I set them up on stools at the counter with an ice cream each (on the house, my mom insisted) and a pad of paper and pens and asked them to write down every idea they had, and anything they overheard people saying, good or bad. When it was quiet, we would chat a bit, but I had to stay behind the counter in case a customer came in. It was hard for me to watch Tamiko and Sierra out there, heads bent together; I wished I could join them. It was always the three of us before.

The best thing about the day was that people loved the ice cream, and I was super-proud. But I started to notice a funny thing: people didn't know what they wanted. Sometimes people would come up, all excited to try something new, but then they'd just chicken out and default back to basics and say, "Oh, you know what? I'll just have chocolate chip in a cone." It made me sad that people weren't willing to take a chance on something new and different—because, hey, you never know! Maybe the new thing would be even better than the old one. Or maybe you'd love them both! I promised myself I'd think about this later when I had some peace and quiet.

The traffic kept coming, which was good for business and bad for time with friends. Tamiko and Sierra were so close—right in front of me!—but I was scooping and sprinkling and had both hands busy as I tried to keep up with the orders. Suddenly Tamiko and Sierra spun around.

"Kenz!" cried Tamiko.

"*Niña!*"

There she was again—the girl from the mall. Tamiko and the other girl raced across the shop to hug each other. Thankfully, Sierra did not. Whether that was because she was eating ice cream or not wanting to hurt my feelings, I wasn't sure, but I appreciated it either way.

"Come meet Allie!" said Tamiko happily.

My palms were damp, and I gulped hard as they headed toward me. I plastered a fake-ish smile on my face (it was the best I could muster) and waited.

"Hi," said the girl. "I'm MacKenzie. I've heard so much about you. Your friends miss you so much. It's nice to finally meet you."

"Hi," I said. "I'm Allie."

We looked at each other for an awkward second. MacKenzie was very pretty, with beautiful pale skin and some freckles, like mine, sprinkled across her upturned nose. She had hazel eyes and dimples, and something about her smile just made her look like she was a nice person.

"Okay, you two weirdies," interrupted Tamiko. "New friend, old friend, no one's replacing anyone, no one needs to fill anyone's shoes. Let's just all be friends."

I burst out laughing, and so did MacKenzie. "Tamiko!" I cried.

"What? I broke the ice!" she said. "Or should I

say, ice *cream.*" Then she laughed at her own joke.

I shook my head. "You are too much."

Tamiko continued. "Oh, hey. I forgot to mention this to you, Allie. MacKenzie's a huge Anne what's-her-name fan, like you."

"Anne Shirley?" I said eagerly. "Anne of Green Gables?"

MacKenzie nodded vigorously and pointed to her bright red hair. "With hair like this, how could I not love her?" She grinned. "My mom loved the books so much growing up because she has red hair too. She prayed I'd be a redhead like Anne, and she even named me after her: MacKenzie Anne!"

"No way!" I said reverently. "You are so lucky! Which book in the series did you like reading the most?"

MacKenzie shook her head in embarrassment. "I'm a terrible reader. It's just really hard for me. Sierra keeps wanting me to work on Book Fest with her, but I just can't spare the time; I need it for my homework. My mom has actually read all the Anne books to me aloud, and I've seen all the movies."

I was really glad I wasn't being replaced by her at Book Fest. That would have been tough. "It's so nice to meet you," said MacKenzie. "Oh, and could I please have a peppermint shake?"

"Of course!" I said, and I happily set about making it. MacKenzie left after finishing her shake and said again it was nice to meet me. I said the same.

As the next hour or so wore on, people's beach days ended and we got slammed. Like, really slammed. At that point my mom and I got overwhelmed, and Tamiko and Sierra offered to help. They washed their hands and sanitized them, then threw on some starchy white aprons and jumped behind the counter to serve ice cream. It was sometime during this rush that Amanda and Eloise from Vista Green came in with Amanda's little sister. I was so happy they had accepted my invitation to come—it meant a ton to me—but I couldn't really talk. They got their order filled by my mom and then popped over to say hi to me after.

I quickly introduced them to Tamiko and Sierra, who were really sweet to them, and I felt a happy, warm feeling about where all my friendships were heading. Now all of my friends had met, and I had finally met MacKenzie.

At the end of the day my dad came back from running errands and insisted that my mom, my friends, and I take a break. Things had slowed down a lot, and though we anticipated an uptick again later, we gratefully accepted. My dad threw on an apron, and my mom and I made ourselves an ice cream, and we all sat down for a few minutes at the table.

"Great job, Mrs. S.!" said Tamiko.

My mom smiled a weary but pleased smile at us all. "It went pretty well, didn't it?"

"*Really* well," said Sierra.

"I guess I need to rethink my staffing requirements," said my mom, rubbing her forehead with the palm of her hand while she closed her eyes. "At least on weekends."

"Yeah," I agreed. "This is definitely not a one-lady job."

"Girls, I can't thank you enough for pitching in today like that," said my mom to my friends. "I'm going to pay you for your time." She stood and went to the cash drawer.

"No! Please, Mrs. S. It's on the house," joked Tamiko. "You don't need to pay us. Our parents would kill us if we took money from you on opening day."

My mom laughed. "Okay. Well, then free ice

cream for a week. How does that sound?"

"Be careful what you wish for," cautioned Tamiko, and we all laughed because we knew Tamiko could eat a week's worth of ice cream in a single day.

My mind was spinning. It was so fun hanging out with my besties like old times, and I couldn't bear how lonely it was without them. I thought back to my conversation with Sierra about needing a regular hangout time each week, and suddenly I had a great idea!

"Hey, Mom? What if the three of us worked for you, say, every Sunday?"

"*Ooh*, that would be awesome!" said Sierra.

Tamiko nodded. "Super-fun. As long as we could keep the baseball game on in the back so I could check it from time to time." Tamiko was a baseball nut; she and her grandfather in Japan video-chatted every week during baseball season to discuss their fantasy teams.

My mom stood still, thinking.

"Hmm, Mom? What do you say?" I asked.

"Well, every week is a big commitment. And you have homework and activities, and—"

"You don't have to pay me!" I said. "I'm your kid.

You could just pay them. It would be great!"

Mom laughed. "It's not just the money, Allie."

"Mama?" I said, looking into her eyes. "Please, Mama? I miss my friends. And this way I could still see them every week. Plus we would be *helping* you!"

My dad came out of the back room and exchanged glances with my mom. His eyebrows went up as if to say, *What's going on?* I looked at him pleadingly.

"It would be a great way to learn about a business, and we'd learn new responsibilities."

"Well," said Mom, "first we'd need to check with Tamiko's and Sierra's parents. Then we'd need to make sure that your homework is done and that working here every Sunday wouldn't get in the way of other commitments you all have."

"And that you can make the commitment weekly," said Dad, and Mom nodded.

"That's a lot of ifs," said Tamiko.

"Well, if we get past all those ifs," said my mom, "then we could do a trial run next Sunday. Ten dollars an hour each. If it works out, then you can do the Sunday shift."

The three of us squealed and hugged. "Awesome!" I cried. Then I ran and gave Mom a hug.

"I need to talk to your parents first, though."

Tamiko, Sierra, and I squeezed one another's hands. This could be great! We'd all be together every Sunday. We'd be having fun, plus we'd be making money, too! What could be better than that? Things were finally starting to look up for me. Suddenly life seemed as sweet as a chocolate cone again.

CHAPTER EIGHT
BOOK REVIEW

Colin was grinning as I joined him on the bus the next morning. I had to admit, I was pretty wiped out from being on my feet all day the day before. I couldn't believe my mom had to get up and do it all over again, but she was so excited that she didn't even mind.

Colin held up his hand for a high five, and I smacked it. "Awesome opening!" he crowed.

"Thanks," I said. "The whole day was a whirlwind."

"The store is going to be a huge success. I want to do an article about it in the school paper, with a photo of you at the store. I'm pitching the story at the editorial meeting today."

"Wow! Cool! Thank you!" I said, beaming. That

kind of publicity would sure help bring kids into the store.

"The flavors are awesome," said Colin. "I loved the Lemon Blueberry that I got, but there are so many more I'd like to try."

I smiled. "It's funny you should say that. I've noticed that certain kinds of people just get excited and go for it. They want to experiment and try everything. Other people get overwhelmed with the choices and end up kind of copping out and picking something really basic."

"They don't know what they're missing!" agreed Colin.

I decided to share an idea I'd had the night before while I'd been reading before I went to sleep. "I was thinking, it would be cool to have a little question ready for people, to help loosen them up when they're having trouble ordering. Like, 'Who's your favorite fictional character?' And then I could suggest something based on that!"

Colin laughed. "That's an icebreaker, for sure. So if I said 'Harry Potter,' you'd say?"

I scoffed. "Too easy! Butterscotch Chocolate Chunk, of course. Try someone harder." I laughed.

As Colin thought, suddenly the word "Molly's" caught my ear from somewhere in the bus. It was the Mean Team, seated a row ahead of us across the aisle. Colin and I exchanged a glance and listened in.

"It's the hot new thing," one of them was saying. "It's going to be the new hangout, for sure."

"Everyone's talking about it today, but *I've* known about it for a while. I didn't have time to get there yesterday, but I'm going as soon as possible. I want to get some pics on my feed."

"All you care about is social media, Blair! I just want to try the flavors. I looked at the menu online, and they look delicious."

"Well, I heard the founder is a rock-star chef from New York City."

"No, I heard she's from Paris," cut in Palmer.

I shook my head slightly and giggled as I looked at Colin. He just raised his eyebrows and shook his head.

At lunch I sat with Colin, Amanda, and Eloise, and they were all raving about the store. Colin said he'd gotten the green light to do the article and wanted to start right away, so I texted my mom to see if it was okay for me to be interviewed. She agreed, reminding me to make sure I emphasized that everyone was welcome, there was something for everyone, and that everything was made from handwritten family recipes—all-natural and no preservatives.

Colin asked me a lot of questions about the store; how my mom gets her ice cream flavor ideas (One time—for her Cereal Milk flavor—it was from me and Tanner drinking the milk from our fruit-flavored cereal. Another was from a dessert from France she read about where a chef paired strawberries with balsamic vinegar.); and what had inspired the store's design. I mentioned that my mom used to be a financial officer. Colin stopped me. "Really?" he asked.

"Yeah," I said. "At my dad's company. Then they decided to get divorced, and she wanted to try something she had always wanted to do."

"That's really cool," said Colin. "I mean, not the divorce part."

"No," I said. Things had been so busy, I hadn't thought too much about the divorce. We were all just kind of living life like it was the new normal, after all.

"Divorce is hard," said Colin, looking down. "My parents got divorced a long time ago, but it's still tricky."

"'Tricky' is a good word for it," I said. Suddenly

I wanted to ask Colin a lot of questions. "It just happened right before school started."

"Oh, wow, so that's why you're in a new school?" asked Colin. I nodded. "Well, let me know if you want to talk about it. Right now, though, I have to get this interview done."

"Shoot," I said.

He grinned. "Okay, so is the intent of your mom's place to give the kids a hangout after school? Is she trying to make it a social spot?" I thought about that for a second, especially after hearing the Mean Team talk about it.

"I think the intent is to sell really yummy ice cream," I said, thinking of my mom. "But it's definitely going to be the after-school social spot. And the best part is, *everyone* is invited." I thought of the Mean Team.

I guess it was unavoidable that I would have to deal with the mean girls at the shop sooner or later. That afternoon, after school, I walked straight to Molly's when I got off the bus. My mom was working—tired but happy—and there was a small but steady trickle of customers, just enough for one person to handle.

I checked in on my group chat with Tamiko and Sierra, as we had been doing every day after school at this time, but they didn't reply. I felt a little pang, but I didn't freak all the way out. I did some homework for a bit, but I was restless, so I made myself a small scoop of Banana Pudding ice cream in a cup and sat down to cast a critical eye around the shop. What did it look like to strangers? People who didn't know my mom or have the same taste as her? Was it welcoming? Appealing?

As I let the cool banana cream slide down my throat and I chewed on the salty-sweet Nilla wafers that were chunked through it, I decided the store was objectively beautiful and welcoming but maybe a little cold. It needed a tiny bit more personality to show through. I eyed an empty built-in bookshelf to the side of the window counter, and the wheels started spinning in my head.

"Hey, Mom?" I said during the next lull. "What if I brought in some books—some picture books, and kids' novels, and maybe a couple of books for grown-ups—and filled the bookshelf over there with them? People could borrow books or just look at them or read them while they're eating their ice cream."

My mom looked at the shelf with her head tipped to the side. "I had originally been thinking of doing jars of colorful lollipops there for display, but we could try books," she said. "Actually, I really love that idea, Allie. It would make the store more . . ."

"Homey!" I said, smiling.

"Yes!" she said.

I couldn't wait to curate the shelf with a selection of books I thought would appeal to customers—I might even try to look for books with ice cream themes. Maybe I'd even have a chance to make book recommendations as I served ice cream!

I was picking up my cup and used napkins when the bell above the door jingled. I turned, and there was the Mean Team.

My stomach dropped. On some level I'd known they were coming and that it would likely be soon, but it had seemed sort of unreal, like a distant possibility.

They looked at me and were also shocked, I think. Blair's eyes widened and then narrowed, seeing me in my apron, and Maria glanced at me and gave a half smile. Palmer kind of waved, but it was so fake, she could have been waving at her own reflection in the mirror behind me.

As they walked toward the freezer cases, the bell jingled again and lots of customers—little kids with parents, other middle school kids, a landscaping crew—all poured in at once.

"Allie! I need you!" called my mom.

"On it!" I said, and I turned my back to the Mean Team and went to wash up. I spun around to help the first customer, and it was Blair. Her eyes widened. "You *work* here?" she said.

"Yes," I said, smiling tightly. "Actually, my mother owns the store."

She raised her eyebrows and looked at the other mean girls. "Okay. I'll have a Lemon Blueberry scoop and a Balsamic Strawberry scoop in a cup. Not too big."

Please, I corrected her in my mind automatically, then turned to prepare her order. I could see in the mirror to my right that they were having a silent conversation with gestures and facial expressions, but when I turned to present the ice cream to Blair, they all acted natural.

She looked at the cup in her hand. "You didn't spit in it, did you?"

I was shocked. "What?!"

269

The other girls looked uncomfortable, but Blair looked at me again. "Did you *spit* in my *ice cream*?"

"Blair, come on," said Palmer. "She's just kidding," she said to me nervously.

I saw my mom glance over to see what was going on, but I didn't meet her eye. I stared levelly at Blair.

"I would never do anything to an ice cream except make it as delicious as humanly possible," I said in my calmest voice. "This is my family's store, and my great-grandmother's name is on the door. Anyway, who would spit in someone's ice cream?"

Maria tittered. "Blair would!"

I looked at Maria carefully. "Maybe you need a new friend, then."

Blair scoffed. "I was only kidding. And I wouldn't spit in someone's ice cream, anyway, Maria. Thanks a lot. How much do I owe you?" She smiled at me, but the smile didn't reach her eyes. I could tell she was embarrassed.

"It's on the house," I said, thinking of the phrase "kill them with kindness." It was one of my dad's favorites. "What can I get you two?" I turned my full attention to Maria and Palmer, as if Blair didn't exist.

"No, I'm happy to pay," Blair protested, but I

waved my hand without even looking at her.

"It's a write-off. A marketing expense." I'd heard my mom say that about free samples, and I felt super-sophisticated saying it, like a real businesswoman.

"Okay, thanks?" said Blair skeptically. I could tell she wondered why I would do something nice for her when she'd been so mean to me, but I had to think about what was good for Molly's.

Palmer was all charm now. "Could I please try the Banana Pudding in a sugar cone? It sounds delicious!"

"It's my favorite flavor of the day," I said, acting cheerful.

"Is there a tip jar?" asked Blair, waving a five-dollar bill at me.

All I needed was a tip from Blair. "No. But thanks anyway." We hadn't done that yet; my mom wasn't sure she liked the idea.

I presented Palmer with her order and asked Maria what she wanted. "I don't know. I can't decide. Maybe I'll just have vanilla."

As I'd been telling Colin, I really felt bad when people didn't go for something interesting at our store. It wasn't that our basic flavors weren't good; they were delicious. It was just that it usually seemed like a person picked them because the person was intimidated or uncreative, either of which could have been the case here. It was time to try my idea.

"Okay, wait. I'm going to help you pick a more interesting flavor by giving you our ice cream personality test. Who's your favorite character, from a book or movie?"

"What?" Maria was confused.

"Just work with me. Who?"

Blair and Palmer exchanged a giggle.

But Maria rose to the challenge. "Um, I guess Harriet the Spy?"

"Harriet? Seriously, Maria?" Blair laughed. Maria's face was red, but she stood her ground.

"Yes. It was my favorite book when I was little."

"And it's a great one," I agreed. "Okay, Harriet loved tomato sandwiches. We haven't made tomato ice cream yet, but another thing Harriet loved was cake and milk, every day after school, right?"

Maria's eyes lit up. "Yes! At three forty every day!"

"Yes. So why don't you channel Harriet and try our Devil's Food flavor? It's a plain cream base with chunks of double-chocolate cake in it—cake and milk, get it?"

"Okay!" said Maria. I could tell she was glad to be guided into a more interesting choice, and I was proud that my strategy had worked the first time, and on an enemy, no less!

"And I think you should drink it, in honor of Harriet. A Devil's Food milkshake, with one of our extra-wide straws, coming up."

"Perfect." Maria's eyes shone with satisfaction, and when I presented the shake to her and she sipped it, she closed her eyes and hummed with happiness. "This is so good!" she said.

"And so is Harriet the Spy," I said. "One of my faves."

Once they all had their ice cream, Blair turned to me.

"Bye, Allie," she said, and they all left.

"Bye. Thanks for coming in," I said with a wave. I turned to my next customer, my heart pounding in my chest.

I couldn't believe I'd just had the courage to stand up to a bully! Not only that, I'd definitely won that round. What's more, my new ice cream recommendation strategy had worked! And the funny thing was, the first person I wanted to tell about it was Colin.

That night my mom came into my room for a chat. She wanted to know what had happened with the girls at the store—she'd sensed something was amiss, but she'd been too busy to come over and check in. When I told her how I'd handled it, she scooped me up into a huge hug.

"Allie Shear, you're the best!"

"Mmmsh!" I said, my voice muffled in her shoulder. Maybe it was babyish to like a hug from your mom, but this one felt extra good.

She let me go and smiled at me, and her eyes were a bit moist. "Dad and I have really put you kids through a lot, and you've both handled it so well. I'm so proud of you."

"Thanks, Mama. I'm proud of you, too."

"And I just wanted to let you know, I've run the numbers, and I think it would be a great thing if you and Tamiko and Sierra came to work with me at the shop."

"Mom!" I dive-bombed her with another hug.

"Okay, but hang on," she said, holding me off at arm's length. "I need to discuss this with Tamiko's and Sierra's parents. It's on a trial basis. I need to see that you girls are taking it seriously, and I will pay you. If it works, you can come every Sunday. That way you can help me out and learn some responsibility in a job, but you can also see your friends."

"Thank you, Mom. We're going to do a great job! And look—" I gestured to the milk crate of books I'd pulled from our collection to put on the shelf at the store. "Those are for our customers. Maybe you can bring them tomorrow in your car, and I'll arrange them when I get there after school."

She ruffled my hair. "Perfect. Thanks, sweetheart. Love you."

"Love you too, Mama."

As soon as she left the room, I lunged off my bed for my phone and texted Tamiko and Sierra. I still hadn't heard from them since our after-school check-in time. Where were they?

CHAPTER NINE
A TASTE OF RESPONSIBILITY

When I woke up the next morning and still hadn't heard from Tamiko and Sierra, I was upset. I turned my phone on and off. Still nothing. I didn't want to get crazy, but I started to feel forgotten. As I waited for the bus, I called Tamiko's phone, and she finally picked up.

"Ali-baba!" she cried.

"Where have you guys been?" I asked.

"Oh, Sierra totally dropped the ball on the Book Fest plans, unsurprisingly, so she roped me and MacKenzie into bailing her out. We were at MacKenzie's until so late last night, I barely had time to get my homework done. I'm sorry I didn't reply yet about the store. That's great news. We do have a Book Fest meeting on

Sunday, but it should be fine. I don't think it will run too long."

I stared at the phone in my hand, unable to comprehend what was happening, on so many levels. Sierra had gotten Tamiko to work on the Book Fest? I'd tried for two years to get her involved, and she wouldn't budge, saying she didn't like books and wanted to save the trees they were printed on. And why had they all been at MacKenzie's? Shouldn't they have worked on it at school, with Mrs. Olson?

My stomach churned and my jaw clenched as the bus rolled up. I didn't even know what to say to Tamiko, so instead I just said, "What? I can't hear you! Bad connection," and hung up, my hands shaking.

I trudged up the bus steps, and as soon as I hit the aisle, I heard someone calling my name.

"Allie! Over here!"

"Allie!"

It was the Mean Team, waving me over to join them.

Just behind them, across the aisle, was Colin, smiling and waving.

As I drew near the mean girls, Blair patted the seat next to her, smiling. "Come. Right here."

Still angry from my phone call with Tamiko, I was

in no mood to play nice. I smiled a tight smile and shook my head. "I'm sitting with my friend Colin over there. He's right past *the pool*," I said, and kept walking. I wondered if they remembered the pool prank they'd played on me the first day.

The girls were silent as I joined Colin. They remembered.

"Hey," I said, settling in.

"Hey," he said. "I don't mind if you sit with them."

I sighed. "Thanks. I'd rather start my day off with someone nice."

He rolled his eyes. "Yeah. But it might not be a bad strategy to sit with them sometimes, you know? Like, keep your friends close but keep your enemies closer?"

We laughed. "Thanks," I said. "But not today, that's for sure. Today I kind of just want things to be normal, not different."

I was really upset about Tamiko and MacKenzie and Book Fest, but before I knew it, it was almost Sunday again and time to have my first official afternoon as an employee of Molly's, with Tamiko and Sierra. On Saturday night, we had a check-in by phone.

"The Book Fest committee meeting is at eleven

thirty tomorrow," said Tamiko. "If we're not finished in time for us to get to work at one, we'll just leave early."

"Yup," agreed Sierra.

"Okay, guys. Just remember, this is our test. We've got to do a good job or my mom won't take us seriously." I really did not want to mess this up, for our sakes and my mom's.

Sierra nodded on my tiny phone screen, with big, earnest eyes. "Yes, Allie. I'll make it! I'm saving up to learn mountain climbing. I said I'd join the mountaineering club at school, so I need all the gear—and I really need the money."

Tamiko and I sighed in exasperation, and Tamiko said, "Well, I need it for my toilet customization fund."

"Tamiko!" I laughed. "I was joking, remember?"

"One person's joke is another person's treasure!" said Tamiko.

"Okay, wait. Before you hang up, Allie," said Sierra. "Um, how many volunteers do you think we need for Book Fest?"

"Well, how many do you have?" I asked.

There was a brief silence. "Um, three? Me, Tamiko, and MacKenzie?"

My eyes nearly popped out of my head. "Sierra!

You'll need at least ten kids to lug in the boxes and set up the books on all the tables. Then a rotating schedule of two per shopping session—they can miss sports for it but no academic classes. Then you need at least fifteen kids to clean up: to repack the boxes, throw away the empties, break down displays, whatever. I guess it could be the same fifteen to twenty kids, but . . ." I paused. "Have you made an announcement in assembly?"

"Oh, Allie," wailed Sierra. "I wish you were here to do it. You're so good at all this. Oh, why did I ever say yes?"

Tamiko and I glanced at each other as Sierra buried her head in her hands. This was how it always went: Sierra would overcommit, and Tamiko and I would bail her out, with mixed results.

I began to walk them through what they needed to do, and I forced Sierra to take good notes on what I said. For goodness' sake, I didn't even go to their school anymore and I felt like I was still running Book Fest. The funny thing was, I didn't miss it as much as I'd thought I would.

On Sunday, Dad dropped me off at Molly's at twelve thirty. He reminded me that I needed to treat this as a real job, not just as catch-up time with my friends, and that Mom was really counting on us. "Promise, Allie?" he said.

"Scoop's honor," I said, holding my hand to my heart, and he laughed.

"Mom told me about what happened with the girls from the new neighborhood," said Dad. I was surprised. I mean, I knew Mom and Dad still talked, but I didn't know how that was going to work. I guess they had to talk about me and Tanner.

"I know it's hard," Dad said, "but—"

"I know, I know," I said. "Better. Better. Better." I sighed.

"Well, yes," said Dad, "but I was going to say that it's going to take some time. And that even if I don't live in the house with you all the time, I'm still here if you need me."

I realized that I hadn't actually seen Dad too much this past week. It had gone by so fast. I thought about him in his apartment by himself and wondered if he was lonely without us.

"Now," he said, hitting the auto-unlock in the car, "go forth and scoop."

"Will do!" I said.

"And if you encounter a bully," he said, turning serious, "then just—"

I waited.

"Cone them with kindness."

"Dad!" I sputtered, and giggled. He grinned. I scrambled out of the car.

I waved to Mom, who was with a customer, and headed to the back of the store. I tied a crisp white apron at my waist and washed up.

We were at the lunchtime lull, as my mom had come to call it. Noon to one thirty was a great time for her to return calls and get some business stuff done, since it was always quiet while people were off having their lunches. Then we'd get hit hard for an hour from one thirty to two thirty. After that, business would slow to a trickle, and then we'd get really socked at four o'clock as people left the beach or came home from soccer games or whatever. By five thirty things were usually quiet again, though there was an after-dinner rush on Fridays and Saturdays.

I checked my watch as a customer with two kids walked in. It was twelve fifty-three, and there was still no sign of Tamiko and Sierra. I was stressed and annoyed. Were they going to let me down?

I finished up with the lady and her two kids, and while they sat to eat, I peeked at my phone, which I'd tucked into my back pocket. As luck would have it, my mom walked in from her back office right then.

"Allie! Remember what I said! No phones on duty!"

"Sorry! I just was checking this once . . ." I didn't want to finish my sentence and highlight the fact that Tamiko and Sierra were late. But luckily I didn't have to! Tamiko came bounding into the store in a T-shirt she'd made—it had pictures of sprinkles and ice cream cones all over it, and it said *Molly's* in flowing script across the back, in the same exact font as my mom's store window.

Luckily, the awesomeness of the T-shirt distracted my mom from the fact that it was now exactly twelve fifty-nine. While Tamiko washed and aproned up, I turned to help another customer. By the time Tamiko was at my side and my mom had gone back to the kitchen, I was able to huff, *"Where is Sierra?"*

Tamiko rolled her eyes. "She'll be here shortly. I finally insisted I had to leave, and I said she should do the same, but she had 'just one more thing' to do."

"Annoying," I said. "I knew that was going to happen."

Tamiko laughed. "Didn't we all! I promise, Allie, I'll be here early from now on."

I squeezed Tamiko in a sideways hug. "Thanks, *chica*. Or *niña*. Whatever you go by these days."

"I like to go by 'Allie Shear's best friend,'" Tamiko said.

It made me feel better to hear that.

It wasn't until one twenty-five that the jingling of the door caused me to look up from the banana split I was making. In walked Sierra, red-faced and huffing. She raced into the back to ditch her stuff, then raced behind the counter, strapping on her apron as she came.

"Wash your hands!" hissed Tamiko. I was glad she'd said it and not me.

In a panic, Sierra knocked over a metal milkshake canister that was mostly empty but dirty, so it splattered chocolaty milk all over. Mom was working the cash register and glanced over. As Sierra bent to clean it up, I could see she was crying.

I squatted down next to her so that the customers couldn't see me. "Sierra. I'll clean it up. Go take a minute in the bathroom to calm down, okay?"

She nodded and fled while I heaved a heavy sigh. Soon the customers had all been helped, Tamiko and I had cleaned everything up, and Sierra emerged, calmer and clear-eyed. She came behind the counter and washed up again.

I wanted to be mad at her—mostly because this happened all the time—but now that I wasn't with her all the time, I could see that things were a legitimate challenge for her in a way they weren't for me and Tamiko. Time management, planning, organization of materials—Sierra couldn't do it alone.

We couldn't really have a conversation while we worked, so we didn't address anything about Book Fest or Sierra's shortcomings as an employee. But we did end up having fun.

Tamiko's sassy personality was great with customers. If they ordered something that she thought was too plain or boring, she'd push them to be more adventurous, always making them laugh in the process. Like when a bald, middle-aged dad came in and copped out by ordering a vanilla shake, Tamiko leaned over the counter and said, "Dude. What would your seventeen-year-old self say to you now if he saw you ordering a vanilla shake? Come on. You owe it to yourself to have a little more fun than that. I bet you had a wild youth!" The guy roared with laughter, and he changed his order to a triple banana split! If I had one complaint about Tamiko, it might be that she spent *too* much time with each customer. The line grew pretty long at one point, and I had to nudge her to move her along.

Where Tamiko was jazzy, Sierra was sweet. She was good with the little kids who dropped their ice cream, soothing their tears as she replaced their cones. She was great with grandmas who wanted to chat a lot about the weather. If she had one flaw, it was probably that she made the scoops too big; she was too generous with the product. But I didn't want to be harsh on her on her first real day, especially not with the beginning she'd had. Plus, Mom was really the boss, not me. And so far at least, Mom seemed pretty pleased. She kept looking over and smiling at us. Maybe because I was smiling a lot too.

My best idea of the day was that I put a tiny pinch of sprinkles on top of each ice cream when I made it. It started by accident, when I thought someone wanted sprinkles, but they stopped me, so only about twelve sprinkles landed on top of their ice cream. The customer laughed it off and called it "a little sprinkle of happy."

For the rest of the day, the girls and I would put tiny smatterings of sprinkles on each ice cream and say, "Here's a sprinkle of happy!" and people loved it.

As our shift drew to a close, there was a bit of a lull. We helped my mom load her ice cream into the deep freeze in the back of the store.

"Good start today, girls. I appreciate your being on time and working so hard."

The three of us exchanged uneasy glances. Had she not noticed that Sierra had been almost half an hour late?

"Next week I'll probably assign you some tasks that you can rotate through. Two people on the counter and one doing other stuff, like cleaning the fridge or smashing cookies for toppings."

We all agreed, and then Tamiko spoke up. "Mrs. S., I had a few ideas for some ice cream designs. Would you let me try some next time if I sent you some photos to show what we could do?"

"Sure, Tamiko. Thanks. If we can do them economically and it doesn't take too long or make too much of a mess, I'd always be up for trying cool new things."

"Great! Because I have tons of ideas for rainbow-dipped cones, and unicorn sundaes, and mermaid pops—"

"Okay, okay, I get it!" said my mom, putting her palms in the air in surrender.

We all laughed. Tamiko was never short on ideas.

"All right. Then let's say I'll see you three back here next Sunday at twelve forty-five. That way you're all set and ready for a one o'clock start. If tardiness stays an issue, this won't work."

I cringed. I guessed she *had* noticed Sierra's late arrival. Sierra blushed and nodded, but Tamiko lightened the mood by saying, "We love our sprinkle Sundays, don't we, girls? Hey, get it? Sprinkle *sundaes*?" We all laughed. "We're the Sprinkle Sunday sisters!" Tamiko added, and we all dove in for a group hug, including Mom.

We hung up our aprons and helped ourselves to an ice cream each while we waited for Mrs. Sato. I showed Tamiko and Sierra the book corner Mom and I had arranged. So far it seemed like a good idea. Right then one woman was reading *Olivia* to two kids as they ate their ice cream. And earlier in the day I'd seen a little girl pick up a copy of *Anne of Green Gables* and not want to put it down when they left, which had made me really happy.

"Oh, I remember this book!" said Sierra, picking up a picture book. "I used to love this one."

Just then the bell over the door jingled, and we all looked up. In walked the Mean Team, and my heart dropped as they sauntered over to our table.

Blair cast an appraising eye over the group of us and sighed, shaking her head. "Still reading little kids' books, Allie?" she said, and snickered.

Tamiko bristled, but I put a hand on her leg to shush her.

"These are my friends, Blair. Why do you want to come in here and be mean to us?"

"It's a free country," said Blair with a shrug. Suddenly my mom came out from behind the counter and was standing by our side. "Hi, girls. What's going on? Can I help you with anything?"

I kept my eyes locked on Blair. "Nothing. Blair was just about to apologize, and then she was going to leave. Palmer and Maria want ice cream."

"Okay," said my mom, gathering Palmer and

Maria, one under each arm. "Let's get you girls something."

Alone, Blair's courage faltered; you could just see it evaporate. She looked at Palmer and Maria, who were both engrossed in choosing a flavor.

"It's not so easy being alone, is it, Blair?" I said quietly. "Imagine being the new girl at school and being alone. We don't have to be friends. But you can't come in here and insult me. I think you should leave now." Blair held my gaze for a few seconds, and then she turned to her friends.

"Palmer? Maria?" she said, but they ignored her.

She stood awkwardly for a minute in the middle of the store, and then she turned on her heel and left. As the door whooshed closed behind her, my friends cheered.

I was shaking, but I felt good. Sierra hugged me, and Tamiko patted my back.

Palmer and Maria had just paid, and they came back over to our table. Mom was hanging back, but close enough to hear.

"Sorry about Blair," said Palmer. "She's going through a bad stage, since her parents are getting divorced. Things are rough for her right now."

"There's no excuse for being mean," I said. "My parents are getting a divorce. It's hard, and sometimes it seems unfair, but it doesn't mean you can treat other people badly. Nothing gives you that excuse."

Maria leaned in to see the book. "Oh, I loved that one," she said, sighing. "I used to read it all the time."

"Me too," said Sierra.

"I think I still have my copy," said Maria.

"Oh, you totally do," said Palmer. She turned to us. "Maria has all of her books organized in her room just so. She never gets rid of any of them."

I tilted my head and looked at Maria, seeing her a little differently.

"Well, they're like old friends," she said, grinning. "And we don't get rid of old friends, do we?"

"We sure don't," said Sierra, giving me a squeeze.

"Well, thanks for the ice cream," said Palmer.

"See you at school, Allie," said Maria. And they left.

Sierra burst out, "Oh, Allie, you're just like Anne Shirley!"

I laughed a little. "Not really, but thanks for the compliment."

CHAPTER TEN
BOOK FEST

I avoided the Mean Team all the next day, even when Palmer and Maria shot me friendly and apologetic looks as I walked quickly past them on the bus. I sat with Colin at lunch, then raced to the library to help Mrs. K. start pulling books that hadn't been checked out in at least five years.

After school Sierra's mom picked me up, with Sierra and Tamiko in the car. It was just like old times! I had offered to help Sierra get organized for Book Fest, and she had gratefully accepted.

"Allie, Sierra told me how you had a showdown with the mean girls at the ice cream parlor. I'm so proud of you!" said Dr. Perez in the car.

"Thanks," I told her. "One of the hard things

about owning a store is that you have to let in any-one. It's not like you're inviting friends over to your house or something. It's open to the general public all the time."

"Yeah, even when the general public are jerks!" said Tamiko.

"You're right," Dr. Perez agreed. "But it's all about how you treat them and react to them. And you reacted beautifully."

Sierra's twin sister, Isabel, was home already, playing a video game.

"Hey, Isa!" I said, crossing the living room to give her a hug.

Isa was nice, but she'd gone in a totally different direction from Sierra. She was very focused and ath-letic; she was so good at soccer that she played on an all-boys high school travel team, the only girl. We used to be closer when we were little but had kind of drifted apart in recent years. We caught up for a few minutes, and I asked if she could volunteer to help with Book Fest. She said, "Sure!" It was a little odd that Sierra hadn't even asked her, but things were sometimes weird between them.

Up in Sierra's room I got out some graph paper and began making a few checklists. One was a timeline of what had to happen over the next few days, since Book Fest started Friday and ran through early next week. Another was a timeline for setup day, and another for breakdown day.

I had Sierra make a list of people she had asked to volunteer, and it was woefully short, so I had Ms. Social Media, Tamiko Sato, begin a campaign to recruit people on SuperSnap and anywhere else she could think of. Within half an hour we had ten kids; within an hour we had twenty.

"Wow! You make this look so easy, Allie!" said Sierra admiringly.

"It doesn't take a lot of time to get organized," I said. "You just need to know what you need. And I've done it before many times, so I have an idea."

I made a checklist of supplies (box cutters, large contractor garbage bags, a couple of cases of water for the volunteers, pens, and more).

After an hour and a half, Sierra was visibly more confident. The systems were all in place, Tamiko had assigned all the volunteers their time slots, and my work was done. But it was bittersweet leaving them when my dad pulled up at six. I didn't want to go.

Sierra could tell that I was a little down as I left. "We miss you, Allie. At least we still have Sprinkle Sundays, right?"

"As long as you're on time this Sunday, we will!" I joked.

Tamiko gave me a squeeze before I got into the car. It was unlike her to hug me, so I laughed and said, "What's the occasion?"

"You're a good friend," she whispered. "My hugs are like unicorns: they appear rarely and under very special circumstances. I know it's hard for you to work on this and not be able to go, and I'm sorry."

I took a deep breath. "It's okay. Really. I think it was maybe the planning and hanging out with friends part I missed the most."

Tamiko gave me another squeeze, and I left.

That night I cried a little in my bed as I was falling asleep. I tried to think of Anne Shirley for inspiration, but honestly, sometimes Anne Shirley just needed a good cry too. I fell asleep dreaming of unicorns and friends and ice cream and better things.

When the bell for gym class rang on Friday, I stood up from my desk in English and stretched. It would feel good to run around for a little while.

As I gathered my things, Colin sidled up to me. "Hey, Allie, I was wondering if you might want to do some book reviews for the paper? And maybe you could do an ice cream pairing with each one at the end."

I was so pleased! "Sure, Colin. Thanks! That would be really fun! What a cool idea."

He smiled and shook his head. "It was actually Maria's idea, if you can believe it. She explained in our editorial meeting how you'd done it for her, and we all thought it sounded really good. She even suggested a name for the column, Get the Scoop. Pretty cool, right?"

"Wow. Wonders never cease," I said. How interesting!

"Yeah," he said. "You know she really loves books too, right? She reads all the time. Anyway, I'll see you Sunday at Molly's!" He waved and left for his next class. Colin was coming to take a picture of me at the store to go with the article he'd written. "See you Sunday" had a nice ring to it. Maybe Molly's would be the next great hangout, for all my friends, old and new.

I felt a warm glow as I left Ms. Healy's room. When I stepped into the hall, there stood Mrs. K., dressed in a black sheath dress, with big fake pearl earrings, and her hair up in a bun. Her arms were crossed, and she appeared to have car keys in her hand, which she jangled at me.

"Okay, let's go. Got the permission. You need to stop by the office to sign out. Gather your things," she said, and she began walking toward the office.

"Um? What?" I scurried after her as she climbed the stairs. "Where are we going? I have everything I need." I always packed up before English because I liked to leave school straight from gym.

She didn't even turn around. "Book Fest. Let's go. I need to see it. Mrs. Olson invited me."

I stopped, stock-still, on the stairs. "Wait, *what*? You know Mrs. Olson?"

Mrs. K. kept walking, rounding the stairs and heading into the hallway, so I chased after her. "Come along. She and I were roommates in graduate school when we got our library degrees. I guess you could say she's my best friend."

Whaaaat? "Oh my gosh, so that's how you knew who I was when I came?"

"Yes. Mmm-hmm. She told me her favorite student was coming here."

"Why didn't you tell me?" We'd reached the office, and I quickly signed out. I noticed that Mom had already signed the permission form.

"Oh, didn't I tell you? I thought I had. Let's go. This way."

The trip to my old school was brief, and Mrs. K. and I chatted the whole way. It turned out she was also friends with Mrs. O'Brien at the bookstore. By the time we reached my old middle school, it had sunk in that I was actually going to Book Fest! I couldn't wait to surprise my friends.

In the lunchroom I ran into tons of kids and teachers who were happy to see me. Mrs. Olson gave me a huge hug and kept saying how much she missed me and how she appreciated my helping with Book Fest even though I'd left the school. I felt like a returning celebrity. Tamiko and Sierra screamed when they saw me, and we did a three-way dance, until I noticed MacKenzie standing to the side, and I thought, *Why not?* and grabbed her into our group to dance with us.

They had to hustle because the sixth grade was coming in for their shopping session shortly, and the author Maya Burns was arriving any minute, so they left me to browse or help as I wished. The only bummer was that I barely had any money. If I'd known I was coming, I would have brought my ice cream money from Sunday and my paltry savings.

When I looked up from the newest Cupcake Diaries book, my eyes went wide.

Maya Burns was crossing the room quickly with a huge smile on her face and a Molly's milkshake cup in her hand!

"Look!" said Sierra, spotting it at the same time as I did. We laughed like crazy.

"No way!" I said.

Just then a hand on my back pushed me into the line to get books signed. I looked up. Mrs. K. was handing me two copies of Maya Burns's book to get signed. "But I didn't bring any money," I said.

"Mmph, you bought this already," said Mrs. K.

"What?" I looked up, confused.

Mrs. K. smiled. "One for you and one for the library. You get both of these signed for me, okay?" Then she walked over to talk to Maya Burns.

Sierra stepped in line in back of me and said, "Oh, darn. Did you already buy her book? Because I bought you a copy this morning. I was going to get it signed by her and give it to you to say thanks for helping me with Book Fest." She handed me a copy of the paperback Mrs. K. had just given me.

"Oh no, me too!" said Tamiko, slipping a copy to me. "But mine's just because we miss you!"

We all laughed, and I thanked them gratefully. "This might be the best day of my life," I said.

"We know that, silly. You always love Book Fest," said Tamiko, whacking me on the shoulder (which was much more Tamiko's style than a hug).

Sierra sighed and shook her head regretfully. "I love it, but there is no way I'm running it next year," she said.

And then it was our turn at the table. As soon as we reached Maya Burns, Tamiko blurted, "That's her family's ice cream parlor! And we all work there on Sundays!" She gestured to the Molly's milkshake.

"Sprinkle Sundays!" I cried, and we all high-fived.

Ms. Burns was super-nice and friendly, and we chatted quickly as she signed the book for the library, then the copy Sierra had given me, which I was going to take to the store, and then the copy Tamiko had bought me, which I was going to take home to read. That left one copy. Maya Burns looked at me. "Should I make this out to someone special?"

I hesitated.

She tilted her head. "What's your favorite book?" she asked.

"*Anne of Green Gables*!" I said quickly.

"Oh, that's one of my favorites too!" she said. Then she scribbled "To a Kindred Spirit" in the front and signed her name. She winked as she handed it to me. "You never know when you'll find a kindred spirit to give this to," she said. "Sometimes they aren't that far away."

A kindred spirit. . . . Who knew there would be so many of them for me to find? Sure, I had my family and Tamiko and Sierra and Mrs. Olson. Now I also had Mrs. K., Ms. Healy, and even Colin maybe. But someone who loved books as much as I did . . . someone who loved Anne. Suddenly I knew—this book had to be for MacKenzie. You just never knew when you'd find a kindred spirit.

As Sierra, Tamiko, and I were saying our goodbyes, Mrs. Olson and Mrs. K. darted to the table to say hi. I could hear Mrs. K. asking Ms. Burns to come to Vista Green for a visit, and Ms. Burns saying, "Sure, that would be lovely."

My friends and I chatted for a little bit longer, and then my mom texted to say she was outside to pick me up. We were going out for a casual family dinner with my dad, and I was looking forward to it.

"Get psyched for Sunday, Sprinkle Sisters!" said Tamiko.

"Sprinkle Sundays with my sisters," cheered Sierra.

"See you Sunday!" I called out. See you Sunday. Sundays with my Sprinkle Sisters. It had a really nice ring to it.

"Maybe we could do something like this at Vista Green," Mrs. K. said to me, "but maybe a little different. Maybe a little better."

"I'm all for that," I said. "A little different, but better." I hugged the book to my chest. A new book from one of my favorite authors! I couldn't wait to read it.

I thought about all the recent changes in my life. It was almost as if I were a character in a book. Maybe not Anne Shirley or Hermione Granger, but still interesting and exciting. What would the next chapter be in the life of Allie Shear? I couldn't wait to find out.

DON'T MISS BOOK 2:

CRACKS IN THE CONE

My best friend Allie squeezed my hand. "Happy Sprinkle Sunday," she whispered to me. Then she whispered the same thing into our other best friend Sierra's ear. I could sense both the nervousness and the excitement in Allie's voice. *Sprinkle Sunday*, I repeated in my head. It was finally here. And I did mean finally. I felt like we'd been waiting *forever*—even though it had only been a week since the last time we had all been here.

Allie's mom, Mrs. Shear (or, as I called her, Mrs. S.), had opened an ice cream shop after she'd divorced Allie's dad, and Mrs. S., Allie, and Allie's little brother had moved to another town. It was a whole lot of change, especially for Allie. But we were all really happy when

Mrs. S. offered the three of us (that's me, Sierra, and Allie) jobs at the ice cream store every Sunday. That was why we called ourselves the Sprinkle Sundays sisters.

Aside from our making some extra moolah (which my mom said should go toward a college fund, but I had other ideas) with the new gig, Mrs. S. had given us all cute T-shirts to wear with the shop name, Molly's Ice Cream. (Molly had been Allie's great-grandma, and she'd taught Mrs. S. how to make ice cream and had inspired the shop.) Plus, I got to spend some quality time with my two besties. I'd been super-excited about it all week. Until . . . well, until Sunday morning happened.

I was almost late for work, which would have been bad, because the previous week at our trial session Sierra had been super-late, and Mrs. S. had made it clear that it shouldn't happen again. But I slept through my alarm because I'd stayed up customizing my toilet seat with plastic fish and mermaid charms. It looked really cute, and it was going to make for a funny surprise for my guests. (Don't judge—it was Allie's idea, and it came out awesome.)

Anyway, I woke up to find Mom shaking me.

"Tamiko! You have to get ready," she said.

I groaned and pulled the pillow over my face. "I think there are laws against waking up children by shaking them. It's cruel and unusual," I said.

Mom made a grunty sound. "Well, being late to work on your first day is cruel and unusual. Please get up—and pull your hair back off your face. You don't want to get hair in anybody's ice cream. That would *also* be cruel and unusual."

"I'm up, I'm up," I said. After my shower I quickly made two long braids in my hair and then pulled them back with a ponytail holder. Mom's advice was usually annoying, but she was right about the hair. Nobody wants an ice cream sundae with rainbow sprinkles and Tamiko DNA. Yuck! With a little extra hustle I was able to arrive right on time for our first shift.

After we all hugged hello, we heard a shuffle near the back door. It was Mrs. S., walking in with a tub of ice cream almost bigger than she was.

"Can you girls please help me bring in the ice cream from the van out back?" she asked. "We sold out of seven flavors yesterday!"

The three of us looked at one another. I guess it was time to, you know, work.

"I should have refilled the flavors last night, but

I was just too tired," Mrs. S. continued, and then she turned to Allie. "Your dad was nice enough to bring them over to me today."

Right, Allie's dad. The weird thing about Allie's parents was that they always used to fight when they were married. Not like huge blowout fights but lots of little fights, which made us all squirm. They bickered in front of Allie and her little brother, Tanner, and even in front of Sierra and me. I'm pretty sure you're not supposed to fight in front of your daughter's friends, but we *did* go over to their house a lot, I guess. Nobody was really surprised when they got divorced, except for Allie. It's always different when it's your parents. But now that they were divorced, it was like they were best friends or something. They were super-smiley and helpful to each other. They probably got along better than my own parents, even.

We followed Allie's mom through the back door to the minivan that she used to haul stuff back and forth to the shop. She rented a space in an industrial kitchen somewhere else in Bayville, where she made the ice cream and stored it in a big Deepfreeze. Allie's dad was there now too, unloading the tubs, and Tanner was helping him—or doing Tanner's version of helping, which is to say, he watched us doing everything and complained that it was too hot outside.

"Hey, Mr. S.!" I said. "Hi, Tanner."

Before I could get another word in, Allie's mom took one of the tubs from Mr. S. "Enough talking!" she said. "We don't want the ice cream to melt."

"You heard the boss!" Mr. S. said, and we all laughed. Allie and Sierra grabbed buckets, and we lugged them through the back office and into the front parlor. I dumped the bucket into the bin marked VANILLA in one of the shop's long freezers. A curved glass top was open in the back so that we could scoop, but the glass protected the ice cream in the front from sneezing customers and little kids with icky hands. Besides vanilla, chocolate, and strawberry, Mrs. S. had concocted some truly special and delicious flavors, like Lemon Blueberry, Banana Pudding, Butterscotch Chocolate Chunk, and Maple Bacon.

"There's so much more vanilla than anything else," I said, looking at all the flavors lined up.

"It's Mom's best-selling flavor," Allie said.

"Really? Why would anyone get vanilla when there are so many cool things to try?" I asked.

"You know, I think part of the reason is that even

the basic flavors are amazing," Allie said. "Mom's vanilla is the best vanilla around."

"It is definitely the most vanilla-y," Sierra chimed in. "I love it!"

"Vanilla-y! Is that even a word?" I teased.

"But also I think people just order the same thing out of habit," Allie went on.

"Well, they can eat as much vanilla as they like, as far as I'm concerned," Mrs. S. said, entering the parlor with a tub of ice cream. "They're still giving me business."

"I guess," I said. "But I love all of the exciting flavors. Do you have any new ones coming out soon?"

"I'm trying a new recipe with lavender, but I'm not sure what other flavors to pair with it," she replied. "I don't want it to be too flowery."

"Ooh, will it be purple? That is an awesome color for ice cream," I said, thinking about all of the cool stories people would post with purple ice cream in the frames.

She smiled. "I could definitely make it purple. Hmm. Maybe Lavender Blackberry?"

Then she turned to Allie. "I've got a bunch of ordering and bookkeeping to catch up on, so I'm going to leave you girls out front. You're in charge,

Allie. You know what to do to set up. The afternoon rush will start soon!"

Allie nodded. "We got this!"

Mrs. S. disappeared into the back, and Allie faced us. She had a serious look on her face.

"Okay, here's the plan," she said. "Sierra, you're on the cash register because you're the best with numbers out of all of us."

Sierra gave a goofy salute. "I will make the mathletes proud!" she said.

"Tamiko, since you're such a great people person, you can take the orders," Allie went on. "I'll fill them, and then you can hand them to the customer."

"People person?" I asked. "You mean like a game show host? I can do that." I held up a scooper like a microphone. *"All right, customer seventy-seven, it's time to play Hoop the Scoop!"* I announced, and then pretended to bounce an invisible basketball around on the counter.

"Tamiko! Watch out!" Sierra scolded.

I looked over. The jar with candy buttons was wobbling. I'd almost knocked into it.

"A shaky landing for star people person Tamiko Sato," I hissed in a sports announcer voice, but Allie just sighed.

"Watch out, Ms. People Person," Allie said. "Or else you'll be the one cleaning the entire shop tonight."

"You wouldn't," I said menacingly.

"I so would," Allie said, but this time she was laughing.

Then the three of us cracked up. We actually did have to clean the store—wiping down the counters and tables, sweeping up, and washing out all the scoops—but Mrs. S. had a service come in and do the hard scrubbing, thank goodness.

"All right," Allie said once we caught our breath. "Can you guys help me get more spoons out of the storage room? And napkins. We need to refill the napkin dispensers too. And make sure all the ice cream cups are stacked up and ready."

After refilling one set of supplies, I took my phone out of my pocket.

"I'm going to take some photos and post them," I said. "You know, just to remind people that Sunday is a great day to come out for ice cream."

I dimmed the lights just a *little* to take the perfect snap.

"Okay. Sierra and I can handle the rest of the stuff, I guess," Allie said, but the way she said it, there was an edge in her voice.

Hmm. That was weird. Allie rarely had an attitude. The only time I'd really seen her get mad was when her parents got divorced and told her that she'd be moving and starting school in a new town. And to be honest that was totally understandable, because I'd be really mad about that too. But why was she annoyed now?

I wondered if I should tell her that good marketing is important for any business. I knew that because my brother, Kai, took marketing classes at the high school, and sometimes I helped him study by holding up his flash cards while I painted my nails.

Then I reminded myself that Allie probably wasn't actually mad. Maybe she was just trying to manage Sierra and get everything perfect for our first official day at work. Sierra was my other best friend, but she got distracted a lot and wasn't the most detail-oriented person. Plus she always took on too many things at once. We tried to help her, but sometimes things were a mess. I think Allie and I were both a little nervous about her dropping some ice cream or ringing up someone for five thousand dollars' worth of ice cream by accident.

Still, things were a little different now that Allie went to another school. When we used to see each other every day, we didn't seem to have any problems, but now that we saw her only one or two times a week, things were different. She was still my best friend, but I didn't know every detail of what was going on with her anymore.

I started snapping photos. First I took a picture of the menu sign where the flavors were written in colored chalk. I typed in the caption, **Sprinkle Sundays squad goals: try a new flavor at Molly's #IceCream #Bayville #Yum**, making sure to throw in some hashtags so people knew how to find the store.

Then I started snapping photos of the shop. It was *so* gorgeous that sometimes I wished I could live there. I took a photo of the vintage metal letters behind the freezers, with light bulbs in them that spelled out ICE CREAM. Then I got a wide shot of the parlor, with the cool black-and-white checkered floor flecked with gold; the high counter with stools looking out the window; and the three round, white tables surrounded by wire chairs. The chair cushions had blue- and cream-colored stripes, which matched the awning on the outside of the building.

There was so much to photograph! Above the register, light fixtures that looked like ice cream cones hung down from the ceiling. So cute! Then I moved on to the buckets inside the counter that held all of the toppings that customers could choose to put on their ice cream or have mixed in. I got a close-up of a bin of rainbow sprinkles, and then a jar of red and yellow and green gummy bears, and another one of some glistening blue gummy fish.

Then I grabbed Allie and Sierra and pulled us all together.

"Sprinkles selfie!" I cried, and I held out the phone and clicked.

"Let me see that before you post it!" Sierra said, grabbing the phone from me.

"Don't worry. You look gorgeous," I said, and I wasn't wrong. Sierra had an amazing smile.

I handed the phone to Sierra so that she could see.

"It's not *bad*," Sierra said, looking at it. "Just don't tag me." Then she continued scrolling through the photo feed on my phone. "Oh my gosh, I can't believe that outfit Jenna wore on Wednesday."

"I know! She looked stunning," I agreed.

"Jenna Robinson?" Allie said. "I thought she always wears jeans and sneakers."

"No, Jenna Horowitz," I corrected her.

"Remember her? She was in my fifth-grade class."

Allie shrugged. "So, what was she wearing?"

"A black miniskirt and a long-sleeved white shirt with a collar, and black ankle boots," Sierra reported. "It was so sophisticated!"

"Well, she did copy the whole outfit from the fall cover of *Teen Trend* magazine, so minus ten points for being unoriginal," I pointed out. "But only Jenna would have the guts to wear it, so ten points added."

I liked to pretend to score people's outfits, almost like I really *was* a TV show host.

"Speaking of guts, did you read that chapter about the digestive system in biology?" Sierra asked. "That was so gross. But Mr. Bongort made it really funny, thank goodness."

"Yeah, he was joking around the whole time," I replied. "Cole was picked to reenact the bathroom bit in class," I added for Allie's benefit. "It was hysterical."

"Cole is so annoying," Sierra said. "But it was pretty funny, watching him not be able to find a bath-room fast enough!"

"Well, I wouldn't know," Allie chimed in, and there was that edge to her voice again.

Sierra and I exchanged looks. It was really hard for Allie when she felt left out.

Hole
in the
Middle

Chapter One
Donuts Are My Life

My grandmother started Donut Dreams, a little counter in my family's restaurant that sells her now-famous homemade donuts, when my dad was about my age. The name was inspired by my grandmother's dream to save enough money from the business to send him to any college he wanted, even if it was far away from our small town.

It worked. Well, it kind of worked. I mean, my grandmother's donuts are pretty legendary. Her counter is so successful that instead of only selling donuts in the morning, the shop is now open all day. Her donuts have even won all sorts of awards, and there are rumors that there's a cooking show on TV that might come film a segment about how she started Donut Dreams from virtually nothing.

My grandmother, whom I call Nans—short for Nana—raised enough money to send my dad to college out of state all the way in Chicago. But then he came back. I've heard Nans was happy about that, but I'm not because it means I'm stuck here in this small town.

So now it's my turn to come up with my own "donut dreams," because I am dreaming about going to college in a big, glamorous city somewhere far, far away. Dad jokes that if I do go to Chicago, I have to come back like he did.

No way, I thought to myself. Nobody ever moves here, and nobody ever seems to move away, either. It's just the same old, same old, every year: the Fall Fling, the Halloween Hoot Fair, Thanksgiving, Snowflake Festival, New Year's, Valentine's Day and the Sweetheart Ball . . . I mean, we know what's coming.

Everyone makes a big deal about the first day of school, but it's not like you're with new kids or anything. There's one elementary school, one middle school, and one high school.

Our grandparents used to go to a regional school,

which meant they were with kids from other towns in high school. But the school was about forty-five minutes away, and getting there and back was a big pain, so they eventually decided to keep everyone at the high school here. It's a big old building where my dad went to school, and his brother and my aunt, and just about everyone else's parents.

Some kids do go away for college. My BFF Casey's sister, Gabby, is one of them. She keeps telling Casey that she should go to the same college so they can live together while Gabby goes to medical school, which is her dream. It's a cool idea, but what's the point of moving away from everything if you just end up moving in with your sister?

Maybe it's that I don't have a sister, I have a brother, and living with him is messy. I mean that literally. Skylar is ten. He spits globs of toothpaste in the sink, his clothes are all over his room, and he drinks milk directly from the carton, which makes Nans shriek.

My grandparents basically live with us now, which is a whole long story. Well, the short story is that my mother died two years ago. After Mom died, everyone was a mess, so Nans and Grandpa ended up helping out a lot. Their house is only a short drive down the street from us, so it makes sense they're around all the time.

Even their dog comes over now, which is good because I love him, but weird because Mom would never let us get a pet. I still feel like she's going to come walking in the door one day and be really mad that there's a dog running around with muddy paws.

My mother was an artist. She was an art teacher in the middle school where I'm starting this year, which will be kind of weird.

There's a big mural that all her students painted on one wall of the school after she died. The last time I was in the school was when they had a ceremony and put a plaque next to it with her name on it. Now I'll see it every day.

It's not like I don't think about her every day anyway. Her studio is still set up downstairs. It's a small room off the kitchen with great light. For a while none of us went in there, or we'd just kind of tiptoe in and see if we could still smell her.

Lately we use it more. I like to go in and sit in her favorite chair and read. It's a cozy chair with lots of pillows you can kind of sink into, and I like to think it's her giving me a hug. Dad uses her big worktable to do paperwork. The only people who don't go in are Nans and Grandpa. Dad grumbles that it's the one room in the house that Nans hasn't invaded.

Sometimes I catch Nans in the doorway, though, just looking at Mom's paintings on the walls. Mom liked to paint pictures of us and flowers. One wall is covered in black-and-white sketches of us and the other is this really cool, colorful collection of painted flowers with some close up, some far away, and some in vases. I could stare at them for hours.

I remember there used to be fresh flowers all over the house. Mom even had little vases with flowers in the bathrooms, which was a little crazy, especially since Skylar always knocked them over and there would be puddles of water everywhere.

Sometimes when I had a bad day she'd make a special little arrangement for me and put it next to my bed. When she was sick, I used to go out to her garden and cut them and make little bouquets for her. I'd put them on her night table, just like she did for me. Nans always makes sure there are flowers on the kitchen table, but it's not really the same.

Grandpa and Nans own a restaurant called the Park View Table. Locals call it the Park for short.

They don't get any points for originality, because the restaurant is literally across from a park, so it has a park view. But it seems to be the place in town where everyone ends up.

On the weekends everyone stops by in the mornings, either to pick up donuts and coffee or for these giant pancakes that everyone loves. Lunch is busy during the week, with everyone on their lunch breaks and some older people who meet there regularly, and dinnertime is the slowest. I know all this because I basically grew up there.

Nans comes up with the menus and the specials, and she's always trying out new recipes with the chef. Or on us. Luckily, Nans is a great cook, but some of her "creative" dishes are a little too kooky to eat.

Nans still makes a lot of the donuts, but Dad does too, especially the creative ones. Donut Dreams used to have just the usual sugar or jelly-filled or chocolate, which were all delicious, but Dad started making PB&J donuts and banana crème donuts.

At first people laughed, but then they started to try them. Word of mouth made the donuts popular, and for a little while, people were confused because they didn't realize Donut Dreams was a counter inside the Park. They instead kept looking for a donut shop.

My uncle Charlie gives my dad a hard time sometimes, teasing him that he's the "big-city boy with the fancy ideas." Uncle Charlie loves my dad, and my dad loves him, but I sometimes wonder if Uncle Charlie and Aunt Melissa are a little mad that Dad got to go away to school and they went to the state school nearby.

My dad runs Donut Dreams. Uncle Charlie does all the ordering for food and napkins and everything you need in a restaurant, and Aunt Melissa is the accountant who manages all the financial stuff, like the payroll and paying all the bills. So between my dad, his brother, and his sister, and the cousins working at the restaurant, it's a lot of family, all the time.

My brother, Skylar, and I are the youngest of seven cousins. I like having cousins, but some of them think they can tell me what to do, and that's five extra people bossing me around.

"There's room for everyone in the Park!" Grandpa likes to say when he sees us all running around, but honestly, sometimes the Park feels pretty crowded.

That's the thing: in a small town, I always feel like there are too many people. Maybe it's just that there are too many people I know, or who know me.

Right after Mom died I couldn't go anywhere without someone coming up to me and putting an arm around me or patting me on the head. People were nice, don't get me wrong, but everyone knows everything in a small town. Sometimes I feel like I can't breathe.

Mom grew up outside of Chicago, and that's where my other grandmother, her mother, still lives. I call her Mimi. We go there every Thanksgiving, which I love. I remember asking her once when we were at the supermarket why there were so many people she didn't know. She laughed and explained that she lived in a big town, where most people don't know each other.

It fascinated me that she could walk into the supermarket and no one there would know where she had just been, or that she bought a store-bought cake and was going to tell everyone she baked it. No one was peering into her cart and asking what she was making for lunch, or how the tomatoes tasted last week. Nans always wonders if Mimi is lonely, since she lives by herself, but it sounds nice to me.

Everyone in our family pitches in, but I officially

start working at Donut Dreams next week for a full shift every day, which is kind of nice. I'll work for Dad. He bought me a T-shirt that says THE DREAM TEAM that I can wear when I'm behind the counter.

We have a couple of really small tables near the counter that are separate from the restaurant, so people can sit down and eat their donuts or have coffee. I'll have to clean those and make sure that the floor around them is swept too.

Uncle Charlie computerized the ordering systems last year, so all I'll have to do is just swipe what someone orders and it'll total it for me, keep track of the inventory, and even tell me how much change to give, which is good because Grandpa is a real stickler about that.

"A hundred pennies add up to a dollar!" he always yells when he finds random pennies on the floor or left on a table.

Dad will help me set up what we're calling my "Dream Account," which is a bank account where I'll deposit my paycheck. I figure if I can save really well for six years, I can have a good portion to put toward my dream college.

So we're going to the bank. And of course my

friend Lucy's mom works there. Because you can't go anywhere in this town without knowing someone.

"Well, hi, honey," she said. "Are you getting your own savings account? I'll bet you're saving all that summer money for new clothes!"

"Nope," said Dad. "This is college money."

"Oh, I see," she said, smiling. "In that case, let's make this official." She started typing information into the computer. "Okay. I have your address because I know it. . . ." She tapped the keyboard some more.

See what I mean? Everyone knows who I am and where I live. I wonder if people at the bank know how much money we have too.

After a few minutes, it was all set up. Afterward Dad showed me how to make a deposit and gave me my own bank card too.

I was so excited, not only because I had my own bank account, which felt very grown-up, but because the Dream Account was now crossed off my list, which meant I was that much closer to making my dream come true. I was almost hopping up and down in my seat in the car.

"You really want to get out of here, don't you?" asked Dad, and when he said it, it wasn't in his usual joking way. He sounded a little worried, and I immediately felt bad. It wasn't as if I just wanted to get away from Dad.

"You know," he said thoughtfully, "I get it."

"You do?" I asked.

"Yeah," he said. "I was the same way. I was itchy. I wanted to go see the big wide world."

We both stared ahead of us.

"I don't want to go to get away from you and Skylar," I said.

Dad nodded.

"But think of Wetsy Betsy."

Dad looked confused. "Who is Wetsy Betsy?"

"Wetsy Betsy is Elizabeth Ellis. In kindergarten she had an accident and wet her pants. And even now, like, seven years later, kids still call her Wetsy Betsy. It's like once you're known as something here, you can't shake it. You can't . . ." I trailed off.

"You can't reinvent yourself, you mean?" asked Dad.

"Exactly!" I said. "You are who you are and you can't ever change." I could tell Dad's mind was spinning.

"So who are you?" he asked after a few more minutes.

"What?" I asked.

"Who are you?" Dad asked. "If Elizabeth Ellis is Wetsy Betsy, then who are you?"

I took a deep breath. "I'm the girl whose mother died. I sometimes hear kids whisper about it when I walk by."

I saw Dad grimace. I looked out the window so I wouldn't have to watch him. We stayed quiet the rest of the way home.

We pulled up into our driveway and Dad turned off the car, but he didn't get out.

"I understand, honey. I really do. I understand dreaming. I understand getting away, starting fresh, starting over. But wherever you go, you take yourself with you, just remember that. You can start a new chapter and change things around, but sometimes you can't just rewrite the entire book," he said.

I thought about that. I didn't quite believe what he was saying, though. In school they were always nagging us about rewriting things.

"But you escaped," I said. "And then you just came back!"

"Well, you escape prison. I didn't see this place as a prison," Dad said. "But Nans as a warden, that's . . ."

He started laughing. "Seriously, though, I left because I wanted an adventure. I wanted to meet new people and see if I could make it in a place where everyone didn't care about me and where I was truly on my own. I never had any plans to come back, but that's how it worked out."

"So why did you move back here?" I asked.

"Because of Mom," said Dad. "She loved this place. I brought her here to meet everyone and she didn't want to leave."

"But Mimi didn't want her to move here," I said, trying to piece together what happened.

I had always thought it was Dad who wanted to move back home. Mom and Dad met in college. She lived at school like Dad did, but Mimi was close by, so she could drive over for dinner. Mom and Dad hung out at Mimi's house a lot while they were in college.

"Noooo," Dad said slowly. "Mimi wasn't too thrilled about Mom's plan. She didn't really understand why Mom would want to move out here, so far from her family, and especially where there weren't a lot of opportunities for artists."

"So she changed her mind?" I asked.

I never remembered Mimi saying anything bad

about where we lived, but Dad would always tease her, saying, "So it worked out okay, didn't it, Marla?"

She came to visit twice a year and always seemed to have a good time. "It's a beautiful place to live," she would say, smiling.

"Well," said Dad. "It took Mimi a while to change her mind. But she saw how happy Mom was and how much everyone here loved Mom, so she was happy that Mom was happy. That's the thing about parents. They really just want their kids to be happy, even if they don't understand why they do things. If you decide to move away from here, I'll miss you every day, but if that's what you want to do and that's what makes you happy, then I will be there with the moving truck."

"So if I tell you I want to move to Chicago for college, you'll be okay with that?" I asked.

"If you promise to come home and visit me a lot," said Dad, grinning.

"Deal!" I said.

"I love you," said Dad.

"I love you back," I said.

"Okay, kiddo, let's go in for dinner. Nans goes mad when we're late."

"Dad, isn't it correct to say that Nans gets angry? Because, like, animals go mad but people get angry."

"In that definition, Lindsay, I think that is an entirely correct way to categorize your grandmother when you are late for dinner. She gets mad!"

I giggled and opened the car door.

"Ready, set, run to the warden!" said Dad, and we raced up to the house, bursting with laughter.

Chapter Two
First Day of Work

The plan was that I'd start working at Donut Dreams two weeks before school started. That way I'd get into my regular routine and not have to adjust to a job at the Park and a new school at the same time. For the school year, I'll work after school two days a week and one day on the weekends.

But since much of the waitstaff take vacations at the end of the summer, it was all hands on deck, according to Grandpa, and the whole family was taking full-day shifts at the restaurant.

Mornings were always way complicated because things start early in the restaurant business. Even if the Park didn't open until six thirty in the morning, that meant everyone, including the cooks, the busboys, and the waitresses, got there by five o'clock to start prepping the food, brewing coffee, sorting the daily bread deliveries, and making sure the ovens were on.

Since we own Donut Dreams, everyone just assumes that we eat donuts at every meal, and that they're stacked everywhere in our house. But we actually eat like everyone else, and Nans only lets us have donuts on the weekends, just like Mom did.

So Monday morning I put on my Dream Team T-shirt and got downstairs early. Nans already had my fruit and juice at my place at the table. Since she got up early to make the donuts, by the time Skylar and I got up, she joked that she should be making lunch. Dad had to be at the restaurant early in the morning, so after Mom died, Nans was the one who came back home from the restaurant to stay with us when Dad had to leave.

Nans was making me scrambled eggs and I was surprised to see Skylar, still in his pj's, eating his cereal.

"What are you doing up?" I asked. "It's not like you have to go to work today."

"Nans woke me up," he whined. "We have to drive you to work. So even if I don't have to go to work, I still have to get up."

"You can get in the car in your pajamas!" Nans said, exasperated. "I just can't leave you here alone while I run Lindsay to work!"

Skylar rolled his eyes. "Well, can I at least get a donut while we're there?"

Nans sighed. "Sure," she said with a grin. "On Saturday."

It probably seems weird to eat breakfast before you go to work in a restaurant, but working in a restaurant is hard, and you don't get a lot of breaks. It's not like you can stuff snacks in your apron pockets either. You're on your feet the whole time and running around, and you can barely sip a drink, let alone eat. During slow times the staff will grab a plate in the kitchen, but as soon as you have a customer you have to put it down, so no one ever has a leisurely burger or anything.

Nans jingled her keys, and Skylar sighed loudly and pushed back his chair. I took one last look in the mirror before we left, and then Nans drove down the curvy road toward the restaurant.

I could ride my bike to work, especially in nice weather, but Mom would never, ever let us ride on Park Street. She said people went too fast around the curves.

It's kind of weird that even though Mom died, some of her rules are still here, and nobody has tried to get rid of them. At first we did things like staying up really late because everyone was so distracted, and nobody seemed to notice. Plus, there were, like, hundreds of people at the house and stopping in at all hours.

But one night at dinner, Dad said, "Okay, life as we know it is going to be very different, but there are ground rules that stay the same."

After that we had bedtimes and regular meals and all the old rules seemed to kick back in.

When we pulled up to the restaurant, it was six fifteen. You could tell Nans was torn, because she wanted to go in and check things out and get a few things done in the office, but Sky was scowling.

Nans glanced in the back seat. "Sky, do you want to go say hi to your dad?"

But before he could answer, Dad came bounding out of the restaurant. "A fine family morning!" he bellowed, smiling at me. "Look at this wonderful employee on her first day at Donut Dreams!"

He actually looked really proud, and I kind of blushed a little.

"She's going to be spectacular, as always!" said Nans, smiling.

"And I get to see my boy!" said Dad, reaching in to give Sky a squeeze.

"I had to get up early," Skylar whined.

"Good practice for when school starts!" said Dad. "And since you made the very big effort of getting into the car, I have a little treat for you." He handed Skylar a bag.

"Donuts!" screamed Skylar, and Dad laughed.

"First-day-of-work exception," Dad said. "Don't get too used to it!" He gave Skylar a kiss on the head and added, "Have fun at camp!"

Then he turned to me and opened the car door. "And you, my dear, are mine for the day. Let's get to work!"

My cousin Kelsey was also working behind the counter at Dreams, and she gave me a quick wave when I came in.

Kelsey and my other four cousins all work at the Park and Dreams. Kelsey is only older than me by a month and a half, but she always tells people I'm her younger cousin.

"You know what to do?" asked Kelsey.

I nodded and slipped behind the counter with her and put on an apron. Dad was talking to the manager of the restaurant about something, so I turned around and stared at the rows of donuts, making sure they were all lined up and that the shelves were clean.

When Mom was alive I went home right after school, but after she died, Dad would pick Skylar and me up and bring us to the restaurant so we could be near him. We'd hang out at a table and do our homework or color for a few hours before Nans would take us home for dinner. I had watched the counter at Dreams for a few years, so now I knew exactly what had to be done.

If you look around, a restaurant is kind of a fascinating place. It's usually busy—if it's a good restaurant, that is—and there are people sitting and talking about stuff, and if you pay attention, you can learn a lot. And most people don't stop talking when someone comes over to the table. So even if I helped clear a table or dropped off a glass of water, I could really get an earful. That's what I loved most, picking up little pieces about people that you wouldn't normally know.

Grandpa loves to go around and talk to everyone,

and he stops and chats with the regulars, especially the ones at the counter in the morning. He knows everything that was going on in town, but he never spilles it to any of us, which drove Mom crazy.

"Oh, come on," she'd say. "I know they were probably talking about it at the Park. What's the dirt?"

And he would just smile and shake his head and say, "I just pour the coffee. What do I know?"

But Grandpa never misses a beat, so you have to be on your toes. I once saw him correct people for not properly wiping down a table, or not setting it right, or sloshing a glass of water when they put it down.

I know that he likes things tidy, which is hard when you sell donuts, because some of them have sprinkles or are crumbly. So when you lift them off the tray, you get crumbs everywhere—on the shelf, on the floor, and sometimes on the counter.

At Dreams there's a lot of wiping and sweeping, because if Grandpa sees sprinkles all over the glass counter, he won't be pleased. He'll say, "Is that counter eating those sprinkles?" So the first thing I did was wipe down the counter, which was already clean.

"Ugh," whispered Kelsey, "it's the East twins."

The East twins were running up to the case and

putting their fingers all over the glass front. The two boys were adorable, but every time they came in, they made a huge mess.

"Hi, Mrs. East," said Kelsey. "What can we get you today?"

Mrs. East always looked like she'd just run through a windstorm. There were always papers coming out of her bag, and her clothes were usually wrinkled or stained.

But she was really nice, and after Mom died she made us a lot of dinners and brought them over. She even came over with a picnic lunch one day for me and Sky and took us to the park.

"Oh, let me get the boys settled here," she said, lifting them into chairs. "Jason, please stop hitting your brother!"

"That one, that one!" the boys started yelling, waving their little hands at the donuts.

"Boys!" said Mrs. East. "Use your manners! And Christopher, stop screaming!"

The boys scrambled off their chairs and ran back to the counter. Luckily, there was no one else waiting, because it took them a full ten minutes to choose their donuts.

I had one hand over the chocolate iced one when Christopher yelled, "No, no, no, not that one!" and I had to move my hand around the shelf until it was hovering over the "right" one.

"Thank you," said Mrs. East. "You girls are amazingly patient! And I'm more frazzled today than usual. We just got back from vacation with my mom, and even though we love them, moms can be such a pain sometimes. Right, girls?"

She looked up as she was handing us the money for the donuts and froze. Her eyes went wide as she looked at me, remembering, and then her hand flew over her mouth.

Kelsey shifted from foot to foot nervously.

This happens a lot. People will say things and then be really scared that they said the wrong thing in front of you. Before Mom died, even when she was sick, all of a sudden everyone was really careful about what they said around me. For a month after Mom died, my friends wouldn't even talk about their moms in front of me.

I talked to Aunt Melissa about it, because she was who I went to for a lot of stuff these days.

"Honey, people are trying to be considerate. But

sometimes you have to help them, too," Aunt Melissa told me.

Poor Mrs. East looked a little like she might cry. Kelsey looked at me expectantly.

"Yeah, you should hear Kelsey complain about Aunt Melissa," I joked.

Kelsey opened the cash drawer and smiled. "Yeah, but she's got nothing on Nans, and you basically live with Nans."

We laughed, but Mrs. East still stood there, silent. I could tell she still felt awful.

"That'll be five fifty, please," said Kelsey, and Mrs. East suddenly looked down and realized she still had the donut money in her hand.

"Oh thank you, honey," she said.

She took the donuts to the boys, who shoved them into their mouths in five seconds flat. Then she walked back over and grabbed some extra napkins.

"Sometimes you take things for granted," she said to me, I guess as an apology. "How was your summer, Lindsay? You excited for your first day at Bellgrove Middle School? Oh and the big Fall Fling is soon, right? Did you do any dress shopping this summer?"

Fall Fling is, I guess, a big deal. It's the fall dance at

the middle school, and everybody goes. I think they go because there's not much else to do, but kids start talking about it around the Fourth of July.

My BFF, Casey, had already started looking online for a dress, and she's been poking me to go shopping. The thing is that shopping for school is a little weird these days. Usually Aunt Melissa takes me and Kelsey to the mall that's an hour and a half away and we stock up, or we just order stuff online.

"I'm not ready to start thinking about school," I said. "It's still summer!"

"You're right!" laughed Mrs. East. "You enjoy every last drop of summer!"

Then she went over to try to wipe the boys' faces, which were covered in donut icing. It was also in their hair.

"So did you pick out a dress yet?" I asked Kelsey.

"Not yet," she said. "I found a few online that Mom said she'd order so I can try them on. Here, I'll show you."

She grabbed her phone from behind the counter, which was a big no-no. Grandpa did not let anyone have a phone when they were "on the floor," which meant out in the open in the restaurant.

"You have to pay full attention!" he'd say.

I hated this rule, because if there was some downtime, it could get really boring.

Dad came over then. "Are you girls doing okay?" he asked, eyeing the mess the Easts were making.

"Yep," said Kelsey. "We've got it, Uncle Mike." She slipped her phone into her back pocket.

"Kelsey, you know the rule," said Dad. "And if Grandpa catches you, it won't be pretty."

"I asked to see her dress," I said, trying to cover for her.

"What dress?" asked Dad.

"The dress she might wear for Fall Fling."

Dad looked confused.

"Fall Fling is a big deal, Mike," said Aunt Melissa, who had come up behind him.

"Oh, so I guess . . . well . . . we'll have to get Lindsay a dress?" he said, and he sounded so scared we all laughed.

But I had kind of wondered about it. I mean, Aunt Melissa usually took me shopping for school clothes, but no one had mentioned dress shopping. There was one store in town that had some fancy stuff, and that's where Casey's mom would probably take her.

"It's covered, Mike," said Aunt Melissa. "You're a great brother, but I would never count on you to pick out a dress."

Dad looked relieved.

"So you bought me one?" I asked, confused.

"Nope," said Aunt Melissa. "Your grandma Mimi did. Actually, she bought ten."

"Mimi?" I asked. "*Ten* dresses?"

"Yes," said Aunt Melissa. "There's some store near her that specializes in this kind of thing. I think she originally bought a dozen, but I told her that was crazy, so she narrowed it down to ten."

"Ten?" yelped Dad.

"Well, she's only going to keep one," said Aunt Melissa. "Unless you can wear more than one dress at a time. Can you, Linds?" she asked, teasing.

"So wait," Dad said. "Lindsay's grandma picked out her dresses? Can't Lindsay pick out her own clothes?"

Aunt Melissa laughed. "Your grandmother has wonderful taste," she said to me. "But there's a lot to choose from, don't worry. We will make sure you love whatever you end up wearing. Plus, she's insisted on bringing them when she comes, so she'll—" She stopped midsentence. "Oops."

"When is she coming?" I asked.

"Melissa!" said Dad. Then he sighed. "Okay, Mimi is coming for a surprise visit. Or at least it was *supposed* to be a surprise. She wanted to be here for you guys on the first day of school."

That was a little weird.

"Well, you know, it's a big deal, especially because you're starting middle school. She wanted to be here," said Dad.

"We're going to have a little dress party," said Aunt Melissa. "Kelsey, Molly, Jenna, and I are coming, and Nans, of course. Plus Aunt Sabrina and Lily. And we thought we'd invite Casey, too."

Aunt Sabrina is married to Uncle Charlie, and she's my cousins Lily and Rich's mom.

"I'm not invited?" asked Dad.

"Definitely not," said Aunt Melissa. "We already have too many opinions with that crew."

"My little girl is going to a dance," said Dad, and he got a little teary.

"Is anyone working today or should we all have a cup of tea?" asked Grandpa, whispering loudly behind us.

"It's okay, Dad," said Aunt Melissa. "We just had

a five-minute family huddle about scheduling." She winked at us.

"Yep," said Dad, taking her cue. "And here's Lindsay reporting for her first day at Donut Dreams."

Grandpa beamed. "There's always room for family in the Park!" he bellowed. "Now get back to work, everyone!"

After we cleaned up from the East twins, which required sweeping and mopping the floor and cleaning the table and chairs they'd sat in, it was a little slow.

The lunchtime crew was getting busy on the other side of the restaurant, and I saw my cousins: Jenna, Kelsey's older sister, and Lily in their waitress uniforms, serving table after table.

Jenna, Lily, and Lily's older brother, Rich, were the only ones allowed to wait on tables, because they were old enough. Molly, Kelsey's other sister, was a runner, which meant she filled the glasses at the tables, brought extra ketchup or hot sauce if someone asked for it, and replaced a napkin if someone dropped it on the floor—stuff like that. Then Kelsey and I were on the Dream Team. One day Skylar would probably work here too.

We got a little busier after lunch, when people would buy a donut to go. Kelsey and I had a good rhythm together, with one of us putting the donuts in a bag and the other one ringing up the customers and keeping the line moving. (We knew some of the regulars' orders already.)

Principal Clarke, who was the principal of the middle school where I'd be going, smiled at me as she came up in line.

"Well, I think you'll be joining us soon, Lindsay," she said.

"Yes, ma'am," I said. "Looking forward to it!"

"Oh, I can't wait to have you. It's going to be a great year!" She watched as Kelsey packed her dozen donuts. "I'm headed over for a meeting now and thought I'd sweeten up some of the teachers!"

"Well, donuts usually do the trick!" I said.

I wondered about the teachers. Some of them were friends of Mom's. But even if you know someone, they can act totally different when they're in front of a classroom.

After Principal Clarke left, Kelsey whispered, "The sweetest donut in the world won't sweeten Mrs. Gable up."

I giggled because she was right.

Mrs. Gable taught at the middle school and also happened to be my next-door neighbor. She was what Nans called "a prune." She was always complaining about things and was never really friendly.

Dad always shoveled her walk and helped rake her leaves anyway, which I thought was nice, since she was always yelling over the fence that Sky and I were making too much noise in the backyard.

Eventually, we slowed down again. We had to run an inventory report, which showed how many donuts and which kinds we'd sold, so that we could plan better and not run out. But since Uncle Charlie made the system automatic, we did that in about a minute.

Kelsey and I leaned on the counter. "Are you nervous about middle school?" she asked. "Because it's different."

"Not really," I said. "How different can it be?"

"You wouldn't think that much, but it is," said Kelsey. "At least that's what Jenna tells me."

I raised an eyebrow.

Jenna always acts like she knows everything, and Kelsey and her sister Molly always believe everything she says. Since Jenna is already in high school, they act like she's the queen. Jenna's always been supersweet to me and I love her, but sometimes her know-it-all attitude can get a little irritating.

"So according to Jenna, how is it different?" I asked.

"Well," said Kelsey, "for one thing there's more homework. And you move around from class to class a lot more."

I expected those things. I mean, last year Mrs. Graves told us every single day, "You'll see next year in middle school . . . the teachers won't tolerate anything less than your best. And there will be a lot more work!"

And moving around from class to class? It might be nice to get a bigger change of scenery. I still wasn't worried.

"So what kind of dresses do you think Mimi picked out?" asked Kelsey.

"Don't know," I said, starting to wonder myself. "There are lots more stores near where she lives, so she probably has a range, right?"

Kelsey shrugged. "Well, there's definitely more there than there are here. I mean, there's only one dress store in town. So you're lucky, because your dress will probably be really different from everyone else's."

"Yeah," I said, perking up. "That's true, and pretty cool."

Dad came over just then and whispered, "Elbows off the counters, girls, and look alive . . . or Grandpa will eat you alive!"

We giggled and stood up straight.

The main restaurant always had customers, but Donut Dreams definitely had busy times and not very busy times. We swept the floor again and moved the donuts around on the shelf, but there wasn't a whole lot to do.

I felt bad because my other cousins were running around the restaurant. It wasn't East boys' level of crazy, but my friend Hannah's three year-old brother, Tristan, could be a handful, and he kept dropping his silverware on the floor. Molly would have to scoot over, pick it up, and bring him a new fork or spoon.

Mrs. Wood was always really nice, but even she was getting tired of Tristan's behavior.

"For goodness' sake!" she yelped. "No more forks! That's it!"

Molly froze, a new fork in hand.

"Molly, honey, you can leave that with me, and

when Tristan starts behaving, he can have his fork," Mrs. Wood said.

Molly put the fork on the napkin, as Grandpa taught us to do, and skittered away. She shot us a look across the room and rolled her eyes.

I wasn't really sure why Molly was a runner and Kelsey and I were "on the counter," but that's the way it was set up.

Maybe because Molly is technically a little older than us, even though we're all in the same grade at school. Molly was adopted, and right when she came home with Aunt Melissa and Uncle Chris, they found out they were having a baby, and that was Kelsey.

But even though Molly is ten months older, a fact she likes to point out a lot, Kelsey and Molly are pretty much the same age. Grandpa used to call them the "almost twins" until last year, when Molly threw a fit about it.

"That one has sass," Nans said, when Molly exploded at Grandpa.

"She has spunk, and we love her for it," said Aunt Melissa. "And she's right. The girls aren't twins."

Molly's spunk might be the other reason that she wasn't working behind a counter. I could totally see her saying to the East twins, "Just pick a donut already!"

Plus, Molly has a lot of energy, and she doesn't mind running around.

Donut Dreams closed at six o'clock every day. Nans said you couldn't really keep donuts fresh past that point, and not a lot of people eat donuts at night, which is a strange but true fact. It got really, really slow in the afternoon, so I took my break.

When I came back to the counter, I worried a little bit because in our family we always talk about "business" and whether "business is slow" or "business is good." Busy was always good, slow was not.

Jenna dropped off a tray full of food to the Woods' table, then came over to us.

"How are you doing, girls?" she asked. "Can you spare a cinnamon donut? I'm starving."

Kelsey reached into the case and put a cinnamon donut on a napkin.

"Oh, that was such hard work," said Jenna. "You sure you guys can handle this job?"

"Maybe," I said.

Jenna laughed. "*You* can definitely handle it. My sister Kelsey is not a fan of working."

"Well, it's the end of summer," Kelsey whined. "Everyone else is at the lake today!"

"They've been at the lake all summer!" said Jenna. "How is today any different?" She had a point.

"Because it's like the last stretch of summer that we should hold on to before we go back to school."

Jenna gave her a look.

"Trust me, Kelsey," she said. "You aren't missing anything."

Jenna and I agreed on life here. Jenna was always bored and always planning.

"That one's got her eye on the door," Nans always said, and Aunt Melissa would sigh.

"She has big dreams. But she'll come back," she would reply. "They always do. Just wait and see."

But with Jenna I wasn't so sure. She was constantly talking about moving to Los Angeles, where the weather was beautiful all year. Jenna studied really hard and was always talking about her grades and whether they were good enough to get into a good college.

Jenna took the donut into the kitchen to eat. That was another rule here: no eating on the floor.

I know, it's crazy, right? I mean, we make and serve

food but can't eat in front of the customers. You'd think they'd want us to advertise that the food is so delicious we eat it ourselves. But on the other hand, I guess it wouldn't be good for a customer to ask us a question and us to answer with a mouthful of donut.

"Is Mom taking you home after work?" she asked Kelsey.

"I think so," said Kelsey. "But we have to wait for Molly's shift to end too. That's another hour."

"Well, maybe Uncle Mike can drop you off," said Jenna. "I think Lily is driving me, or maybe Rich."

Lily and Rich were both older, and both of them had their driver's licenses. Rich was the oldest cousin, and Skylar was the youngest. Nans joked that her two grandsons bookended the girls in between.

At big family dinners, I always felt a little sorry for Rich because he was definitely outnumbered, but Sky loved him and followed him everywhere.

Finally it was closing time, which meant we had to clear the shelves, clean the counters, empty the trash, and close out the register. Grandpa didn't like us to close out until actual closing time, because he said it turned away customers if they thought they needed to rush before you went home.

So Kelsey and I watched until the clock said six o'clock on the dot, and then we sprang into close-mode. We made a good team and played Rock-Paper-Scissors to see who had trash duty, which was the worst.

You had to empty the trash, throw the bag into the Dumpster in the back, then lug the trash can into the parking lot and hose it down. Even though there should have been just napkins and cups, there was always something really gross in the trash can. One time I had to scrape out gum, and it was awful.

"Great job today, girls!" said Dad as we signed out.

Everyone who worked at the Park recorded when they started working and when they stopped. Aunt Melissa was a stickler for records, and she was always complaining that someone didn't log out.

"Ready to do it again tomorrow?" asked Grandpa.

Kelsey sighed. "Ugh."

"Hey, young lady," said Grandpa. "You should consider yourself lucky to have a job!"

"Grandpa, I am!" she said, pouting. "But it's the last few days before school starts!"

"And then what happens?" Grandpa teased. "The big bad school monster comes out?"

Kelsey laughed. "Grandpa! We will have homework and we have to sit in school all day and not do fun things like swim in the lake and stay up late!"

"Oh, my poor, poor granddaughter," said Grandpa. "Are you allergic to work? Because if you are, we may need to kick you out of the family!"

"Dad!" said Aunt Melissa. "You can never kick anyone out of this family!"

"Especially not me!" said Kelsey.

She was right. Kelsey was always Grandpa's favorite. It wasn't like he didn't love all of us, but there was something about Kelsey that allowed her to act in a way that would have made Grandpa very prickly with the rest of us.

Nans said that it was because Kelsey was named after Grandpa's mother Katherine, and that Kelsey was very much like her.

"I'm taking the girls home," said Dad. "Melissa is waiting for Molly to finish her shift. I'll be back soon."

Kelsey and I followed him out to the car. We had been inside for most of the day, so the sun felt especially hot and bright. We blinked as we walked.

"Melissa said I could drop you at the lake if you wanted, Kels," said Dad.

"I can't go like this!" Kelsey said. "I'm in my work clothes."

"But it's just the lake," Dad said.

"Uncle Mike, you can't go to the lake in work clothes," said Kelsey. "Besides, everyone is probably headed home now anyway."

Dad shrugged. Our town isn't that big, but it's kind of spread out in parts, so there are a bunch of us who live five minutes away and then there are people like Kelsey, who live on the other side of the lake.

Some people have boats and just row or drive across the lake instead of taking a car. There have been a lot of stories about kids taking boats out at night, and Dad has already hammered it into our heads that it's too dangerous to do that.

At Kelsey's house, Uncle Chris opened the door when he heard the car pull up and waved to us.

"See you tomorrow," I said to Kelsey as she opened the car door, and she sighed.

It was still pretty sticky and hot. I guess a lot of people were on vacation, because the town seemed quiet, which was kind of nice.

"So how was your first day?" asked Dad as we drove away from Kelsey's house.

"Pretty good," I said. "A little slow."

"Yeah," said Dad. "Time of year. You'll see, it will speed up. That's when the days go a lot faster."

Dad and I drove in the quiet. It was nice having this time with just him, without Skylar or Nans or Grandpa or a million other family members. I actually didn't mind the slow pace of the day. I hoped things didn't speed up too quickly.

Chapter Three
My BFF Is Back!

I didn't have to worry about things going quickly, because even though the next day was kind of slow at Donut Dreams, it had a nice rhythm.

Kelsey and I were pretty good about splitting the "ick" stuff, as we called it, like hosing down the mat behind the counter or making sure the chairs were clean underneath (you wouldn't believe). I liked chatting with the customers, and I knew almost everyone who came in.

After a flurry of morning customers, I had a second to sip some water. I was itching to check my phone because I knew my best friend, Casey, was coming home today, and I couldn't wait to see her.

But even though my phone was in my apron

pocket, Grandpa had been especially vigilant this morning, and I didn't want him to catch me using it.

Grandpa has been telling every customer that he now has six out of seven grandchildren working at the restaurant.

"One more and it's a full house!" he'll say.

I cannot imagine Sky working . . . at all. He'd probably complain the entire time and try to eat all the donuts.

On the one hand, it is nice to work with my family because we help each other out. One day, while here after school, Lily dropped a huge tray she was carrying, and it made such a loud crashing sound that everyone stopped talking and stared at her.

In a flash Molly, Jenna, and Rich ran over to help her, and they got everything up off the ground in record time.

Another time crazy Mr. Brown, who is known to have a temper, yelled at Jenna for not toasting his bread well enough, and Grandpa walked over and said, "Hey, Ed, are you yelling at one of my favorite granddaughters over a tuna sandwich?" and calmed him down right away.

Family always has your back, and while Grandpa

can be tough, he is also pretty protective of us.

I was busy wiping down the counter when I heard someone scream, "I'M BAAAAAACK!" That could only be one person: Casey, my best friend in the entire world! We've been friends since we were born, because we were born exactly one day apart and were in the hospital together.

She has gone to sleepaway camp for the past few summers, which generally makes me miserable because I miss her so much. At her camp you can't have computers or phones, so she can't e-mail me, let alone text me, and I hate not being able to talk to her. Casey sometimes sends postcards, but it's not the same thing.

I spun around and Casey charged at me, hugging me over the counter.

"So how much did you miss me?" she asked.

"A lot!" I said.

"I need to know everything that I missed this summer!" she said.

I blinked. "Seriously? You missed nothing, Casey. You know that!"

"Really?" she asked. "I was hoping something exciting might have happened."

"Um . . . no," I said.

"Well, you got a job!" she said, grinning. "Spin around and let me see your uniform."

I spun around, pointing to the DREAM TEAM on the back of the shirt.

"Nice, nice," she said.

"Casey!" Kelsey squealed, coming back from the kitchen.

She was so happy to see Casey, she almost dropped the tray she was carrying.

"I have returned!" said Casey dramatically.

"Wow, you look different," said Kelsey.

I looked at Casey. She did look different.

First of all, she was wearing a little makeup, which was surprising because I knew her mom hadn't let her wear any before the summer. She also seemed to be a few inches taller.

She was wearing shorts and a T-shirt, but she looked . . . well, more put together or something, not like she just threw clothes on, which I knew for a fact was what she usually did. And they were usually clothes she had stashed under her bed. She had on a cute pair of sandals, and her toes were painted purple with glitter. Her hair, which was usually in a ponytail, was down and bouncy and curled like she'd just had it styled.

"Did you just get your hair cut?" I asked.

"No, but I used a blow-dryer," she said.

"You used a blow-dryer in August?" I asked.

Normally, I only blow-dried my hair when it was freezing cold and Nans was yelling that I couldn't possibly go outside with wet hair or it would freeze on my head.

"I have been dying for those sandals!" said Kelsey. "But Mom won't let me get them. Did your feet grow too or can I borrow them?"

"Kelsey, are you taking the shoes off poor Casey as soon as she returns to our fine town?" asked Dad, who was grinning.

He loved Casey and came out from the kitchen to say hello the minute he heard her voice. "Hey, Case. Did you have any big summer adventures?"

"I did!" said Casey very seriously. "I had some monumental softball games."

Then she burst out laughing. "It was great. I had a lot of fun, and it was nice to get away."

I'll bet, I thought.

I had asked Dad if I could go to summer camp,

but he wasn't too into the idea. I made a note to myself to start bugging him about it early for next summer. Maybe he'd change his mind next year.

Casey's phone buzzed, and she looked at it with a giant smile on her face. I had never seen her smile like that before.

"Who's bugging you besides me?" I asked.

"Oh, just someone I met at camp," she said. "His name is Matt."

Matt?

"You have a boyfriend?" Kelsey yelped.

"He's not really my . . . ," said Casey. "Well, he's kind of . . . I don't know. Summer's over, and he lives far away, so . . ."

My head was spinning a little. We barely spoke to boys. I mean, we spoke to them, but we had never looked at our boy *friends* as potential boyfriend material.

"You came home from camp with a boyfriend?" Dad asked. "Well, that's it. Lindsay is never, ever going to camp now!" He laughed.

"Daaaad," I said, crossing my arms.

"Who has a boyfriend?" asked Lily, whizzing by. "Oh, Casey!"

She gave Casey a squeeze and winked. "Well, I'd say that sounds like you had a good summer!"

"I did!" said Casey, and then her mom came in.

"Hey, I said you could run in, honey," Mrs. Peters said, exasperated.

Then she saw me. "Oh, Linds, I've missed you!"

"You missed Lindsay more than you missed me!" said Casey, all huffy.

"Well, she doesn't give me as hard a time as you do," said Mrs. Peters, embracing me in a big hug.

Mrs. Peters takes Casey to camp and then goes to visit her mother, Casey's grandma, for the summer. Casey's grandma moved to Arizona so she could be warm all year, which drives Mrs. Peters crazy because they don't get to see her a lot.

"How is Granny?" I asked.

"Good, good," said Mrs. Peters. "She sends her love and said we should all come see her when it snows, because she'll be at the pool!"

"Ooh, that could be fun," Casey said, her mind already whirling.

"Casey, the dog is going nuts in the car," said Mrs. Peters. "We were on our way back home, but you know we *had* to stop and see Lindsay first!"

"Well, I am the main attraction of the town," I said, grinning.

"Of course you are," Casey said. "Okay, I'll come over later."

"Casey, you just got home, and Dad and I would like to have dinner together as a family!" said Mrs. Peters.

"Okay," said Casey. "After dinner, then!"

"Can I have you for twenty-four hours?" asked Mrs. Peters. "Seriously, Casey. You and Lindsay have plenty of time to catch up."

"Fine!" said Casey. "At least I can text now. I'll TTYL, Linds!"

I gave her another quick hug, and she was halfway out the door before she whipped back around.

"Oh my gosh, I missed the donuts almost as much as you! We need four, please!"

I smiled, because I knew that she liked cinnamon, Gabby liked old-fashioned, and Mr. and Mrs. Peters liked powdered jelly. I carefully put them in the bag.

"Those are on the house!" Dad called. "Welcome back, Casey. We missed you!"

"Thank you," said Casey. "I promise I'll eat them all, even the ones for my parents!"

Dad laughed, and Casey and her mom rushed out.

I was so glad to have my BFF home. I missed having Casey as my go-to, because she just always knew what I was thinking or how I felt about things, and I didn't need to explain everything to her. She just got me.

On the other hand, Casey seemed different. I mean, a boyfriend was a big deal. Who was this guy Matt?

Maybe Jenna was right. Maybe middle school *was* going to be different.

Chapter Four
Early Dismissal

At eleven o'clock the next Monday morning, Dad sauntered up to the counter and asked if I wanted the rest of the day off.

"Really?" I asked, surprised.

"Yep," said Dad. "We leave at noon."

"Wait," I said. "Leave for where? To do what?"

"Special surprise!" Dad called over his shoulder.

"No fair!" said Kelsey. "I get stuck here and you get a day off?"

I didn't know what to say, because it actually didn't sound very fair.

"You can leave too," said Rich, who was walking over wearing a Dream Team tee. "I'm covering the counter from noon to six."

"Yes!" Kelsey yelled, and pumped her fist. "Lake bound!"

The next hour actually sped up because we were crowded, and I felt bad about turning over the counter to Rich. I guess more people were coming back from vacation because the Park, Donut Dreams, and even the town itself was busier.

My next customers were Mrs. Ellis and her daughter Elizabeth, aka Wetsy Betsy. I mean, it's terrible that we're friends and I still think of her as Wetsy Betsy, but I can't get it out of my head.

It's not like anyone really calls her Wetsy Betsy, except for Mitchell Stewart, who is kind of a bully anyway. "Hey, Wetsy!" he'll say when he sees her. She just ignores him, but I'm sure it bothers her.

"Hi, Lindsay!" Elizabeth said.

I smiled back at her. "Hey, Elizabeth."

"How has your summer been, Lindsay?" asked Mrs. Ellis. "Did you enjoy the rec classes as much as Elizabeth did?"

Elizabeth and I—along with most of the kids— went to the camp that the town ran for a few hours every morning. We hung out at rec because we both liked the art classes, and Elizabeth was really good at ceramics. She helped me work the wheel so I could make a bowl for Nans.

"It was pretty good," I said. "I wish summer was twice as long, though!"

"I do too!" Mrs. Ellis said. She worked at the high school, so she had most of the summer off too.

The thing I've learned about working in a restaurant is that people generally want to talk to you. I guess it's polite? They can't just say, "Give me that donut," so they say, "Oh, it's so hot out that I decided to treat myself to a donut and cool iced tea to wash it down. Isn't it just so hot?" So I end up talking about the weather a lot.

"Pretty soon it will be Fall Fling, and I can't believe you girls are starting up with all that soon!" said Mrs. Ellis.

Ugh, Fall Fling again.

When you live in a town where nothing ever happens, little things are a big deal. But I wasn't sure what she meant by "starting up with all that." Starting up with what? Getting dressed up? We did that already on holidays and for family things. Last year was Nans and Grandpa's fortieth anniversary, and we all had to get really dressed up. Dad even wore a suit.

Hole in the Middle

"Enjoy the last of summer, dear!" Mrs. Ellis said.

Elizabeth waved. "See you at the lake!" she said.

Here's the thing: everyone goes to the lake. But nothing really happens at the lake. We all take our towels and phones and some of us bring books, and everyone sits around talking to each other. If it's really hot, we'll jump in, and some kids play volleyball in the water, but mostly it's a lot of just hanging out. On a beautiful day it's really nice, but it also gets pretty boring by the end of the summer, with all of us running out of conversation and just staring out into the lake.

The lake was a big deal this year because it was the first year that me and my friends were allowed to go without an adult. There were lifeguards there, but the lifeguards were mostly the older brothers and sisters of my friends.

Everyone is always so intent on being there, though. It's like buying tickets to a show, but there's nothing on the stage, you know? Everyone just ends up watching each other, even though we've all been staring at each other for years.

I guess there's one thing that has changed. When we used to go with an adult, we'd sit with them. Kids hung out with their families. Since we're going with friends now, we're all arranged in slightly different circles. All the middle school kids sit together with the high school kids mostly at one end of the lake.

Without Casey this summer, I mostly sat with Kelsey and her BFF, Sophia. Sometimes Molly would hang out with us too. I guess it is weird that Molly and Kelsey have totally separate friends, since they are sisters and in the same grade, but they are so different that it makes sense.

Kelsey likes to think she's friends with everybody, and that everyone likes her. She always cares about what people think, and she is obsessed with being in on everything.

I still remember the fit she threw in third grade when she wasn't invited to Anna's birthday party. It turns out she was; Anna had just accidentally dropped Kelsey's invitation on her way to school.

Molly is much more of a free spirit. She could not care less what people think about her, and pretty much always says what's on her mind, which does tend to get her in trouble. Nans says she has absolutely no filter from her brain to her mouth. But Molly is also a lot of fun, and she's the first one to organize a kayak race across the lake or a s'mores contest to see who can build the biggest one.

She's really good with little kids, too, so they're always running over to her at the lake. Molly says that when she's old enough she's going to babysit instead of working at the Park, but Aunt Melissa says, "Molly, family first. If we need you, we need to know you'll be there."

There are only twenty-five girls in my grade, so the truth is, even if we split ourselves up, we are all kind of forced to hang out together. There are a ton of cousins and one set of twins, so there are also a lot of people related to each other. My point is, you can't really get away from anyone. Sure, I'm going to avoid some of the meaner girls, but at some point I'm going to be in class or on a team with them.

"Okay, Rich," said Dad. "You got this?"

"I got it," said Rich, eyeing the door because a bunch of his friends from the soccer team had come in and were swarming the counter.

"Hiiiiiii, Lindsay!" called Mason R.

There were three Masons on Rich's team, so they went by Mason R., Mason L., and Mason B.

Mason R. leaned over the counter. "Hey, can you

give me a dozen donuts even if I only pay for a half dozen?" He smiled.

I smiled back. "Nope," I said.

Mason R. laughed.

Rich's friends always tried to get us to give them free donuts. Uncle Charlie brought them to every game, and each of those guys ate about four. Uncle Charlie joked that the soccer team would eat us out of business.

"Get out of here, Linds," said Rich, "before they try to get you to sell them the whole case at half price."

Dad was waiting for me off to the side of the counter. "Okay, Pops," he said to Grandpa. "We're off. I'll see you later tonight!"

Grandpa gave me a quick hug. "Are you sure your grandma Mimi's plane is on time?" he asked, looking at his phone.

I looked at Dad. "Mimi's plane?"

"Pops!" Dad yelled.

I giggled. I guess Grandpa had just ruined some sort of surprise!

Chapter Five
Grandma Mimi

"What?" said Grandpa. "She already knows her grandma Mimi is coming!"

I laughed. "Well, I didn't know she was coming *today*!" I said.

"For goodness' sake," said Dad, throwing up his hands. "No one in this family can keep a secret!"

Grandpa looked around. "Well, no one told me this was still a secret. They just told me her whole trip was a secret but Melissa spilled!"

Dad shook his head. "Okay, Lindsay," he said. "I thought it would be nice to pick up Grandma Mimi from the airport, so we have a ways to go. Let's get out of here before Grandpa and the family also tell you what I'm getting you for your birthday and every other secret we still have." Then he laughed. It was hard to stay mad at Grandpa for long.

The airport is about two and a half hours away, in St. Louis. Sometimes Dad takes us to St. Louis for a weekend, which is a lot of fun. It's so crazy different there, with so much more to do. It's weird that you can get in a car, drive, and end up someplace that's so different from where you started.

"I figure we'll get there in time to pick up Grandma Mimi," Dad said, heading out to the highway. "Then we'll have an early dinner and head back."

"We're having dinner in the city?" I said, realizing I still had my Donut Dreams T-shirt on with a pair of shorts.

Dad usually wore a nice button-down shirt to work with pants and nice shoes, so he always looked a little dressed up to me. And Mimi was always, always dressed up. No matter where she was, she always had lipstick on and some kind of jewelry. I tried to picture Mimi on the plane like a lot of other grandmas, wearing sweatpants and a sweatshirt, but I just couldn't do it.

"Mimi wants to take you on a little surprise excursion in St. Louis," said Dad. "And Uncle Charlie wants me to meet with one of our vendors for the restaurant, so I'll leave you guys to it. Then I'll pick you both up for dinner. Okay?"

"Sounds great!" I said.

Some people might think it's strange that I am looking forward to hanging out with my grandma, but I love being with Mimi. It was the rest of the family that sometimes annoyed me.

Dad is always on time for everything, so of course we got to the airport a little early. I watched people lugging bags or rolling suitcases, and I wondered where they'd been or what adventure they were heading off to.

"What's one place that you've never been that you'd like to see?" I asked Dad.

Dad and I did this a lot, asking things like, *If you could eat only one thing for twenty-four hours, what food would you choose?*

"Hmm," Dad said. "Well, Europe was wonderful, but if it has to be someplace I've never been, I think I'd love to go to Japan."

I nodded. I always forget Dad had traveled a lot with Mom, before she got sick.

Mom lived in France for a year during college,

and when Dad went to visit her, they traveled all over Europe.

"But you know I'm not a big traveler," said Dad. "I like being home. It's fun to see other countries, but I miss home when I'm away."

"Did Mom miss home when she was living in France?" I asked.

"Well, she definitely missed her family and her friends," said Dad. "And me!" He laughed. "But I think she liked learning how people lived in different cities. To some extent she had to learn how people lived in our town too."

I thought about that. "You mean like how we pronounce certain words?"

"Well, that, yes," said Dad. "But also that everyone eats dinner early or that people think it's rude if you don't say hello when you see them out and about, that kind of thing. When she first moved here, she could not get used to the fact that people would just walk in the front door without knocking first. For about six months, she screamed when anyone came into the house."

I laughed. "Well, to be fair, people only walk in if you've invited them over or are expecting them.

It's not like we just randomly walk into each other's houses!"

"Of course not!" said Dad. "But even then. One time when Casey's mom came over, she startled Mom so much that Mom dropped an entire platter of meatballs and spaghetti she was making for dinner. There was red sauce everywhere . . . even on the ceiling."

I cracked up. "Wow, that sounds like a mess!"

"It was," said Dad. "There was sauce in her hair and dripping from above. And we all laughed at her, and she did not like that one bit!"

I giggled. I was used to seeing Mom covered in paint but not sauce.

Then I spotted Mimi striding toward us. She was hard to miss. Mimi doesn't exactly look like a grandma, or at least not like what most of my friends' grandmas look like.

She wears bright red lipstick that's always perfect—it never smudges, even when she eats (and I've watched her!). She is always what she calls "smartly dressed," which means she's usually in pants, with a nice top and a jacket and heels.

I've never seen her wear jeans, and the only time

she wears sneakers is when she goes for a run, which she does every day. Dad sometimes teases Mimi about wearing sweats, but we all know she doesn't own one sweatshirt.

Today Mimi had on these cool sunglasses and a scarf wrapped around her neck, I guess because she was cold on the plane. Her feet, as always, made a *click, click, click* sound with her shoes.

"Baby girl!" Mimi cried out, and grabbed me for a big hug.

She smelled like flowers. She took off her sunglasses and propped them on top of her head.

"Let me take a good look at you. Oh, you are even more beautiful than ever, and . . ." She looked at Dad. "She's the spitting image of Amy, isn't she?"

Dad smiled. "Well, she's Lindsay, so she looks like Lindsay to me," he said.

"Oh, you know what I mean!" said Mimi. "Lindsay, you look more and more like your beautiful mother each time I see you."

She looked at me for a minute longer. I wondered if she was imagining me as Mom, or Mom with my head. Or Mom's head on me.

"Good to see you, Mike!" Mimi said then, giving

Hole in the Middle

Dad a long hug. "You seem to be faring well."

"I am!" said Dad.

"You know I would have been happy to drive out to you," said Mimi.

"Don't be silly," said Dad as we walked toward the exit of the terminal. "Happy to give you some company on the trip. And we like our city trips, don't we, Linds?" He winked. "It's good practice for when Lindsay leaves us and moves to the big town!"

"Oh?" said Mimi. "There's so much to catch up on! Lindsay, I want to hear everything you're up to! And how is my sweetie Skylar? Did you leave him at home? I was hoping he'd join us!"

Dad grabbed Mimi's bag and we piled into the car. "Well, I didn't think he'd last while you went out," he said as he started up the car engine. "Unless you take him shopping for video games."

"Well, I'm happy to shop for Sky, too," said Mimi, "but all he wears are those terrible athletic clothes. He looks like he's going to the gym all the time!"

"Marla, that's what all the boys wear," said Dad.

Mimi shook her head. "I bought him some button-down shirts," she said. "And a few pairs of pants."

Dad rolled his eyes and smiled at me in the rearview mirror.

"Where are we going today?" I asked Mimi. "Dad said it's a surprise."

Mimi nodded and smiled. "Oh, it is," she said. "It definitely is."

Chapter Six
A Day at the Museum

Mimi typed an address into her phone, and we were off to the St. Louis Art Museum. Before I knew it, Mimi was ready to march me into the museum, but not without first touching up her makeup and hair in the car.

"Oh, I'm such a mess from traveling!" she said.

I tried not to giggle as I looked at Dad, because not one hair on Mimi's head was out of place.

Dad pulled up in front of the museum and let us out.

"Have fun," he shouted as we waved goodbye.

At the entrance, Mimi asked a man at the information desk for "a docent named Ellen Colbert."

The man picked up the phone and made a call.

"She'll be right down," he said.

I turned to Mimi. "Docent?" I asked.

Mimi smiled. "A docent is a museum guide."

A few minutes later a woman came to the desk and said, "Marla?"

"Yes!" said Grandma. "But you can call me Mimi! And are you Ellen?"

Ellen nodded. "I am! Jenny told me you were coming with your granddaughter."

I admired Ellen's black suit and silky white blouse. She wore black patent-leather pumps, and tiny little diamond stud earrings twinkled in her ears. She looked dressed up, yet she still managed to appear comfortable at the same time. Not an easy look to pull off.

Mimi shook Ellen's hand.

"This is my beautiful granddaughter Lindsay," she said, tucking my hair behind my ear. "Look at that gorgeous face!"

"Mimi!" I said, and I could feel my face getting hot.

Ellen laughed. "Oh, that's what grandmas do!"

She led us into the museum and started pointing out all the different paintings.

It was incredible. Even though Mom was an artist, I had never been to an art museum before.

Ellen smiled at me. "We have something here your grandmother has been eager to show you," she said. "She's been calling me nearly every day, asking, 'Is it still on? We didn't miss it, did we?'"

I looked up at Mimi questioningly. She didn't say anything.

Ellen laughed. "I think it's time to tell her, Mimi!"

Mimi nodded and took me by the hand.

"There's a special exhibit here this month," she said. "I'm just so glad I was able to get you here in time before it ended."

Then we walked down a hallway and there was a sign that read, THE ST. LOUIS ART MUSEUM IS PROUD TO HONOR CLAUDE MONET. EXHIBITION ON LOAN FROM THE NATIONAL GALLERY OF ART, WASHINGTON, DC. There was a security guard at the entrance who smiled and nodded at us as we walked in.

I gasped. Monet was my mom's absolute favorite artist. When I walked into the exhibition, I felt like I was dreaming.

"I'm sure your mom must have talked about Monet to you," Mimi said, smiling.

"Oh, you know, just . . . all the time," I said. "I know he painted by observing and using his own thoughts and emotions in his art, instead of drawing things exactly as they were in real life. Is that right?"

Ellen was nodding. She was also smiling from ear to ear.

"Very good! Yes, it's called impressionism, Lindsay," she said.

I walked over to one painting that caught my eye. It was called *Palazzo da Mula, Venice*. It was wonderful. I felt as if I could dip my hand into the cool blue water.

"Mom always talked about Monet and the way he painted water," I said.

Mimi tapped me on the shoulder. "Let me show you one of your mom's favorites," she said.

It was called *Woman with a Parasol—Madame Monet and Her Son*. It was a woman walking through a field of flowers, holding a parasol, with a little boy walking close to her.

As I looked at it, I took a deep breath.

"It's so . . . soothing, isn't it?" I said. "The puffy white clouds, the way her scarf is gently blowing in the breeze . . . I love how everything is so soft, and a little blurry." I gave a little happy sigh. "I could look at this for hours."

"You know, when Monet was alive, his work was criticized," Ellen said.

"Why?" I said. "How could someone not like this?" I pointed to the painting.

"Some critics said Monet's work was blurry not by choice, but because his eyesight was failing," Ellen explained. She shook her head. "They just wanted to criticize his work, instead of seeing the beauty behind it." She sighed. "Monet is one of my favorites too."

"Which goes to show you should do whatever you want when it comes to art," Mimi said. "Paint how you love to paint, write what you love to write, sing what you want to sing!"

She turned to me. "The point is, you're never going to make everybody happy, Lindsay, so it's important that you make *you* happy."

I nodded. "Thanks, Mimi."

Of course all this made me think of my mom. She always painted what made her happy. I pictured her sitting by her easel, softly humming as she mixed colors from her palette.

I remembered one time when she had just finished a painting; I caught her looking at the final product, her head tilted slightly to one side, with a small, satisfied smile on her face. "I can never get it exactly the way I see it in my mind, Linds," she told me. "But this one is close."

Monet painted a lot of water lilies, but there were other paintings I found equally wonderful. Fishing boats, sailboats, cathedrals: they were all beautiful to me.

After I made sure I had looked at every single one, Mimi called Dad to come pick us up, and told him we were going to make a quick stop at the gift shop first. Mimi bought me an art book all about Monet's paintings. It was pretty expensive.

We met up with Dad and got into the car, and the minute he saw the bag from the gift shop, Dad immediately whipped out his wallet, thinking I had asked Mimi to buy the pricey art book for me.

But Mimi waved her hand, shooing him away, saying it was a gift and her treat.

After some protest, Dad eventually put his wallet away. "But I'm paying for dinner," he said. "No arguments. It's not up for discussion."

Mimi nodded seriously. "Yes. Food I'll let you pay for," she said. And we all laughed.

Dad and Mimi and I stopped at a restaurant Dad wanted to try for dinner, and he went to talk to the manager while Mimi and I settled into a booth.

"I worked up an appetite," said Mimi.

I realized I was pretty hungry too. I looked at the menu, which was huge, and everything sounded good.

"Okay," said Dad, sliding into the other side of the table. "There are a few things I'd like to try, so let me know if there's anything that catches your eye. Otherwise I'll order for everyone."

"That makes it easy," said Mimi, and she slapped her menu shut and slid it to Dad.

Dad ordered enough food for about ten people.

"Uh, Mike, it's just the three of us, right?" asked Mimi.

"It's market research!" said Dad.

It was strange to be in a restaurant that wasn't the Park. I noticed how busy the staff was, and, because it was a big restaurant, they really had to move fast to get from the kitchen to the tables.

It was also weird to be out to dinner and not see one person we knew. I wondered if you could spend a whole day in a city without seeing anyone you had ever met before. You would be totally anonymous.

I wondered if that was good or bad. You could pretty much do what you wanted to do, but then again, if you didn't show up somewhere, would anyone know? What if you needed help and didn't know anyone to ask? What if you just wanted to see a friendly face but all you saw were strangers?

It was also a little weird being someplace with just Mimi and Dad. After Mom died, it seemed like three of us (me, Skylar, Dad), went everywhere together.

When we were a family of four, I didn't really notice when Mom was out or Skylar was off doing something. And since Dad worked a lot, there were a lot of times it was just Skylar, me, and Mom.

Now I'm always aware of where Dad and Skylar are, and it's like I'm constantly looking around for Sky if he's not with us. If I moved to the city, it would just be Dad and Sky back home.

For some reason that thought made my throat feel a little funny. Maybe without the two of them, I would be lonely.

Dad must have read my mind, because he said, "Ah, it's strange not to have Skylar here, but Mimi, you should consider this your last meal with no whining while you're visiting."

Mimi laughed. "Oh, Sky is a good kid," she said. "I can't wait to see him. But today is about Lindsay!

Tell me about middle school. Are you excited?"

Here we go again, I thought.

"Not really," I said. "It's a new school but the same kids, so not much is different."

"Oh!" said Mimi, surprised. "Your mom spoke so highly about the school, though. It has wonderful programs, especially for art. And some of her friends still teach there, right?"

I nodded.

"Well, Carla teaches there," Dad said. "You remember her, right, Mimi? And Laurie is still the assistant principal."

"Laurie is Casey's mom," I said.

"Of course!" said Mimi. "I remembered that. It will be a little weird for Casey then, right?"

I remembered talking about it with Casey before she left for camp, when she was packing up her stuff and there were clothes thrown all over her room. I knew she was not too happy to have her mom at school with her.

"I mean, I'll see her every day, all day!" she said, flopping on her bed. Then she sat up. "Oh, I'm sorry," she said. "I'll bet you'd do anything to see your mom every day."

I was quiet for a second, which I can only do with Casey. Usually I'd just quickly say, "Oh, it's okay" to get the awkward moment over.

But Casey understood. She tilted her head and waited for me to think it through.

I thought about how I'd feel if Mom was my principal. She'd always know if I got in trouble, if there was a test, if I was talking to someone or not.

"No, I get it," I said. "I mean, yes, of course I'd do anything to have my mom back. But if she was here and things were normal, I would not be too happy having her watch me all day."

Casey sighed. "That's why Gabby liked high school so much. She got rid of Mom on an hourly basis!"

"But it's not just you," I said. "Jessica Walsh's mom is a teacher there, and Jake Todd's dad is a science teacher. Claire's mom works in the lunchroom, and Richie Miller's mom works in the office. Almost every teacher or staff person there has a kid who goes through that school at some point. . . ."

"True," said Casey. "It's totally worse for Claire. I mean, her mom is probably not going to let her eat only french fries for lunch." She giggled.

"I know!" I said.

"'Claire, you come back here and get milk and some fruit!'" Casey imitated in a high voice.

"'And you sit with those nice kids over there!'" I imitated in a high voice too.

We collapsed into giggles on the floor.

"Well, thank you for showing me that someone always has it worse," said Casey.

"It is my duty as your friend to always make you feel better!" I said.

She smiled. "It's going to be a long summer without you, Miss L.!" she said.

"Don't worry," I said, laughing. "You're in for an even longer year with me when you get back."

"Ugh!" said Casey, and then she hopped up. "Okay I can only take three books, so help me decide here!"

We spent the next hour debating the books Casey had on her shelf until her mom peeked in and said, "Ladies, I can assume you're having a good time, but need I remind you that someone named Casey has to be packed and ready to go in the morning? The very early morning?"

Then we got down to business, with me calling out the things that were on Casey's packing list and

Casey folding them up and stuffing them into a giant duffel bag.

That day seemed like a long time ago now, especially with the first day of school right around the corner. Maybe everyone was right. Maybe middle school would be different. Maybe everyone was worried about it for different reasons. Maybe I should be worried about it.

On the car ride home I looked out the window at the lights of the city as they disappeared behind us. As much as I loved the city tonight, I was glad to be going home, where Sky and Nans and Grandpa were waiting for us and where I knew tomorrow morning I'd have a text from Casey.

Chapter Seven
Middle School Musings

Sure enough, the next morning there was a text from Casey, asking me what time I would be home from work. I texted her back, put on my Donut Dreams shirt, and went downstairs, where Nans and Mimi were already having coffee.

"Ready for work?" asked Nans, putting a plate of scrambled eggs in front of me. "Mimi is going to wait until Prince Sky wakes up, so I can drive you to the Park and get some things done in the office."

"Thanks," I said.

I looked from Nans to Mimi and smiled at them as I ate. It was nice having both grandmas here at the same time.

"Okay, all done! Reporting for duty," I said,

finishing up my breakfast. Mimi reached over to clear my plate.

"I can do it," I said. I didn't want Mimi to do any extra work for me.

"Oh, you get to work, honey. I'll clean up," said Mimi.

Nans raised an eyebrow but didn't say anything.

She would always say, "I am not a waitress in my own home!" whenever one of us didn't clear our plate and scrape it off before we put it in the dishwasher.

"Should I pack a snack in case you get hungry?" asked Mimi, opening the fridge.

"Uh, Mimi," I said. "I'm going to work in a restaurant. Where there is, um, a lot of food."

She spun around. "Oh, right," she said. Then she laughed. "That would be like bringing books to a library!"

"Kind of," I said.

Mimi was not the type of person to ever sit down. After dinner Nans and Grandpa would sit and talk while they had coffee or tea. When we were at Mimi's house in Chicago for Thanksgiving, she would jump up and clear the table and start cleaning the kitchen. I never saw her sit around, really. She always had projects, as she called them, or "tidying up" around the house. There was never anything out of place at Mimi's house, so she must spend a lot of time tidying.

"Well, have a good day, Lindsay," said Mimi. "I know you'll do a great job!" She gave me a kiss, and I followed Nans out the door.

When we got into the car, I said, "Nans, Mimi tried to send food to a restaurant!"

"Well," said Nans. "She means well. She doesn't know how to help when she comes, so you can't really blame her. Plus, walking into the house is hard for her, Linds. She misses your mother so much."

"Why would she miss her more at our house than at her house?" I asked, puzzled.

"Well," said Nans. "Your mom really made that house your family's home. Her stamp is all over it, from the garden in the back to her studio, to the mural she painted in Skylar's room. It's hard to be there and not think she's going to come around the corner."

"You know she's not going to come around the corner!" I said a little loudly, and Nans glanced at me.

"Well, I think Mimi does too," she said slowly. "But maybe part of her hopes that when she comes to visit, your mom will be there, just like she used to be."

For a while I thought Mom would reappear. Every day I'd wake up and think, *Maybe that was just a nightmare*, and she would be downstairs making me French toast. But after a few months, I stopped thinking that.

"Do you think she likes coming here?" I asked.

"Your grandma? Oh, very much," said Nans. "She just loves seeing you and Skylar and spending time with you. Right after your mom died, she thought about moving here because she missed you so much."

"She did?" I asked, surprised.

"Yes," said Nans. "But she was still working then, and her life was really in Chicago. So she made a promise to herself to visit as often as she could."

Just then a car pulled out in front of us really slowly, and Nans tapped the brakes.

"Holy moly!" she said. Then she peered over the steering wheel. "Is that your cousin Lily?" she asked.

I looked at the car. "Probably," I said.

"I am going to have a serious talk with her and with Charlie," Nans said. "She can't possibly think it's okay to drive like that!"

Lily was a really bad driver. Grandpa made her

park in the back of the restaurant, away from any customers, because in the first few months after she got her license, she hit two parked cars.

She didn't drive fast and she was a really nervous driver. She said she didn't like driving near any other cars, but of course, that was often unavoidable. Usually Uncle Charlie drove with her.

Nans went on and on about Lily's driving until we got to the Park.

"Lily!" she said, rolling down the window as we pulled in. "Young lady, we are going to talk about your driving!"

Lily sighed, and I gave her a look as if to say *sorry*, but I also took it as an opportunity to hurry in.

Every morning Grandpa sits at the podium right before we open and watches everyone come to work. He knows who gets there on time and who slides in. He notices if you are trying to eat a bagel while you're setting up or if your uniform isn't clean.

"Hello, lovely Lindsay!" he boomed, and I gave him a hug before I tied my apron.

Then I got out the glass cleaner and started polishing the case, even though it was already gleaming. I saw Grandpa glance over and smile.

Kelsey came streaking in a few minutes after me. "Grandpa the Great!" she said, saluting him. "Reporting for duty!"

Grandpa smiled and gave her a wink.

Kelsey went to put her bag in a locker in the back and then came bounding back.

"Okay, I want to hear all about your trip," she said.

"I'll show you," I said, noticing that Nans and Grandpa were going over the specials for the day.

I slipped Kelsey my phone. She flipped through the pictures of the art, her eyes getting bigger and bigger.

"This is so cool, Lindsay! I can't believe you got to see all this. I'm totally asking Mom if she can take me to this place."

"It was kind of fun," I said. "Ellen, the woman who worked as a guide at the museum, showed me some really amazing things."

Kelsey nodded.

"Kelsey . . . alert!" I hissed, and she shoved the phone in a drawer.

Dad and Grandpa were headed over. "Okay, guys, we have a special order today," said Dad. "The track team ordered three dozen donuts for the first track practice of the season." He handed me a piece of paper. "Can you pack up the boxes with everything they ordered? Someone will run them over at eight."

Grandpa looked over my shoulder at the order. "Looks like we're going to need some refilling of the shelves, Jane," he called to Nans.

Nans looked over and nodded, then headed back to the kitchen. Kelsey and I smiled . . . fresh donuts out of the fryer are the most delicious thing ever. I knew I'd have to elbow her to get back to the kitchen to "pick up the refills" and snag a freshly made donut.

Everyone was setting up their stations, and by six thirty we were ready to go, with the first customers coming in at 6:31. The regular breakfast customers have been coming for years.

Mrs. Selling was walking slowly, using a cane, and Rich offered her his arm to lean on. "Mrs. Selling, can I help you to your usual table?" he asked.

Mrs. Selling smiled at him.

"Coop, your grandson is just a gem," she said to Grandpa.

Our family's last name is Cooper, but everyone calls Grandpa Coop.

"Well, he learned from the best!" Grandpa said.

"The crew is all here!" Mrs. Selling said, looking around. "You're a lucky man!"

"I am," said Grandpa. "I am!"

Then he grabbed a coffeepot to start pouring everyone's morning cup.

Grandpa knew how everyone liked their coffee: with milk, with sugar, or with nothing added. The regulars didn't even have to ask him; they just sat down and he came over with their cup and saucer.

Suddenly we heard a crash, and everyone turned around to stare. Dropping things in restaurants is always the worst, especially if it's crowded. Everyone just stops and I imagine you must feel like you want to sink into the floor.

Usually what goes down is either silverware, which makes a loud racket, or worse, a dish or glass, which shatters. If there's food on a plate, it makes a huge mess. This time it was a tray, and of course, it was Lily who had dropped it.

I love my cousin, but Lily is a bit clumsy. Uncle Charlie always jokes that to have Lily work as a waitress means ordering an extra set of dishes, because she breaks so many.

Rich and Molly rushed over to help, and I heard

Grandpa sigh as he strode over with a broom.

"Poor Lily," whispered Kelsey.

"I know," I whispered back. "So embarrassing!"

Lily is really pretty and smart. She has long, wavy dark hair and bright red lips, even without lipstick, and everyone always tells her that she looks like Snow White. Someone passing through town told her she could be a model if she wanted to, in New York. But Lily really wants to be a nurse like her mom, my aunt Sabrina.

"So what outfit are you wearing for the first day of school?" Kelsey asked.

"I don't know," I said. "I haven't really thought about it. Plus, it will still be hot."

Kelsey tilted her head. "Then can I borrow one? I want to wear something new!"

"Sure," I said. "But I just don't get dressing up for the first day. We'll probably see everyone the day before school starts. So why would you dress up the next day, just to see the same people at school?"

Kelsey paused. "Well, I don't know. I guess it's like Thanksgiving or a holiday. I mean, you see your family all the time, but for certain things you just dress up."

"Yeah," I said. "That makes sense."

Kelsey looked at her watch. "This is going to be such a long day. I almost wish school had started already!"

We packed up all the donuts for the order and stacked the boxes into bags.

"All set?" asked Dad, glancing in.

"Yep," I said. "Ready to go."

"Okay, I need someone to run these over to the high school," Dad said, looking around.

"I'll go!" said Lily.

Uncle Charlie, Dad, and Aunt Melissa all said, "No!" at the same time, and Lily stomped off, looking hurt.

"Jenna!" Uncle Charlie called. "Delivery!" He tossed her his keys. "And hide the keys from your cousin!"

Nans came out of the kitchen.

"What did you say to Lily to upset her?" she asked Uncle Charlie.

Kelsey and I saw our opening. She grinned at me and nodded, and I skittered into the kitchen to grab the fresh donuts from the rack.

Lily was sitting on a stool in the corner, her lip quivering.

"Are you okay?" I asked.

She sighed. "I don't think I am cut out for waitressing," she said, shaking her head.

Nans strode back in.

"Lily," she said, "we're going to put you up front at the host station today. Do you have your regular clothes instead of your uniform?"

"Well, I have clothes to change into for after work," said Lily, grabbing a skirt and a top out of her locker and holding them up. She showed us a pretty pink top and a black skirt.

"That'll do," said Nans. "Change and then up front you go!"

Lily didn't need to be asked twice. Rich subbed in as a waiter, and Lily managed the podium up front.

She was really friendly and so chatty that people didn't even mind waiting for a table during the lunch rush. Plus, she knew exactly where everyone liked to sit. She even helped Mr. and Mrs. Block load their son Preston into his high chair.

"He never goes in without a fight!" Mrs. Block said. "You have the magic touch!"

"There's a place at the Park for everyone," said Grandpa, giving Lily a hug on her way back to the podium. "We just needed to find the right one."

Then he spun around at me and squinted. "Lindsay Cooper, you have powdered sugar on your nose, young lady!"

I looked at Kelsey, and she started laughing. "You got caught, Linds!"

"Eating the profits!" said Grandpa, pretending to yell. He acted as if he was mad at us, but he was just kidding.

☀ ☀ ☀ ☀ ☀

Dad dropped me off at Casey's house after my shift ended. We had a few days left before school started. Casey's mom was at school, helping to get everything ready.

"She's in a crazed place," said Casey. "Back to school is always nuts in my house. Dad is busy too, with everyone's back-to-school visits."

Casey's dad is a doctor, and he takes care of just about everyone in town. My aunt Sabrina is a nurse in his office. She met Casey's dad when they both worked in the same hospital, and she invited him and his wife to a birthday party she was having for Uncle Charlie. That was how Casey's parents met.

Aunt Sabrina likes to say, "It's a good thing they came to my party!"

Casey led me up to her room, which is generally pretty neat, unless you open her closet or look under her bed. I looked around, and either I hadn't noticed it last week or she just put it up, but there was a picture of a boy on the bulletin board above her desk.

Usually she just had pictures of the two of us goofing around, and there were a couple cute family photos from when she was little.

But the boy photo was a new addition.

"Who's that?" I asked.

"Oh . . . ," she said. "That's my friend Matt."

"Your friend?" I asked.

"Well, I guess . . . I don't know."

"Is he your boyfriend?"

"Mom won't let me have a boyfriend yet," Casey said. "We're just pals."

I nodded, but I was a little confused as to why she had his picture up. I decided to let it go for now.

"Kelsey keeps asking me what I'm wearing on the first day of school," I said.

"Why?" Casey said. "What's the big deal?"

"Exactly!" I said, relieved.

I feel like Casey is the one person who really sees things the same way I do.

"I'll probably wear these pants," said Casey, pulling a pair out of her closet. "They're light cotton, so they'll be okay even if it's still hot out. And that top . . . now where is it . . ." She was pulling things out from under her bed. "Oh, here it is!"

It looked like a regular outfit to me.

"Do you think middle school is going to be different?" I asked.

"Well, everyone says it is," she said. "It's a different building, and we walk around to our classes and have lockers, so in that way it will be different. And we get split up into different classes, so there's that."

"But I mean, *we* won't be different, right?"

"You and me?" she asked. "Like, am I going to change overnight?"

I laughed. "No, well . . . maybe? It's just that everyone is making such a big deal about it and I think it's just . . . school starting."

"Well, I guess there's only one way to find out," said Casey.

I nodded, and we heard the front door open.

"Casey?" Mrs. Peters called upstairs.

Hole in the Middle

"Up here with Lindsay!" Casey called down.

Mrs. Peters came upstairs. She looked tired.

"Well, we are set," she said. "School is ready for you. Now are you ready for school?"

Casey laughed. "No! I need more summer!"

"You know what?" said Mrs. Peters. "After today, so do I."

We followed her back downstairs and she made us a snack, just like she did when we were in first grade: sliced grapes, cheese on crackers, and what she calls banana boats, which are sliced bananas with peanut butter on top.

"Mom, how is middle school going to be different?" Casey asked, her mouth full of crackers.

"From your old school?" Mrs. Peters asked. "Well, it's a different building and a different schedule, moving around from class to class, and that takes some getting used to."

Casey looked at me. *Just as we'd thought.*

"But at this age kids are trying new things and changing, too. You might find your friends going off in new directions," Mrs. Peters said.

Casey and I thought about that for a moment.

"You mean like Brett Carr will suddenly start

playing soccer instead of being a piano genius?" I asked.

"Maybe," said Mrs. Peters. "That's why it's so exciting. You can really start figuring out who you are and what you like."

"What if we already know what we like?" asked Casey.

"Well, some kids do," said Mrs. Peters, "Brett is probably still going to be a piano genius. He's been playing since he was three. But it's always good to be open to new things too. You may not even be aware that you'd love being on the volleyball team until you try it."

I looked at Casey and giggled. She broke two fingers playing volleyball last summer, and she hates it.

"Okay, maybe volleyball is a bad example," said Mrs. Peters, laughing.

I guess I looked a little worried, because Mrs. Peters put her arm around me and said, "But whatever changes, I know you and Casey will always be friends."

"What? Of course we'll be friends always!" yelped Casey. She slid over and threw her arms around me. "Don't try on any new BFFs!"

I laughed and hugged her back. "I won't. You are stuck with me!"

Later that night, I thought about what we'd talked about. I usually fell asleep really fast, but I was tossing and turning, thinking about what Mrs. Peters had said.

What would I decide to do that was different? What if I didn't want to try anything different? I tried to stop my mind from spinning so I could get to sleep.

Finally I decided that even if middle school was different, if Casey was around, it would all be okay. Plus, I had my dreams, and I knew those would never change. The next thing I knew, it was morning.

Chapter Eight
Dress Party or Pity Party?

Mimi had talked about a "dress party" for me since she'd arrived, and even though it made me feel a little squirmy, I figured it would be fun. I don't really like being the center of attention, but I would be with my family and friends. It wasn't like I'd be strutting down a runway.

"It's party day!" Mimi trilled as she came into my room in the morning. "So much fun awaits! But first, work!"

I groaned. A day off would be nice, but the plan was for me to go to work in the morning.

Kelsey beat me to the Donut Dreams counter and was bouncing up and down, she was so excited.

"Do you think your grandma will let me keep

one of the dresses that you don't like?" she asked.

"Uhhhh," I said, unsure.

"I mean if Mom pays for it!" said Kelsey. "Oh, I'm so excited I just can't wait. Aren't you so excited to see what she picked out?"

I started to answer, but Kelsey cut me off.

"I mean, what if you hate everything?" she asked, her eyes getting wide. "That would be a disaster!"

"Well, a flood or a tornado would be a disaster," I said. "Not liking a dress is not a disaster."

Kelsey rolled her eyes at me.

"Okay, okay," she said. "But, like, everyone is going to be staring at you and expecting you to just go crazy over one of them!"

"Kelsey, no one who knows me expects me to go crazy over a dress!" I said, starting to get exasperated. "It's just a dress, and Mimi thought it would be a fun thing because—"

"Because you don't have a mom to take you shopping," Kelsey said.

I stopped stacking the napkins on the counter. "What?" I asked, a little shocked.

Kelsey looked at me. "Well, I mean, that's why we're all making a big deal about it, right? Everyone's mom takes them for their Fall Fling dress, and they thought this would kind of make up for the fact that you can't do that. We're trying to fill in for your mom."

I felt like someone had punched me in the stomach. "Um, I have to go to the ladies' room." I said, and bolted, practically running across the restaurant.

I closed the door to the stall and took a deep breath. It hadn't even crossed my mind that this wasn't a dress party—it was a *pity* party. I felt my cheeks get hot, and I could feel tears welling up in my eyes. My hands were shaking too, and I crossed my arms over my chest to kind of hold myself together.

The door to the bathroom swung open.

"Lindsay?" It was Kelsey. "I'm sorry. I'm so sorry. I think that came out wrong."

I gulped. "It's okay," I said, but my voice was shaking and the tears were starting to come.

"Lindsay, can you come out? We both left the counter, and I'm afraid Grandpa is going to notice," Kelsey said.

She waited a second and I gulped again.

"I need . . . ," I said. "I need a second, okay? Can you cover for me?"

Hole in the Middle

"Of course," Kelsey said. I heard the door shut and then suddenly swing open again, and then she paused. "It's not because we feel sorry for you. It's because we want to help in case you're sad about things."

I nodded, but then realized Kelsey couldn't see me. I quickly wiped my eyes.

The door shut and I heard voices outside. A few minutes later Aunt Melissa came in.

"Lindsay?" she called. "Honey, are you okay?"

"I just have a stomachache," I said.

Aunt Melissa stood right outside the stall. "Sweetie, can you please come out?"

The bathroom door opened again and I heard Jenna and Lily whispering. Goodness, there was nowhere at the Park I could go and be alone!

Aunt Melissa tried again. "Honey, sometimes we all say that Kelsey has no filter, but in truth it affects the whole family. Sometimes things come out really awkwardly or wrong. I'd like to set the record straight."

"Is she all right?" It was Nans, squeezing in.

I sighed. "Please, please can I have a minute alone?" I sniffed. "I just . . . I just need a minute."

"The girl needs some alone time!" declared Jenna.

"Everybody out." They all filed out.

I just needed some air to think a little bit. But how was I going to walk out of the bathroom and look like everything was fine? Or leave my shift?

There was a knock on the door. Again.

"Lindsay, it's Daddy." Wow, he hadn't called himself Daddy in a long time.

"Um, this is awkward, because I can't actually come into the ladies' room, but I'd like to talk to you and not through the door."

I sighed. There was no way I could just slip back to work. I pushed open the door to the stall and looked at my puffy face in the mirror. I threw some cold water on it and patted it dry, which felt good.

When I came out of the bathroom, Nans, Jenna, Lily, and Aunt Melissa were all standing there with Dad, looking anxiously at me.

"This way," said Dad, taking my hand and leading me back through the kitchen.

He opened the back door and a breeze hit my face. Finally, I could breathe. Dad sat down and patted the step next to him. I sat there for a few minutes, just thinking. It was nice not to have to say anything.

"The thing about family," Dad finally said, "is that

they always mean well, but sometimes they don't say exactly the right things. I'm sorry you got upset."

"So are they having a dress party because they feel sorry for me?" I asked.

"No!" Dad almost yelled. "They are having a party because Mimi wants so badly to make shopping for this dress a special experience. She knows how much Mom would care about taking time to make sure you had a dress you loved, and she's trying really hard to make it a memorable thing for you."

"So why didn't Mimi just take me dress shopping?" I wailed.

Dad looked across to the trees at the end of the lot. "I think she's trying to make it a happy occasion. But in truth, it's a sad occasion for her. She feels terrible that Mom didn't get to experience this. And she feels even more terrible that you don't get to have Mom here. So her idea was to have a fun party to distract from the plain fact that everyone is missing Mom."

I was quiet for a few minutes, thinking about that. "So it's actually Mimi who feels sorry for me?"

"Well, not exactly," said Dad. "This isn't a pity party. And it's not even just about one person. It's about feeling bad that someone we love can't be here. Yes, we all feel bad about that. And we feel bad that you're missing Mom. But that's compassion. It's different from just feeling sorry for you. When you're in a family and someone is struggling or feeling bad, your family does everything they can to try to make it better. That's really what this party is about."

"Well, now I feel bad that I just made a scene," I said. "I'm really sorry."

"You didn't make a scene," said Dad. "If you want to do that, just drop a full tray at lunch like your cousin Lily."

I giggled. "Daaaad!"

"I know," said Dad. "It's not nice. And Lily is so kind, so it's especially not nice. But speaking of being nice, you should apologize to Kelsey."

"Why would I apologize to her?" I asked. "She made me feel awful!"

"She didn't mean to," said Dad. "You have to understand that no one has ever really dealt with something like this before in our family. There's no guidebook to say, 'When someone feels like this, you should do that.' People are trying and doing the best they can. Your cousin Kelsey did a lot of the organizing for the party, and she's the one who helped Mimi choose the dresses. She's been working on this for the past month. She really wants it to be a special day for you."

"She has?" I asked.

Dad nodded. "She managed to keep that a secret, which is a pretty big deal."

"Yeah," I said. "Especially in this family."

Dad laughed. "You're right. You can't hide anything in this family, that's for sure. Speaking of hiding, what do you say we get back to work before Grandpa sends out a search party for us?"

I sighed. It was nice just sitting outside.

Dad reached over and pushed my hair off my face. "You okay?"

I nodded and stood up.

When we went back inside, Nans looked up from where she was in the kitchen. I saw Dad nod to her and she nodded back. She didn't say anything, but she watched me walk to the floor. I passed Jenna, who blew me a kiss. Lily tugged on my apron bow as she passed by.

I looked at Grandpa, who was reading something at the podium. He wiggled his finger at me, and I thought he was going to give me the business for leaving the counter. Instead he gave me a giant hug.

"Remember how loved you are," he whispered. Then he went back to reading. "And now get back to work!" he said, without looking up.

Kelsey was reaching for a glazed donut when I got to the counter.

"Hi, Mrs. Lee," I said. "Kelsey is getting you a freshly made one up there!"

Kelsey held a donut, and I opened a paper bag for her to put it in before I rang it up.

"Oh, it's so nice that you girls get to work together," said Mrs. Lee.

"It really is," I said, looking at Kelsey.

Kelsey looked relieved. "Yep," she said. "Because you get to work with people who love you."

"Oh, aren't you girls just the sweetest?" Mrs. Lee said. "You are sweeter than the donuts!"

I giggled as she left. "Kelsey, we are sweeter than the donuts," I said.

"Hmm," said Kelsey. "Like, sweeter than the chocolate ones or the plain ones?"

"Oh, definitely the ones with sprinkles," I said, laughing.

"How about the crème-filled ones?" she asked.

"Yeah, those too," I said. "And absolutely the jelly-filled."

"Ugh, I hate the jelly-filled," Kelsey said. After a minute she asked, "So you aren't mad at me?"

"I'm not mad," I said.

I didn't want Kelsey to feel bad, but I guess she did, because she took out the garbage without even bargaining with me. She also wiped under the tables and chairs. We closed up the counter a little early to get ready for the dress party, and I was waiting for Dad to take me home when Casey appeared.

"Hey, what are you doing here?" I asked.

"Your chariot awaits, madam," said Casey. "We're taking you home." She waved to Jenna and Lily, who appeared with big bags of stuff.

"What's all that?" I asked.

"We are your glam squad," said Jenna. "I'm doing hair, Lily's doing makeup, and Casey is doing your nails."

"Really?" I asked.

"That way," said Lily, "you can see what you'll look like when you're all done up in the dress."

Jenna twirled her keys. "Let's go. I have orders from Kelsey to stay on schedule."

I looked over at Kelsey, who was rolling up the

mat behind the counter. I ran over to her to help.

"Go!" she said, shooing me away.

I gave her a big hug. "Thank you!" I whispered into her ear.

I didn't know what else to say, but I guess it was enough, because she hugged me back and said, "This is going to be such a fun night!"

Then she pushed me toward Jenna and Lily, and Casey grabbed my hand.

"Operation Glam!" said Casey. "Reporting for duty! I hope the Glam Squad is ready, because this one is going to need a lot of work!"

"Casey!" I yelped. "That's not nice!"

She laughed. "I'm kidding, Linds. You're perfect just as you are. Now let's go, Cinderella. The ball is starting soon!"

Chapter Nine
Operation Glam!

"First, a shower," demanded Jenna when we got home. "We start from scratch here."

I wrapped myself in my bathrobe, wondering what else was ahead of me.

Mimi was downstairs setting up and had chased me out of the living room. I noticed that the dining room table was already stacked with plates and teacups. I peeked out the window and saw Dad and Nans unloading boxes of food from the car.

Dad was taking Skylar night fishing, and Sky was so excited he was running up and down the hall and nearly collided with me.

"Watch it!" I said.

He stopped. "Why are you taking a shower at the

end of the day? Are you going to bed early?"

"No," I said. "I'm getting ready to try on some fancy dresses for the Fall Fling."

Sky looked confused. "Well, I'm going fishing, so maybe Dad will let me take a bath in the river!"

"Eeeuuw," I said. "You will take a bath with a toad. That's disgusting!"

"That would be so cool!" Sky said, and ran down the stairs. "Dad! Dad! Lindsay said that maybe I can take a bath with a toad!"

"That's not . . . ," I started to yell after him, but then decided to let it go.

I took a quick shower, and washed and combed out my hair. I wrapped my towel around me and sat down on the bed.

Jenna and Lily both looked at me seriously as if they were about to perform surgery.

"Makeup first," said Lily, and she started dusting powder on my face.

"Not too much!" said Jenna. "Nans will not be happy."

Lily nodded. "She doesn't need much," she said, winking at me. "Because she's naturally pretty."

I blushed.

Then Jenna took out a blow-dryer and a curling iron and was tugging at my hair for what seemed like forever. Casey was carefully putting bright pink polish on my toenails.

I heard the door opening and closing downstairs and started to get a little nervous. "So how many people are coming?" I asked.

"Well, the four of us," said Jenna, "and Casey's mom, Aunt Sabrina, my mom, Molly and Kelsey and Nans and your grandma Mimi."

"And Gabby!" said Casey.

"Right," said Jenna. "Gabby too!"

"Twelve of us?" I yelped.

"Yeah, it takes at least a dozen people to decide on one dress," said Lily, smirking.

Finally they all stepped away, looking at me. Lily reached over and pulled some hair behind one of my ears. Then she nodded at Jenna.

"Okay, go look," said Jenna.

I went over to the mirror. At first it didn't even look like me. Well, it looked like me, but more glamorous. My hair was shiny and wavy and it didn't even look like I had makeup on, just a little pink on my cheeks and lips.

I grinned. "I think I'm ready for my big modeling job!" I tossed my hair and struck a pose.

"We're coming down!" Jenna yelled down the stairs. I heard everybody cheer and applaud.

"We're ready!" Kelsey yelled back up.

Lily helped me into a button-up shirt so I wouldn't mess up my hair, and I pulled on a pair of jean shorts.

I followed Jenna, Lily, and Casey but stopped as I got halfway down the stairs.

The living room was set up like a giant dressing room. The sofa and chairs were pushed along the wall and someone had rolled up the rug. There was a rolling rack like you see in a big store, and it was filled with dresses. Next to the rack was a line of shoes, some of which I recognized as Kelsey's. A full-length mirror was propped up on the wall, and I saw Nans's sewing basket next to it.

There were balloons tied to the chairs, and flowers in bunches on the end tables. It definitely looked like a party.

"Well, come on down, Ms. Lindsay!" said Mimi. "Let the dress games begin!"

I stood next to Mimi, not sure what to do.

"Okay," said Kelsey. "Here are all the selections."

She pointed to the rack. "You decide where you want to start. Then you try on all the dresses until we find the perfect one."

Everyone was looking at me and I felt a little shy.

Mimi pulled out a green dress. "I thought this would be so pretty," she said. She grabbed my hand. "But come look and pick one to start."

I took the one Mimi was holding. "This is nice," I said. It was dark green with light green ruffles on the skirt.

"Okay, that's the first one then!" said Kelsey. She pointed to the corner of the room, where someone had hung a bedsheet. "That is your dressing room!"

"And I am your official dresser!" said Molly. "Some of these dresses have a lot of buttons!"

I giggled and followed Molly to the corner and behind the sheet.

I pulled on the dress and Molly zipped it up. "It fits!" she yelled out.

"Good job on getting the sizing right!" Nans said to Mimi.

"Oh, I'm so glad," Mimi replied.

I looked at Molly. "Well, you have to come out of the dressing room so everyone can see!" she hissed at me.

I took a deep breath and shuffled out, and then Molly pushed me into the center of the room.

"Oh, you are just so lovely," sighed Mimi.

"That's beautiful, Lindsay," said Aunt Melissa.

"I love that color," said Mrs. Peters.

"You look like grass," said Skylar from the hall.

"Sky!" Nans scolded, and everyone started laughing.

"Okay, we're on our way out now and just came to say goodbye," said Dad, pulling Skylar. "Gone fishing! Lindsay, you look beautiful as always, but choose the dress that makes you happiest, okay?"

"And one that doesn't look like a soccer field!" called Skylar.

Everyone cracked up again, and Dad scooted Skylar out the back door.

"Well," I said. "Now all I see is grass."

"No grass dresses!" said Kelsey. "Next!"

Casey tugged at a purple dress. "This is nice!"

"Okay," I said, grabbing it.

Molly helped me get out of the soccer dress and into the purple one, which was a lot more complicated. It had a halter top that tied behind my neck and a zip on the side that was really tricky to pull up. Then there was a light purple sash that tied around the waist.

"What's taking so long?" demanded Kelsey.

"I'm going as fast as I can," Molly yelled back.

"Girls!" said Aunt Melissa.

Molly stood back and scrunched up her nose. "I don't love it," she said. "But go see for yourself."

The skirt swished when I walked out. I wasn't sure what to do, so I stood next to Mimi.

"Well, that's pretty too," she said. Then she steered me to the mirror.

The dress reminded me of something, but I couldn't put my finger on it.

Casey came over and put her hand on her hip, looking at me. "Uh, do you remember that doll you had that you used to tote around everywhere?"

I looked at her blankly.

"Cressida!" said Mrs. Peters.

"Cressida!" said Nans. "Oh my, I remember Cressida!"

"Yes!" I squealed. "She was my favorite doll. She came in a big poufy purple dress . . . oh." I peered in the mirror. "I look like Cressida!"

"You totally do!" laughed Casey.

We both collapsed into giggles.

"Next!" said Kelsey.

Mimi handed me a pink dress while Molly tugged the Cressida dress off me. The pink dress had a long pleated skirt and the body was really fitted. It had buttons that ran up the side.

When Molly was finished fastening the last in the long row of buttons, she tilted her head to the side. "This one has possibilities," she said.

I walked out and over to the mirror.

"Ohhhh," said Mimi. "Oh, that's so pretty. And I love the color."

Nans and Aunt Melissa nodded.

"Try these with it," said Aunt Sabrina, handing me a pair of silver sandals.

Nans, Mimi, Aunt Melissa, and Aunt Sabrina were all smiling, but Kelsey put her hands on her hips.

"It's really pretty," she said. "I love it. But somehow it just doesn't seem like *you*."

"Oh but I like it!" said Casey.

"I feel like there's something missing," said Kelsey.

"Um, guys, I'm right here," I said.

"Yes," said Mimi. "Let's ask Lindsay what she thinks. Lindsay?"

"I like it," I said, watching myself in the mirror. "It's really pretty."

"Well, there are a lot of others," said Kelsey, pointing toward the rack. "You should buy something you love, not something you like."

I looked at the rack, and one dress caught my eye. "Well, I may as well try on a few more," I said.

I toted the one I chose into the dressing room. "Molly!" I called.

"I need a break!" said Molly. "I'm getting a snack! There's food set up in the dining room, people!"

Everyone laughed, and I heard people moving around to the dining room.

At first I felt a little hurt that everyone had abandoned me for some food, but then I thought, *Well, when I put this one on, I can make a grand entrance.*

Chapter Ten
True Blue

I pulled the next dress on myself and easily zipped it up. It felt light and flowy, like I could run around in it if I wanted to. I turned around to leave and I heard a gentle *swish, swish* from the bottom of the skirt, which made me happy for some reason. I felt like I had on a magical fairy dress, like I could float across the room without my feet touching the floor.

Everyone was in the dining room when I came out, so I walked over to the mirror to get a look before anyone else could see.

I stopped when I got close. There was a picture of Mom that we had on a table in the front hall. She was in a cornflower-blue dress, smiling at the camera, her head tilted back and her eyes crinkled up with laughter. It was taken when Mom and Dad were at a fancy party in Chicago, right before we found out Mom was sick.

I looked down and realized the dress I was wearing was the same purplish-blue color of her dress. It made my hair look darker and my lips look brighter. I looked a lot like Mom in that picture.

"Oh!" I heard a gasp behind me. It was Mimi, and her hand flew to her mouth.

Everyone rushed back into the living room and everyone, it seemed at once, said, "Ohhhhh!"

"That's it!" said Kelsey. "That's the magic dress!"

"Oh, Lindsay," said Mimi. "You look so beautiful."

I spun around. "I look like Mom."

Mimi looked startled. Then she smiled. "You do. You look exactly like her, and that color . . ."

"It's her favorite color," I said, remembering. "True blue."

"True blue," Mimi whispered, and I could see her eyes were filling up with tears.

The room was really quiet. Mimi came over and put her hand on my shoulder, looking at me in the mirror. I didn't know if she was looking at me or if she was seeing Mom.

True blue was a color Mom made up. She always said her favorite shade of blue was a little purple, a little white, and a little gray mixed together. She mixed it up on her paint palette and even kept some in a paint jar on her shelf. It was hard to find anywhere, but this dress was the closest to her shade of true blue I had ever seen outside of her paintings.

And suddenly, I missed her more than ever. My grandmothers were here and my aunts and cousins and BFF, but the one person who was missing was Mom, and I really, really wished she were here. I missed her all the time, but at this moment, wearing this dress, it hit me hard that she wasn't here. I started to cry, and I just couldn't stop.

Mimi hugged me tight, then Kelsey and Nans, and Aunt Melissa and Casey. There were so many arms around me that I didn't know whose hands or arms belonged to who. Soon we were a big pile of crying arms.

Finally it was Molly who yelled, "And break!"

We were all so startled we laughed. Casey handed out tissues, and everyone blew their noses.

Mimi cupped her hand under my chin. "You okay?" she asked.

I nodded and smiled. "Mom would want me to wear this dress," I said. "It would make her so happy."

Tears streamed down Mimi's face, but she was smiling. "She would have picked this out herself," she said. "It's the perfect dress for you."

Nans knelt down next to me. "Someone hand me my sewing box."

Jenna passed it to her and Nans started pinning the dress up a little. Lily helped me put on a pair of sparkly sandals, and Jenna pulled my hair so it was half up, half down. I still looked like me, but with a dreamy dress.

"Done!" said Kelsey, satisfied.

Everyone clapped.

"Whoo-hoo Team Dress!" said Molly.

"And now we eat donuts!" said Casey.

Nans and Mimi helped me out of the dress and I slipped back into shorts and a shirt. I followed Nans into the kitchen to help with the donuts.

"Do you know why I love donuts, Lindsay?" she asked.

"Because they're delicious?" I answered, watching her roll out the big ball of dough.

"Well, yes," she said. "But see how I make them?

You use the dough cutter to cut out circles from the rolled-out dough."

I nodded as I watched her. I had seen her make donuts millions of times. She could probably make them in her sleep.

"Each donut is a circle," she said. "You drop the circles in the oil or the fryer and scoop them right out when they're done."

I watched as she tossed the circles of dough into bubbling-hot oil in the pan.

"The thing is," said Nans, "they have a hole in the middle, but they're surrounded by dough." We both watched as the dough bubbled.

"That hole," she began, "reminds me that sometimes there's a hole inside us. Sometimes it gets filled or sometimes we don't notice it as much, but it's always there."

She scooped out the puffed-up donuts with a slotted spoon and laid them on paper towels to drain.

"But there's always dough surrounding the hole." She put down the spoon. "Do you know what I'm trying to say?"

"Sort of," I said. "We all have a hole in us?"

Nans cocked her head. "Sometimes we do.

Sometimes those holes close up and sometimes they get smaller, but they're always there. But no matter what, those holes are surrounded."

"So our family is a donut?" I asked.

Nans laughed. "Kind of. I like to think the donut is more of a symbol of our family. That even when there are holes that can never be filled, there's a lot of sweetness totally surrounding them to help them not get any bigger."

She looked at me like she wanted me to say something, but I wasn't sure what.

"Lindsay," she said, putting her hands on my shoulders and looking into my eyes. "You are surrounded by people who love you. I want you to always remember that."

I smiled. "I will."

"Hey, where are those donuts?" Molly yelled as she stormed into the kitchen.

Nans laughed. "Right here! Right here!"

I helped her pile them on a platter, and Molly carried them out to the table.

When I sat down in the living room, I couldn't help noticing Kelsey sneaking looks at a certain silvery gray dress. She kept walking by it and touching it.

"Why don't you try that on?" I asked.

She spun around. "Me? Oh, I couldn't. These are all for you to try on."

"Well, I already have my dress," I said.

"But it's your party," she said.

"If it's my party, then you have to do as I say," I teased.

"Well," she said, looking longingly at the dress. "This is really beautiful."

"Come on," I said, and pulled her toward the dressing room.

I helped put on the silver dress. It had lots of layers that made it shimmer when Kelsey moved. There were these see-through ruffles that went around the bodice and short sleeves that kind of looked like wings. I stood back.

"Kelsey, you look like a fairy princess," I said.

"Like for Halloween?" she asked.

"No, no, like a beautiful princess," I said. "Go look!" I pushed her out toward the mirror.

"Hey!" said Molly. "Kelsey, those dresses are for Lindsay!"

"Well, I already found mine," I said.

"So the rest are up for grabs?" asked Molly.

"Girls, girls!" said Aunt Melissa. "These were chosen for Lindsay. This is her party. We will find your dresses later!"

"Well, if they like some of these, why not let them try them on?" asked Mimi. "We have so many. Plus, it will save me the trouble of returning all of them!"

Aunt Melissa looked at me. "Are you okay with this? These dresses were for *you* to choose from."

I nodded my head. "I made Kelsey try this one on. She loves it, and look how pretty she is in it!"

Everyone gathered around Kelsey. "It is beautiful on her," said Mimi.

"Well," said Aunt Melissa. "If you don't mind me just buying this from you, then we'll have two girls with dresses for the Fling."

"Two down!" cried Mimi. "And two to go. Casey and Molly, do you see anything you want to try?"

Casey looked at her mom.

"Go ahead," Mrs. Peters said. "If the dress store comes to you, why go to the dress store?"

Casey took the pink dress off the rack. "I know you didn't love this," she said. "But I do. Can I try it?"

I grabbed her hand and pulled her toward the dressing room. "We'll be right out!"

The dress had looked nice on me, but it looked amazing on Casey. Casey's mom pulled it up a little and smoothed down the skirt.

"Oh, I love that on you!" said Mrs. Peters.

"All right, Molly," I said. "Do you see anything you like?"

Molly smiled. "Well, I kind of like the soccer-field dress," she said.

We all started laughing. "So try it on!" said Mimi. "Don't let Sky be your fashion police!"

Molly came out in the dress. She stopped, did a spin, and put her hand on her hip.

"Dahling, I think this might be just fabulous!" she said, and we all laughed.

"You know, it really suits you," said Aunt Melissa, smiling.

"Let me fix your hair," said Jenna, pulling Molly's hair up off her neck.

The green dress looked nothing like a soccer field on Molly; it looked perfect.

"You all need to put on your dresses so we can take a picture!" said Lily.

So we all scrambled into our dresses as Nans scolded us to watch out for all the pins she'd put in them. I was in a blue dress, Casey in pink, Kelsey in silver, and Molly in green.

"It's a rainbow of pretty!" said Aunt Sabrina. "Get in close so I can fit the whole dress into the shot!"

We stood together, arms around each other, smiling.

"Everyone say, 'Fall Fling'!" said Aunt Sabrina.

"Fall Fling!" we all yelled, and held still for about a second.

"Dance party!" cried Jenna, and she put on some music.

We were dancing around while Nans and Mimi shouted at us to be careful with the dresses. But we didn't care. We all grabbed hands and danced, laughing and twirling.

Chapter Eleven
Post-Party Chat

Later that night, my dress was hanging on the back of my door and I could see the outline of it in the dark as I pulled up the covers in bed.

Sky had thrown a fit about going to sleep, and through the wall I could hear Dad reading to him to try to soothe him, even though it was late.

I wasn't supposed to have my phone in my room at night, but I had actually forgotten to leave it downstairs in the charging station, and I was too tired to go back down anyway. I grabbed it and flipped through the pictures Aunt Sabrina sent us from the party. We all looked happy and goofy, and I had to say those dresses looked pretty good on us.

My favorite picture showed me in the middle,

smiling and sort of spinning, with everyone around me in a circle, laughing.

I looked hard at that shot. I realized as I scrolled through that both my grandmothers were there, both my aunts, my BFF, and all my girl cousins. There was one person who was missing, of course, and that was Mom.

Dad knocked on my door. "From what I heard, it was a pretty good party," he whispered, coming in.

By the time Sky and Dad came home, the party had wrapped up and all the dresses had been packed up.

"Dad," I said, then stopped.

"Yes, honey?"

"I missed Mom tonight."

Dad sat on my bed. "I did too," he said. "But I heard your dress was her favorite color." He squinted at it in the dark.

"It's true blue," I said, smiling.

"Sometimes," said Dad, "I'm reminded of Mom in ways that make me feel like she's still here."

"Like a ghost?" I said, alarmed.

"No, no," Dad said. "Like in the way Sky laughs exactly like her, or the way your dress for the dance ended up being her favorite color."

"Nans says that we're like donuts," I blurted out.

"Hmm," said Dad.

"She says that we have holes in us, and I guess for me that hole is where I miss Mom."

"Oh, I see," said Dad.

"But that like a donut's shape, we're surrounded by people, in a tight circle, so that hole doesn't get any bigger."

"That's exactly right," said Dad. "You have so many people who love you. They may drive you nuts, but they love you. And you might not like that they surround you all the time, but they always have your best interests at heart."

I laid back on the pillow and yawned. Suddenly I felt really tired.

"Okay, young lady, it's time for bed." Dad reached over to switch off my night-table light when I noticed a little bouquet of flowers next to my stack of books.

"Hey!" I said, sitting back up.

There were violets and bluebells in a little vase.

"Oh," said Dad. "Sky found those today when we were fishing. We weren't sure where to put them when we brought them home, and Mimi thought maybe you would like them."

I smiled. "They remind me of Mom," I said.

"They do," said Dad, smiling back. "True blue."

"She's still here, sort of," I said, yawning.

"She's always with us," said Dad quietly.

I flopped back onto my pillow. I couldn't keep my eyes open. I knew Dad was still sitting on my bed like he did when I was younger, waiting for me to fall asleep, but I was so tired I couldn't even say good night.

It was nice having him there, and knowing that Sky was asleep on the other side of the wall. Mimi and Nans and Grandpa were all in the house, all of us together, one big circle.

I pulled my blanket tighter, and as my eyelids fluttered, all I saw were shades of blue.

Chapter Twelve
A New Beginning

And just like that, before I knew it, it was the first day of middle school. It was still pretty warm, so I just put on a short-sleeved purple T-shirt that Mimi had bought for me, a silver bangle bracelet, and a new pair of jeans. I wanted to look nice and fresh, but I didn't want to get super dressed up or make too big a deal out of it.

"Well, don't you look beautiful!" Nans said, as I sat down at the kitchen table.

She plopped down a plate of homemade pancakes (my favorite) in front of me, and I saw she had made a smiley face with syrup.

I laughed. "Thanks, Nans," I said as I dug into the pancakes.

She was still staring at me. "Yes," she said, nodding approvingly. "You look perfect. Lovely, but not overly done."

I smiled at her. "That's just what I was going for," I told her.

Then I added, "You remembered Mom used to make pancakes on the first day of school." Nans nodded.

"And she would always say the same thing to me," I said. "She used to tell me to have a great day, and to remember to always be my 'own special self.' It felt a little silly when she kept saying it as I got older, but by then it was sort of like a first-day-of-school tradition, and she had to say it. I made her say it."

I smiled at the memory, but then I was startled to look up and see Nans's eyes filling with tears.

Oh no! That was the last thing I wanted.

Luckily, just at that moment, Skylar came bounding into the kitchen.

"Oh boy, pancakes!" he yelled. "Awesome!"

Nans dried her eyes and put a plate in front of him. She tried to lighten the subject.

"What did your mom say to Skylar on the first day of school?" she asked.

I grinned. "Keep your mouth closed when you eat." Nans laughed.

☀ ☀ ☀ ☀ ☀

When I walked through the doors of Bellgrove Middle School, I paused in front of the mural that my mom's students had made in her honor.

I had been worried that seeing it every day would make me sad, but I actually felt really happy when I saw it.

I noticed that some students had painted in bright, cheery colors, and others had sketched in charcoal. Parts of the mural showed wildflowers in bloom (which my mom would have loved), and another section showed a stormy sky, and then another section showed a rainbow.

Each student painted whatever they wanted and didn't worry about whether it blended in with the rest of the mural. The end result showed so many different personalities and styles that it was all the more beautiful.

I reached out and ran my hand gently across the colors. "Always be your own special self," I whispered. "Thanks, Mom."

Hole in the Middle

In that moment I could feel her presence. Even though I couldn't see her anymore, I knew she was always with me. And I would always have my family and friends to help me through rough times, and make the hole inside me a little smaller.

I took a deep breath and walked into my first class.

Still Hungry?
Here's a taste of the second book in the

series, So Jelly!

I Don't Like Change

My friend Sophia was looking at me like I was crazy. "But you have a job!" she said. "That's so cool!"

I sighed and pushed my bangs off my face. They were really starting to annoy me, and I had to decide if I should just let them grow out or get them trimmed.

"Well, yes and no," I said. "Yes because it's cool to work at Donut Dreams, but no because it's hard work, and I'd rather be doing a lot of other things, like going out for pizza tomorrow with you."

I work at my family's restaurant, the Park View

Table, after school Fridays and one day on the weekends. This week I'm working on Sunday.

Inside the Park there's a donut counter, Donut Dreams, that my grandmother started with her homemade donuts, which are kind of legendary around here. I work at the Donut Dreams counter with my cousin Lindsay.

I don't mind working with my family, but it's hard when my free time is eaten up by work while my friends get to hang out and do things—like how Sophia, Michelle, and Riley were planning to go out for pizza after school the next day.

"Hey! Are you coming with us tomorrow?" asked Riley as she plunked herself down at the lunch table.

"She's working," said Sophia with her mouth full.

"What?" said Riley, and then without waiting for an answer, she called out, "Oh hey, Isabella, over here!" Sophia and I looked up to see Isabella walking toward us.

Sophia, Michelle, Riley, and I have been what my dad calls "four peas in a pod" since we were toddlers. We have other friends too, but everyone knows we've always been a crew. But when school started, Riley was suddenly really into hanging out with Isabella, who seems to be joining us at lunch on the regular.

Whenever I complain about having more people around instead of it just being the four of us, my mom always replies, "When it comes to friends, additions are always okay, but subtractions are not."

So I'm trying to be okay with more friends, but sometimes I'd like to subtract Isabella and just make it Sophia, Michelle, Riley, and me, like it always has been.

Sophia wrinkled her brow a little bit when Isabella sat next to Riley. No one else noticed, but if you've known her for eleven years like I have, you'd have noticed.

Michelle uses a wheelchair, and she wheeled her way over to my side. "Scootch over," she said, and I made room for her.

"Hey, Isabella," Sophia said.

Isabella put her tray down and looked like she was going to cry.

"What's wrong?" Sophia asked.

"You guys, I totally think I am going to fail my coding class," Isabella said. "I just do not get it."

"Bella, it's only the second month of school!" said Riley. "You'll get the hang of it." I had never really heard anyone call Isabella "Bella" before.

"Yeah, chill out, Isabella," Michelle said. "Take a deep breath. It's going to be fine."

"Ugh," said Isabella. "It's just so hard and there's so much pressure. I mean, they all say that everything starts to matter in middle school if you want to go to college!" she complained.

"You still have a long way until college!" I said. "No need to worry about it now. Trust me, my sister Jenna is in high school. That's when the pressure really starts."

That wasn't entirely accurate. Jenna had been talking about college for a good seven years. Jenna is the oldest of my siblings (she's a junior in high school) and a little bossy. Actually she's *a lot* bossy.

She and Lindsay, and even my adopted sister Molly, who is a few months older than me, are always talking about going away to college. My parents are okay with this, but I can tell they don't want us to go too far. Jenna talks about how she wants to go to a school in California, which kind of scares me.

She is also always talking about "getting away" from our small town, like it's some bad place to be. She loves reading about big cities or seeing movies that take place in big cities. One year for her birthday, Jenna asked for a bunch of travel guidebooks to all the big cities in the world, even though she's only been to one of them: Chicago.

I don't understand why you'd ever want to leave Bellgrove. This town is home to me. I mean, sure, it would be nice to go somewhere sometimes without being totally recognized, but then again, seeing familiar people is kind of nice.

I like that the person who cuts my hair has been cutting it since I was a baby; that the librarian, Ms. Castro, has known me since even before I could read; and that every year we do the same things, like go apple picking at Green Hills Orchards in September before we get the same hot apple cider at Corner Stop. I like living within a few minutes of just about every single person in my extended family. All those things to me are not just dull things we're stuck with—they're traditions and familiar people and they make me feel safe.

I know I'll have to go to college in another town because there isn't a college here, but the closest state university, where my mom and dad and aunt and uncle went to school, is about two hours away. Mom keeps reassuring me that I can come home on the weekends if I want to.

When we have these conversations, Jenna just rolls her eyes and says, "Really, Kelsey? Stretch yourself! Open your eyes to new adventures! It's only two hours away!"

But to be honest, two hours away from *everything* I know sounds like plenty of an adventure for me.

"So," Sophia said, jolting me back to the table. "Are you going to try out for the field hockey team like we talked about?"

I nodded. "Yeah, it sounds fun, and Mom really wants me to do something active," I said.

Mom and Dad are always taking us on walks or bike rides, even when it's freezing cold outside. I wasn't too sure how I'd like playing competitively, but I love to be outside, especially in fall when the air turns crisp and smells so good.

"As long as I can still keep my hours working at the restaurant," I added.

"But your grandparents own the place where you work!" Riley said. "I'm guessing they can work with your schedule!"

"You'd think," I said, "but Grandpa is a stickler for not giving us special consideration. We still have to clock in a certain amount of hours, unless our grades slip. School comes first."

"So if you fail a few tests, you can get out of work," snorted Isabella, or *Bella*.

"If I fail a few tests, I'd have a lot more to deal with than missing work," I retorted, kind of snapping at her. I don't know why, but Isabella gets under my skin sometimes.

"Well . . . ," said Riley. She paused, and Sophia and I looked up. "Bella and I were thinking about doing soccer instead of field hockey."

I caught Sophia's eyes, which looked as surprised as mine.

"That's great!" Michelle said. "So now I'll take photos of the soccer team as well as field hockey." Michelle takes awesome photos and dreams of being a professional photographer someday.

Riley bit her lip. "The thing is, I'm not sure I'm great at field hockey, and I know I'm a pretty good soccer player, so I want to try out for the team."

Isabella looked at her and smiled. I had a weird feeling they'd talked about this before. Sophia looked at me.

I shrugged. "Well, you should always do what

makes you happy," I said. "Soph and I will be a team of two on the field hockey team."

Riley looked at me strangely. "Okay," she said. "I just don't want you guys to be disappointed that we all wouldn't be playing field hockey together. But you're right, you have each other on the field."

"Yep, we have each other," said Sophia.

It was quiet for a second, and then Michelle asked me, "So how is work going?"

I shrugged. "It's okay. A lot of the time I'd rather be somewhere else, but everyone in the family works there, so it's my turn to step up. Or at least that's what Grandpa said."

"Do you get to eat the extra donuts?" asked Isabella. "Because oh my goodness, I could eat, like, a dozen of those at a time."

"No," I said. "We donate the ones that haven't sold at the end of the day."

Sophia and I exchanged a smile, because everyone always asks me that question.

People think if you work at a donut shop you eat donuts all day, every day. In elementary school, Joshua Victor asked me if our house was made of donuts.

"Well, you've been known to show up with donuts," teased Riley, and I laughed.

I do try to bring donuts to my friends' houses when we have extra or when Mom brings them home.

"Work perk!" I said.

"Oh, I can almost taste those cider donuts," moaned Isabella. "Shoot, now all I want is a cider donut. It's definitely better than . . . whatever this lunch they're serving is."

"My favorites are the coffee-cake donuts," Michelle said. "And the chocolate ones with rainbow sprinkles. Or the plain glazed ones. Or . . . "

"We get it. You like donuts!" Riley said with a laugh.

Just then the bell rang. We gathered up our stuff and hustled out to our next class.

As we were going into the hall, Sophia grabbed my arm and hissed, "What is going on?"

I sighed and shrugged. "She is really good at soccer," I said.

"Well, Riley may be good at soccer, but she'd better be good at being our friend," said Sophia, and before I could respond, she shot off down the hall.

Isabella, Riley, and Michelle turned in a different direction, heading toward language arts, where they were in a class with my sister Molly. Before they went into their class, I caught Molly's eye as she walked by in the hallway.

It was obvious she could tell something was up. She was looking at me as if to say, *What's going on?*

But I just said, "You'd better catch up to your potential new soccer teammates," and hurried off to my own class.

Middle school was different, that's for sure, and I don't think I like change.

Sisterly Love

My dad is usually home after school. He teaches woodshop at the high school during the year, and in the summer he works for a construction company that his brother owns.

Molly and I dumped our stuff in the cubbies that he built us, kind of like lockers, near the back door and found him in the kitchen, making a snack.

You'd think that because Mom's family owns a restaurant she'd be a really good cook, but she totally is not. She jokes that's why she married Dad, because he can whip up anything and it's always delicious.

I sniffed. "Ooh, popcorn!"

"And hello to you too, honey," said Dad.

He was popping kernels in a deep pot on the

stove, and the kitchen smelled like a movie theater. He pushed a plate of sliced bananas and peanut butter toward us.

"Dad, where are the raisins on top?" Molly asked.

Dad used to call this snack "ants on a log," which we thought was hysterical. He slices the bananas lengthwise, smears on peanut butter, then scatters raisins on top. He used to tell us that they were ants crawling on a banana log. We thought it was funny, but it could also explain why I hate raisins . . . I mean, eww, eating ants! I always pick them off.

"We're out," said Dad. "It's still back-to-school season, and Mom and I have been so crazed and busy we haven't been able to get to the market."

"So, ant-less?" asked Molly.

"Yes, I'm afraid we are out of ants, Molls," said Dad. "So I am making it up to you with some popcorn."

"If we put these on top . . . ," said Molly, cocking her head and thinking.

"They could be clouds on a log," I said, taking a piece of hot popcorn.

"They could be fluffy sheep on a log," said Molly. "That makes more sense. Why would clouds be on a log?"

Dad grabbed the grocery list that Mom kept on the fridge door and wrote *raisins* on it.

"Okay, I'm still finishing up this summer job and I have to install the cabinets I built," he said. "So I'm going to head out until dinnertime."

This year Mom and Dad have been letting us stay in the house without them home, but only during the day. Dad is always here after school, though, which is nice, even if he's sometimes really annoying and asks a ton of questions about our day.

Today, though, Dad was in a hurry.

"Okay, dinner is in the slow cooker," he said, "so whatever you do, do not turn that thing off, or we'll all starve. Mom will be home by five thirty. We both have our phones at the ready, so just text or call if you need anything."

"Where's Jenna?" I asked.

"At work," said Dad. "Wait, is she at work? This new schedule . . . ," he muttered.

He scurried over to the bulletin board in the kitchen, where Mom keeps a monthly calendar and writes down who goes where on each day. Dad calls it the Command Center.

"Yep, yep, she went to work after she had a

student council meeting, and Mom will bring her home when her shift ends," said Dad.

"Dad, did you just lose track of a daughter?" teased Molly.

"No!" said Dad, but we all laughed.

Mom is crazy detail-oriented. Everything at home is organized beyond belief. Like the cans in our kitchen cabinets are basically alphabetized. Her socks are folded a certain way and arranged by color.

Maybe it's because she's an accountant, and, as she says, accountants have to be precise about things because they work with numbers. As the accountant for the restaurant, she makes sure that all the finances are up to date, like the staff gets paid, the bills are paid on time, and at the end of the month the restaurant isn't spending more money than it's making.

Uncle Charlie does all the ordering, everything from napkins to food to supplies like extra water glasses, because in a restaurant you are always breaking glasses. Uncle Mike runs Donut Dreams, where I work. Nans plans out the menus and figures out the daily specials, and makes her special donuts, and Grandpa . . . well, as Grandpa proudly tells everyone, he steers the ship and keeps it on course.

Everyone has their "own lane" as they all like to say, and they say that a lot to each other, as in "Hey, get out of my lane!" when they step on each other's toes. Everyone has a different role, but we all work together.

Dad builds things, so he has to be precise too, but in a really different way. When he's building something, he's all about measuring, and remeasuring, and cutting things accurately so everything fits together. But when he isn't building something he isn't too precise, which drives Mom crazy.

Once he went to pick me up at dance class . . . only I wasn't at dance class, I was waiting for him to pick me up at the library. He also once dropped off Molly for a playdate at the wrong house.

He's always messing up the laundry, too. Just last week Jenna was struggling and trying to get into a pair of jeans until she realized that they were mine; Dad had put them away in her closet instead.

"I have it together!" said Dad, a little indignantly.

"Okay," said Molly. "So you know you have to take me to soccer, right?"

"What?" said Dad, looking panicked.

"Practice starts at six," said Molly. "It's on the board!"

Dad went over to the bulletin board. "Oh . . . yeah, there it is."

Just then our phones lit up with a text message from Mom.

> All good? Everyone home?

"It's like she senses when we need her," said Molly, laughing.

"She probably just wants to check in to see how school was," said Dad.

He texted back,

> All OK.

Molly added,

> Dad forgot soccer.

About two seconds later, Mom called Dad's phone. He picked up immediately and reassured her that everything was fine and that he would be home in time to get Molly to soccer, and that he would take me with him if she wasn't home from work yet. He then left the house to finish his work, and the house was nice and quiet.

Not that my older sister Jenna or Dad or Mom are loud people, but you notice when they are around. I can always hear Mom puttering around the house, or Jenna playing music. Sometimes I even hear Molly practicing with her soccer ball against a wall somewhere, stopping only when Mom or Dad yells, "Molly, cut it out!"

I wondered if our house would still be like this once Jenna left for college, when it would just be the four of us. It seems so weird that she wouldn't be here every day. The thing about having two sisters is that you get really used to having them around.

"Do you ever wonder what it will be like when Jenna moves out?" I asked Molly, who was sitting right next to me at the counter.

She looked up from her phone. "What?" she asked.

"When Jenna goes to college," I said. "When it's just the four of us instead of five, do you worry that it will be weird?"

Molly wrinkled her forehead. "I dunno," she said. "Like will we miss her?"

"Well, we'll miss her, sure," I said. "But I mean,

what will dinner be like without her? What will the weekends be like?"

"Well, the weekends will be easier, because we don't have to worry about making noise and waking her up," said Molly, in her very matter-of-fact Molly way.

This was true. Jenna liked to sleep in on the weekends, and she was always barking at us to keep it down. Molly and I are early risers.

"But won't it be like one person is just missing?" I asked.

I knew Molly wasn't always into these kinds of conversations, so I was pushing it.

"Things change, Kelsey," Molly said in a tone that sounded like she was explaining it to a two-year-old.

"Oh, never mind," I said, and pushed away my chair. Molly was making me feel worse instead of better.

Sometimes getting people to talk in our family was impossible. My cousin Lindsay was the one I used to talk to about everything. We're just about the same age and grew up together, so in a lot of ways we are more like sisters than cousins.

But Lindsay's mom, my aunt Amy, died a couple years ago after being sick for a long time. If you talk to

Lindsay, she doesn't burst into tears or anything, or at least not usually, but I'm always really careful when I talk to her now, especially if I'm talking about my family.

If, say, I complain about Mom, I'm worried that Lindsay is really thinking, *Oh, well, at least you still have your mom.* If I tried to talk to her about how weird it would be with Jenna gone, I'm afraid she would think, *Well, she's just going to college. She's coming back. But my mom isn't.*

Lindsay is actually really sweet, so I don't think she'd think those things on purpose, and she would never say them to me out loud, but there are things I just can't talk to her about anymore.

"You'd better get your homework started before Mom gets home," said Molly.

I looked over, annoyed, and I noticed that while I'd been sitting there thinking, she had already set up her laptop and was typing away.

Molly is only eight months older than I am, but she acts like she is my much older sister. So between her and Jenna, I really feel ganged up on sometimes and like I am the baby of the family.

Jenna and Molly are a lot alike. They are both super organized and they belong to a million different clubs and are always thinking about their next project or what they'll be doing in ten years.

Dad calls me Kelsey Dreamer because I guess I daydream a lot, and I like to take my time doing things. I just don't feel that crazy rushing sense or the competitiveness that Jenna and Molly seem to have been born with.

I opened my laptop, logged in, and clicked over to the homework page and sighed. Ugh. There is *so* much homework in middle school.

There was no way I'd finish before dinner, which I hated. I liked to be able to relax after dinner, and have what Dad calls downtime, when you kind of just do nothing.

I peeked over at Molly. "Do we have to read this whole chapter for history?" I asked.

"Yes," said Molly, her hands flying over the keyboard.

I opened the window and breathed in.

"Ooh, someone is burning leaves," I said. I love that smell.

I positioned my chair so the breeze from outside tickled my face. It was a shame to spend such a beautiful afternoon inside doing homework.

Then I looked over at Molly again. "Did you finish reading it already?" I asked.

"Yeeesss," said Molly with a hint of annoyance, not looking up from her laptop.

"What is it about?" I asked.

"KELSEY!" Molly screamed so loud I jumped. "You have to do your own homework! I'm not going to do it for you!"

"I wasn't asking you to do my homework," I said crossly. "I was just curious."

"If you're curious, then open the book," said Molly, and she sounded exactly like Mom when she said it.

I sat there for a few more minutes, listening to the leaves crinkle in the wind. Dad was going to make us help rake them up on the weekend.

"Kelsey, I can help you if you get stuck, but you have to start and you have to try," said Molly.

"Okay," I said, eating some more popcorn. "This tastes so much better when Dad makes it on the stove than in the microwave," I said. "And it's fluffier."

Molly looked at me sideways. "Thanks for the review, Princess Popcorn," she said.

I snickered.

Molly looked over and giggled too. Then she

grabbed a handful and chewed. "You're right," she said. "This does taste good."

She glanced over at me with a mischievous twinkle in her eye that I know well and said, "Sheep on a log! Well, what if those sheep *flew*?"

Then she hurled a fistful of popcorn at me.

"MOLLY!" I screamed, shaking popcorn from my hair but laughing.

I tossed some down the back of her shirt.

"Oh, it is *on*, Princess Popcorn!" she said, and showered me with half of what was in the bowl.

We were both throwing the popcorn and cracking up when we heard my mom say, loudly, "Girls, what on earth is going on in here?"

Jenna peered around her. "Are you maniacs having a popcorn fight?"

We both said, "No!" while popcorn fell from our hair, and we tried not to giggle.

Mom sighed and handed me the broom and Molly the dustpan. "I don't even want to know. And I don't want to see anything either . . . please clean up this mess."

I started sweeping and Molly scooped up the piles, but we couldn't stop laughing.

"Sheep on a log!" Molly whispered, trying to stifle her laughter.

"What are sheep on a log?" asked Jenna.

"What happens when you don't have ants," I said, and Molly started to laugh even harder.

"What?" asked Jenna, but she started to laugh too.

Sometimes that happens when we're all together. We just start laughing and we can't stop, sometimes over something silly and sometimes over nothing at all.

Mom looked at the three of us cackling and threw up her hands. "I don't get it," she said. "But the sound of you three girls laughing is always the best."

Molly and I settled down and cleaned up and Jenna started to set the table. I felt another surge—this was so nice—the three of us together with our own secret kind of language.

Why would you ever want to leave it? I just wished it could stay this way forever.